AMALIE SKRAM (1846-1905) is one of Norway's major nineteenth-century novelists. Her turbulent early life in the bustling seaport of Bergen, and then travelling the world as the wife of a ship's captain, gave her ample material for her studies of contemporary society. The two novels in this present volume, *Sjur Gabriel* and *Two Friends*, are the first two of a four-novel cycle called *The People of Hellemyr*, a Zolaesque portrayal of the doomed attempt of a family to escape the vicious circle of poverty and crime. Some of her other novels focus on women's struggles against restricted freedom and stifling convention; also published by Norvik Press are *Lucie* (1888), *Fru Inés* (1891) and *Betrayed* (1892), all translated by Katherine Hanson and Judith Messick.

JANET GARTON is Emeritus Professor of European Literature at the University of East Anglia, Norwich. She has published several books about Amalie Skram, including a biography, *Amalie. Et forfatterliv* (2011) and an edition of Amalie and Erik Skram's letters, *Elskede Amalie* (2002). She has also translated many Norwegian and Danish writers, including Jan Kjærstad, Cecilie Løveld, Henrik Ibsen, Kirsten Thorup and Herman Bang.

Sjur Gabriel and Two Friends

by
Amalie Skram

Translated by Janet Garton

Introduction by Gunnar Staalesen

Norvik Press
2026

Norvik Press Series B: English Translations of Scandinavian Literature, no. 89.
ISBN: 978-1-909408-75-3.

Norvik Press
Department of Scandinavian Studies, UCL
16-18 Gordon Square, London, WC1H 0AG, UK
Website: www.norvikpress.com
E-mail address: norvik.press@ucl.ac.uk

Managing editors: Elettra Carbone, Sarah Death, Janet Garton, C. Claire Thomson.

Cover image: *Handel fra båtene, Bergen*. Photographer Knud Knudsen, Bergen University Library.

This translation has been published with the financial support of NORLA (Norwegian Literature Abroad).

Contents

Introduction

The Legacy of Hellemyr

'From that day on both husband and wife at Hellemyr drank.' It is with this often-quoted sentence that Amalie Skram ends the first volume of her series about the people of Hellemyr, *Sjur Gabriel*. It would be hard to say it more concisely and baldly; with these eleven words she describes an entire family's tragedy. The past has caught up with them, and future generations will carry the burden onwards. Reduced to its essence, that is what this series is fundamentally about: the inheritance of sin, both socially and genetically, and how difficult it is to break the pattern and shape one's own life.

In my opinion, the four novels of *The People of Hellemyr* constitute the most important fictional creation in Norwegian literature, a work which, if it had been written in English, French or Russian, would have been a world classic just as self-evidently as the great novels of Dickens, Hugo, Austen or Dostoevsky. As recently as March 2002 the Danish author Kirsten Thorup expressed it thus in an interview in the Norwegian newspaper *Dagbladet*: 'In *The People of Hellemyr* she is every bit as good as Balzac.'

To a far greater degree than many of her contemporaries, Amalie Skram can still be read with the same enjoyment today, over a century since the books were written. She brings to life the fates of her characters, with an impressive ability to capture them in a few short sentences, often cuttingly ironic, with lifelike dialogue, dramatic incidents, striking characterization and colourful townscapes. This has made her into one of the authors in Norwegian literary history who even today can claim the largest readership – and thus assured her a place amongst the greatest Norwegian writers.

Amalie Skram wrote a number of important novels. In her writing she shed a penetrating light both on women's fates and on the state of marriage in the nineteenth century. Four of these novels have been translated into English: *Constance Ring* (1885), *Lucie* (1888), *Fru Inés* (1891) and *Betrayed* (1892). With her two so-called 'novels of madness' from 1895, *Professor Hieronimus* and *At St. Jørgen's*, she made a considerable contribution to the treatment of the mentally ill in Denmark. Nevertheless, there are few people who would disagree that the four books about the family from Hellemyr – *Sjur Gabriel* (1887), *Two Friends* (1887), *S.G. Myre* (1890) and *Descendants* (1898) – are her crowning achievement. Nowhere else is the full depth of her talent so clearly displayed. In this work she makes full use of memories, experiences and impressions from her Bergen childhood and upbringing, sets up a broad canvas and paints it in striking colours, both light and dark.

Her childhood in Bergen was marked by abrupt changes in her family's social status, with a father who had high ambitions but went bankrupt more than once. Despite that, she had a much better education than girls from her social class could normally expect in the nineteenth century. Amalie Alver was her name, and she was born in a house in one of Bergen's narrow alleyways, Apotekersmuget, on 22

August 1846. But it was in Strandgaten, the town's busiest trading street, that she lived for most of her childhood, before the family made several moves around the same area, ending up at the top of Cort Piils smug. There she lived for the last years of her young adulthood, until in 1864, at the age of eighteen, she married the ship's captain Bernt August Müller, who was nine years older than her.

On her daily walk to and from the girls' school out in Dreggen she would pass the central districts of Torvet and Tyskebryggen (the fish market and the Hanseatic warehouses on the wharf), observing life in the harbour and in the town's teeming business district. She would have seen characters like 'Tippler Tom' and others on the way to buy drink with a flock of kids on their heels, watched the barriers at the quayside rise and fall, followed the sailing ships on their way in and out; all the teeming life of the ancient trading town of Bergen. And the pictures must have stayed with her, because when she sat down many years later in Copenhagen to write her Hellemyr books, they surfaced again and became living poetry, sensually recreated with smells and colours, and with visceral evocations of rain and frost, sun and wind.

But it was not just sensory impressions and childhood memories of the town that Amalie Skram drew on when she wrote her four Hellemyr novels. It is generally agreed that in these novels she wrote more intimately than anywhere else in her fiction about her own family history, not least the fate of her father, Mons Monsen Alver. Perhaps it was precisely this which drove her to complete the series; for it is striking to see how quickly she wrote at the beginning and what a struggle it became later on, as she got closer to her own time and her own personal experiences.

On several occasions Amalie Skram told the story of how she got the idea for the Hellemyr books. In 1887 she wrote to her fellow writer Jonas Lie: 'I was writing a story about a boy who suffers a great deal in his youth, and dies as a student at the age of 18. When I had got some way into the narrative, I had to describe the past life of his parents as well. So I started again with them, thinking that I would publish the book as two independent volumes. Then when I had written quite a bit about the parents, I needed to include their families' histories, so I jumped right back to the boy's parents' grandparents, who are Sjur Gabriel and Oline.' And in a letter to her second husband, the Danish writer Erik Skram, she wrote in 1898: 'You say that there is no composition in *Descendants*. I only wish you had given me an example of what you meant, so that I might get some glimpse of understanding. (…) But don't forget that the "composition" begins right back with *Sjur Gabriel*.'

The first two volumes, *Sjur Gabriel* and *Two Friends*, were both published in 1887. They can be read as independent novels, the first as an intimate naturalistic drama, a Greek tragedy transposed to the west coast of Norway, the second as a thrilling yarn of life at sea.

In *Sjur Gabriel* we meet the husband and wife whose actions create a kind of pattern for the fate of the coming generations in the family of poor peasants from Hellemyr, 'five kilometres north of Bergen (or half a mile using the old system of measurement)'. In *Two Friends* we follow Oline and Sjur Gabriel's grandson Sivert on his flight from Bergen as cabin boy on the barque named Two Friends. Despite the fact that the descriptions of life at sea can be both tough and brutal, they are nevertheless imbued with so much humour and with so many lighter moments that this book remains in the memory as the most upbeat of the four Hellemyr novels. The connection between the two books rests largely on the figure of Oline and the scourge she represents for Sjur Gabriel in the first and Sivert in the second.

From book to book in the Hellemyr series Amalie Skram broadens her perspective. *Sjur Gabriel* is a tight-knit personal drama, with its focus on the unhappy couple at Hellemyr and their children. Poverty and toil, alcoholism and sickness provide the background for her portrayal of life on the barren smallholding north of Bergen. Yet in spite of that, the warmth between Sjur Gabriel and his youngest son Little-Gabriel lights up the story. Little-Gabriel's fate shows how cruel and tragic life could be for the poor. The final chapter of *Sjur Gabriel* is one of the most powerful scenes in the author's whole production.

Large sections of *Two Friends* also take place within a kind of closed room, on board the ship, with Sivert as the central character. The author herself had experienced storms and tempests on her voyages with her first husband, and she recreates these in the novel with arresting intensity. In addition we are given lively depictions of life in Jamaica, in which she does not mince her words when describing the sailors' visits to one of the local brothels – a passage which must have aroused indignation in her home town, populated as it was by sailors' families.

It is only in the following two novels, *S.G. Myre* and *Descendants*, that Amalie Skram broadens her perspective fully. Now she shows us a full-screen image of Bergen, from the poorest districts to the richest, from school and daily life, in work and at play, with the inexorable rhythm of life as a kind of leitmotif: from one death to the next, right up to the final crescendo on the last pages of Descendants.

On reading it through again one is struck by how tightly composed this series is, how the themes return time and again, as in a powerful dark symphony, how motifs which are announced in the two first books are taken up again later and amplified to full strength, in this shocking masterpiece of the human tragedy.

Gunnar Staalesen

Sjur Gabriel

1

On the rocky slopes five kilometres north of Bergen (or half a mile using the old system of measurement) there lived about sixty years ago a peasant farmer called Sjur Gabriel.

The farmland he owned was so wretched to look at that it was practically a wilderness, and the house he lived in was no larger than a crofter's hut.

As well as a wife and five children he had four cows, seven sheep and a pig to provide for.

The farm was called Hellemyren, meaning the stony bog, and it lived up to its name. The whole area consisted of rocky hillocks and boggy meadowland, fenced in by the black, barren mountains and the dark green sea.

As a sideline he busied himself with fishing. Often he went out at night in the little tarred rowing boat with one of the older boys, who were around nine or ten, usually in rainy weather, because that's when the fish were most likely to bite. Then the next morning he rowed the five kilometres into town, where he sold the catch for a few ort.* Fish was cheap in those days. Coalfish and large cod could be bought for four to ten ort apiece.

His wife Oline was brought to bed of a child around once a year. After a little over twelve years of marriage she had borne nine children. The last four had died, with the result that her youngest child, Little-Adna, as she was called, was five and a half.

These days, as she was not nursing a baby, Oline sometimes came along when her husband went fishing. She always had a lot of luck when it came to getting the fish to bite, and in addition she was as sturdy a rower as any man, despite the fact that her body was as small and thin as that of a fifteen-year-old lass.

But the additional income provided by her assistance was most often swallowed up by liquor. For she had the habit of having one too many, the moment there was the remotest opportunity. It didn't matter in the slightest what Sjur Gabriel tried to do about it, she always managed to conceal some fish on their trips to town, which she then sneaked off with on the pretence of some errand or other, in order to sell it in one of the narrow alleys leading down to the quay,* or in the drinking den close by.

One Friday they hadn't started fishing until after midday, so they didn't get to town until between five and six in the afternoon. To make up for that, sales were brisk and they got rid of all the fish in an hour or so.

Sjur Gabriel had kept an eye on Oline the whole time, and issued strict instructions that she was not to leave the boat. He wanted to see if it would be possible just once to get back home with her in a sober state. His son Jens had been sent up to the baker's to buy some rye cakes for them to take home.*

Now Sjur Gabriel was sitting with his back to Oline on the foremost thwart, talking to a man in the neighbouring boat who had some large pollock he had not been able to get rid of.

Oline was sitting on a plank in the stern, leaning forward with her elbows on her knees and her chin in her hands. With her expressionless little child's face and the black headscarf tied tightly around her forehead she looked like a half-grown lass who had dressed up as a woman for a joke.

She peered from side to side with a calculating glance,

without moving her head. The boat was moored by the Triangle,* and the steps up to the jetty were so close that you could step onto them from the boat.

She stood up cautiously, then stood still for a moment, watching her husband's back with fearful eyes and grimacing mouth. Then she slowly bent down and picked up something from the bottom of the boat which had been hidden under her skirt while she was sitting. It was a bundle which was wrapped up in a blue-checked kerchief and knotted together for carrying.

She stood still for one more moment, calculating. Then with a sudden jump she leapt up onto the gunwale and from there onto the steps.

Quick as lightning Sjur Gabriel had turned round, and supporting himself by the knuckles of his right hand on the thwart, propelled himself into the stern in a single jump; bracing one knee against the gunwale and thrusting out his arm after Oline, he managed to grab hold of her skirt.

'Where d'yer think you're goin'!' he snarled with suppressed anger, jerking at her skirt.

Oline grabbed hold of the railings in order to stop herself tumbling backwards, and at the same time pulled with all her might to break free.

'Stand still, or I'll rip your skirt! I said where d'yer think you're goin'?'

Oline gave up. She muttered something about going up to see Guri, who worked at an inn in one of the alleyways.

'Wha've yer got in tha' bundle?'

It was her boat jacket, she explained. It was torn at the seams, and she was going up to Guri's to borrow needle and thread to mend it.

Sjur Gabriel ground his teeth and snarled an oath.

He had seen that the bundle was moving.

'Give it 'ere,' he said curtly, and pulled so hard at her skirt that Oline slipped down a couple of steps.

'Tek the 'ole lot then!' She raised her arm with the bundle, which she had been trying to keep behind her back the whole time, and hurled it with all her strength into the bottom of the boat.

Sjur Gabriel turned round instinctively to see where it fell, and as he did so he lost his grip on her skirt.

The next moment Oline had leapt up the steps, run across the Triangle and slipped into the alleyway like an eel.

'Devil tek the woman,' muttered Sjur Gabriel, when he saw that she had gone. 'Dunno when we'll see *'er* again.'

He took off his sou'wester, scratched his head, put it on again, spat into the sea and then busied himself untying the bundle, where he found two pollocks and a medium-sized cod wrapped up in the jacket.

'Would yer b'lieve the cunnin',' he said in a low voice, and remained leaning over the half-dead fish with his arms on his knees and his hands hanging between his legs.

'How much for that pollock, you *Stril* down there in the boat?'*

Sjur Gabriel looked up and saw a housemaid with a scarf round her head and a basket on her arm; she was leaning out over the railings of the jetty looking at the fish, which were beating their tails feebly against the unfamiliar homespun of the jacket.

His expression did not flicker as he dropped his head again.

'Can't you answer me, you country lout! How much d'you want for your pollock? Can you 'ear me? Are you deaf and dumb, you idiot *Stril*?'

Sjur Gabriel did not condescend to speak.

The girl took a newly-bought twig brush out of her basket, leant so far out over the edge of the wharf that she was balancing on the railings, struck the edge of Sjur Gabriel's sou'wester with the end of the brush, and yelled: 'Are you asleep or is that hat made of lead? What do you want for that pollock, you *Stril* bumpkin? Answer me, or I'll set the police on you.'

'*Stril* bumpkin yersel', yer lazy townie,' said a shrill cross voice, and a boy in a knitted cap and a grey homespun jacket with pewter buttons, with a wooden box in his hand,* hopped from the steps into the boat. 'We're no' *Stril*,' he went on defiantly, trying to grab the brush, 'we're from 'Ellen up north.'

'What do I care,' came the pert reply from the girl, who was flushed after her exertions. 'I should think *Stril* are jus' as good as anyone else.'

'What d'you want for the pollock, you from Hellen up north, then?' she said again.

'Ten shillin' apiece,' came the surly reply from Sjur Gabriel.

'Are you mad *Stri*- I mean: man? You can't be serious! – I'll give you two!'

Sjur Gabriel did not move.

'All right, three!'

No answer.

'What, d'you want more 'an three? Shame on you! Tiddly little things like that, one of 'em's no bigger 'an a baby roach.'

She waited a moment.

'Oh come on, be reasonable *Stri*- you from Hellen up north. No-one's goin' ter give you any more for those miserable tiddlers. – People ain't stupid.'

'One of 'em's a cod,' Sjur Gabriel remarked steadily.

'Well then the price is even more cheeky – such spineless li'l cod! All righ', listen – I'll give you seven shillin' for the lot, tha's far too much, but I 'aven't time to stand 'ere arguin'.'

'It'll 'ave to be eight.'

'Not likely. – D'you think I'm daft? Seven, not a cent more.'

'You can't 'ave 'em for less.'

''And 'em over then!' she shouted crossly. 'I can tell you, you'll be waitin' a long time afore anyone gives you blood money like tha' for such rotten sprats.'

She reached into her basket and took out a twist of grey cartridge paper, which she opened, and which contained a few dirty, corroded copper coins.

Slowly and deliberately Sjur Gabriel shifted the fish onto a hank of woven willow, twisting the ends together to make a handle. Then he stood up, climbed up onto the thwart and held out his hand for the money.

The girl counted the shillings one by one, loudly, down into his hand.

Only then did Sjur Gabriel hand over the fish.

'Rotten *Stril*!' she shouted, crowing, as she left, 'once a *Stril*, always a *Stril*!' She gave a cackle of laughter as she hurried off.

Sjur Gabriel gave no sign that he had heard, as he began to get the boat ready for departure.

'Where's our ma?' asked Jens.

'Ran off – dunno where she went.'

He glanced out over the Triangle and then peered up the alleyway. After that he bent down to pick up Oline's jacket, throwing it into the stern, and then sat down to bale out the boat.

Jens fastened a new willow thong to one oar to replace one that had snapped, and tidied up the anchor rope at the bow so that it lay in a neat coil, all the while constantly checking the Triangle and the steps. When there was nothing more for him to do, he stood wide-legged in the bows with his hands in his trouser pockets and his face turned towards land. His expression was melancholy, the look in his eyes restless and tense.

When the boat was emptied of water, Sjur Gabriel threw the bailer behind him, pulled some chewing tobacco out of his waistcoat pocket and bit off a piece. Then he sat there chewing with his hands braced on his hips, staring in the same direction as the boy. Now and then he sighed heavily, muttering, and shifted in his seat. Daylight was beginning to wane, but the moon was out and the weather was calm.

Eventually he stood up.

'Stay 'ere in't boat,' he said to Jens, without turning round. 'I'll be back soon.'

Then he stepped over onto the steps, climbed slowly up them, and disappeared from Jens's view between the porters and ferrymen who were standing around in groups in the Triangle.

2

A little way up the alley Oline entered a two-storey house with a notice over the front door which announced:

Lodgings
Two shillings a night; with hot coffee four,
with breakfast six. Dinner etc.
on request. Alcohol for sale:
beer, brandy and more

In the passage, which smelt of cheap spirits, there was a staircase straight ahead, and two doors, one on each side; the one on the left was wide open. On the right-hand door was a notice: Public Bar. From behind it could be heard the noise of husky voices laughing and hooting and bellowing, thunderous bangs on the table, and shouts that sounded like threats or howls.

Oh won't you tell me where Rubakken lives,
Rubakken lives, Rubakken lives,
Yes he lives in Norway in a stabbur,
In a stabbur, in a stabbur,
Hi fiddle-de-dee, hi fiddle-de-dee!*

The verse was sung in a falsetto woman's voice, accompanied by a splashing, scouring sound, and through the open door of the saloon Oline could see in the middle of the floor the back of a broad-hipped girl in peasant clothes, with her feet in a couple of clogs from which her heels stuck up. She was on her hands and knees between a bucket of water and a wooden box of sand, scrubbing the floor energetically with a rough floorcloth. There were double bunks made of unvarnished wood along all the walls, some with woollen blankets and bolsters covered in sacking, others with merely a layer of straw in the bottom. Beside the beds stood long benches which were wet and shiny from recent scrubbing. A large number of spitoons overflowing with disgusting slops were stacked up one on top of the other around a crooked stove with a cooking plate and a whitewashed base, which was plastered with spills of innumerable shapes and sizes. On one of the benches there stood an oil lamp with a red flame which flickered in the draught each time the door to the bar opened.

"'Ard a' work, I see,' said Oline, walking across to stand beside the scrubbing girl.

'Folk from Hellemyr in town again,' answered Guri, without pausing in her work.

'Jus' a quick trip,' Oline nodded, thrusting her hands beneath her apron and rubbing them together.

Guri stood up, pulled the bucket and sandbox a bit further along, got down on her knees again, sploshed water onto the floor with the cloth, sprinkled sand over it and started scrubbing violently once more.

'Fine weather today,' remarked Oline, as Guri stopped scouring and plunged the cloth into the bucket to rinse it.

'You don' say,' was the answer.

'Many lodgers?' asked Oline after a while.

'Cram full every single night.'

'Mus' be, I s'pose.'

'D'you wanna sit down?' asked Guri, as she stood up again in order to move to a new piece of floor.

'Thanks anyway. – Can't stay, I've ter be off straigh' away.'

'S'pose you must. – It's gettin' dark.'

'Still, there's a moon, y'know.'

'Aye, s'pose there is – good to 'ave a moon when you're a' sea.'

Oline's hands became more and more restless. It looked as if she had a kitten under her apron.

'I'd best be off then,' she said, but sat down instead on one of the benches.

'What've you done with Sjur Gabriel?' asked Guri, after nothing had been said for a while.

'On't boat,' answered Oline. The next time the scrubbing stopped for a moment and it was quiet she went on: 'We came in wi' a few fish we'd caught.'

'Is tha' so.' Guri looked as if she had said something most profound.

'Now I was gonna buy some li'l things to tek 'ome for't kids.'

'Sounds good.' Guri wrung out the cloth so that water streamed from it.

'Trouble is I'm short of a few shillin's.'

'Shillin's is what you need,' Guri answered with the same profound expression.

'Tha' Sjur Gabriel is so tight-fisted, y'know. I can't get a single penny ou' of 'im.'

'Is tha' righ'?' – said Guri in a tone of voice as if she had heard some good news.

'Menfolk, they've their own ideas, they get set in their ways an' you can't shift 'em,' Oline went on, 'so wha's a poor woman to do now an' then bu' find 'er own way ou'?'

'True enough.' Guri shook her head slightly.

'But wha's to be done when you've no money?'

'No, tha's no' easy,' Guri agreed. 'Wha's to be done?'

"F only there were someone t'lend me money.'

"F only.'

"Cos I've got summat to pawn.'

'Let's see then!' Guri exclaimed eagerly, dropping the floorcloth and straightening up with her hands on her hips.

'There's this bib 'ere,' said Oline, unhooking her bodice and pulling out a breastpiece embroidered with coloured pearls.

'Come over 'ere, you're too far away.'

Oline went over to her.

Guri's eyes opened wide, sparkling, as she saw the multicoloured glittering pearls which covered the material, embroidered on scalloped borders and on a gleaming hexagonal star in the middle; it was edged and lined with bright yellow calico.

"Ow much d'you want?'

'An ort.'

'It's not worth tha', said Guri, turning her attention to the floor again.

'Not worth it! It cost me an 'ole three ort and twelve shillin.'*

'Tha's as may be, back then. – Now everythin's much cheaper. I bet I could pop over and buy a new one f'r an ort up the street at Ma Weistendal's.' Guri slopped water onto the floor, and looked as if she had dismissed the whole idea.

Oline went over towards the door. 'I'll not let it out of my 'ands for less,' she said.

Guri watched her out of the corner of her eye, but carried on scrubbing more energetically than ever.

Oline had second thoughts.

"Ow much'll you give me then?' she asked, returning to stand next to Guri.

'Twelve shillin'', she answered indifferently.

'Shame on yer!' cried Oline, nudging her half-jokingly with her foot. 'Bu' all righ' then, twelve shillin'll 'ave to do. Let's 'ave the money, I'm in a tearin''urry.'

Guri brushed the thick brown water off her arms and shook her hands, scattering drops all around, dried her hands on her apron and picked up the breastpiece which Oline gave her between the tips of her thumb and forefinger.

'I'll 'ave to go up to my clothes chest,' she said. She took off her clogs and ran up the stairs.

Whilst Guri was away, Oline shuffled around restlessly. She went over to the window and peered out through the small misted panes, looked longingly across the passage at the door to the public bar, sat down on the bench and then got up again to listen.

At last she heard the stairs creaking as Guri came quickly down.

''Ere you are,' she said, giving Oline a silver twelve-shilling piece.

'Thanks for tha', then,' said Oline.

'Well, thank *you*,' answered Guri cheerfully. 'Jus' 'ope you ain't sorry for it la'er, 'cos you know you'll never afford to ge' it back.'

'I'm allus sorry, for everythin' I do – and everythin' I don' do. That's jus' 'ow i' is.' With that, Oline took hold of the iron door latch on the heavy door with its panels decorated with crosses, and pulled it to after her.

'No need to shut the door!' shouted Guri, who had bent to her work again.

'You'll 'ave cold air blowin' in on yer,' answered Oline, making haste to shut it.

Once she was in the passage she walked along to the

space under the stairs like someone who knew where she was going. Here she lifted up her skirts and felt along the inside of her underskirt, finally pulling a three-quarter pint bottle out of a pocket, grimacing to help it along. She held on to it with her teeth whilst she shook out her skirts and bent her knees a few times to make them fall into place. She concealed it beneath her apron, peered out cautiously and then crept soundlessly past the stairs along to the door of the bar, opened it quickly and went in.

The room was of the same size and shape as the one with the beds. Under the windows, which were half covered by green-painted shutters, and along the walls, there were long tables of unfinished wood, standing on trestles which were roughly held together by nailed crossbars bearing the marks of dirty boots. On the longest wall, which had grey panels, hung iron whale-oil lights which looked like small oil lamps. On the benches along both sides of the tables sat customers with glasses of brandy and tankards of beer in front of them. Some of them were debating together with sage expressions, others were quarrelling noisily and exchanging threats at close quarters. A few were snoring with their arms and heads resting on the greasy table. The air was filled with a choking stench of brandy and whale oil and homespun cloth.

In the middle of the floor, which was covered in brown puddles of tobacco juice, stood a thickset figure in a waistcoat and grey spotted woollen undershirt hanging down over his trousers. His ruddy face was so swollen that his squinting eyes were almost invisible. On the back of his jacket was fastened a layer of roughly-stitched pieces of cloth with a patch of leather on top, which was worn shiny by use. Over his shoulder he carried a porter's rope with a loop reinforced with iron, which hung down behind him like a trailing scarf. His unkempt hair stuck out in all directions and made his head look shapeless and inordinately large. Around him stood a group of more or less drunken peasants, as well as a few men in a similar attire to his. He was talking and telling tales in a hoarse voice which every so often was reduced to a strenuous whisper, imitating other speakers, intermittently roaring with laughter and waving his arms about furiously.

Oline stole across the floor to his left towards the counter, where a tallow candle was burning in a pewter candlestick. There stood the innkeeper, a middle-aged, well-built fellow with fat beardless cheeks. He was wearing a dark blue knitted sweater which seemed to have been pulled on over a large assortment of other clothes, a white drill apron looped around his neck, and a red-and-white-striped knitted cap on his head.

'Gabriel's Oline's in town today then,' he said, making a poor effort to speak the country dialect, and nodding with an indifferent expression.

'Tha's righ',' answered Oline, pulling out the bottle and putting it on the counter.

''Ow much?' he asked, picking it up.

'I reckon it was 'alf a pint Sjur Gabriel said.'

The innkeeper went over to a side table, inserted a funnel into the neck of the bottle and picked up a half-pint pot, which he filled from a keg.

'Well, I c'n tell you a story,' the man with the porter's rope started up, 'ha, ha, hee, hee!' He was acting as if he was unable to speak for laughing, whilst waving his arm about as if he was trying to hit something invisible, all the time staggering slightly from side to side so as to keep his balance. 'I met t'Archdeacon on t'corner o' t'market, so I says to 'im, 'scuse me, Reverend, I says, hee hee! – 'ee went white as a sheet. – 'Ee knows me, you see, 'ee's afear'd o' my sharp tongue, ha ha! 'Ee made as if 'e 'adn't 'eard, the rogue! But I followed 'im an' caught up wiv 'im. 'Scuse me, I says again, 'cos you 'ave ter be p'lite, don'cha, an' I doffed me cap, pssh,' he raised his wavering arm to his head to show how he had greeted the vicar. 'May I 'ave a serious word wiv you, Reverend? No, says 'ee an' 'urries off. Me after 'im. 'Ere's you a servant of the Lord, Reverend, and don' want to 'ear a serious word? I says. – Then you should'er seen 'im!' The porter emitted inarticulate grunts of laughter and shifted his weight forwards and backwards, his body at a rakish angle as if he was the whole time on the point of falling over.

The others laughed along with him and asked what happened next.

'I jus' wan'ed ter say fank you, Reverend, I says then, for the luvly sermon you preached las' Sunday. – If everyone lived by wha' you says, they'd all be repentent sinners, jus' like you an' me, Reverend.'

He laughed again, so hard that he almost choked; his listeners joined in. Some of them bent forwards and slapped their knees loudly, acting as if they were on the point of expiring.

''E's a one, our Tippler Tom! Bloody good fella!' shouted one of them.

'Well look oo's 'ere, i's our li'l 'oman.' The porter's drunken voice took on a caressing, seductive tone.

'Where've you come from, li'l mamma?' He staggered after Oline, who was quickly making for the door with the bottle under her apron, and grabbed her by the shoulder.

Oline pulled herself free with a jerk and muttered something that sounded like a dog snarling before it bites, as she reached out an arm to take hold of the latch.

'Come 'ere, li'l mamma!' shrieked the porter, distorting his crooked blue lips into a wet smile, as he lifted one leg in the air as if to perform a Halling leap,* and swung Oline's arm to and fro so that the joints creaked.

'Let's 'ave your fist, an' we'll tek a turn on t'dance floor!'

'Le' go o' me, le' go o' me, you villain!' Oline forced the words out in a whistle, grinding her teeth as she twisted and turned to get her hand free, hunching her shoulders to protect herself.

The onlookers laughed and called out to indicate their interest and applause. The innkeeper watched with arms folded, leaning against the bottle-lined shelves along the wall behind the counter, eyebrows arched and his thin mouth puckered in a melancholy pout.

Finally Oline managed to get her hand free. At the same moment the porter lurched towards her, almost toppling over. She raised her arm and curled her fingers into claws, thrusting her jaw forward so that she looked like a wild beast; then with all her strength she bored her nails into the face of her opponent, leapt to one side as nimbly as a cat, heaved the door open and fled from the house. As she went she could hear the crash of something heavy falling, mingled with shouts and laughter and general tumult.

3

She ran across the market square in her homemade leather clogs, which were lined with a layer of straw, and didn't slow down until she was sure she was not being followed. The moonlight fell across the centre of the row of houses on one side of the square, whilst the other side was dark.

Oline stood still by an open warehouse door and peeped in. A large wide shape which was hanging by a rope was being raised slowly upwards towards a rectangular opening in the roof, though which a faint light could be seen. From up above she could hear someone heaving and pulling, as they called repeatedly: 'Hey – up, hey – up.' She went inside and slipped quietly behind the door, pulled the cork out of the bottle, put it to her mouth and drank.

Ooh, how good and warm it felt. She patted her chest as the strong liquor burnt her throat and made her mouth water; she hurriedly swallowed it down. Then she drank again, and felt so happy and light-hearted.

'Hm, hm,' she whispered to herself – 'nivver seen anythin' like it' – she burst out laughing, and bent in two in her efforts to make no sound. 'Dancin' hallin' wi' the old 'oman. Come 'ere, li'l mamma!' – she imitated the porter's voice. 'You got li'l mamma you did, you ol' devil.' She laughed again until she had tears in her eyes. – 'I'd like to 'ave seen 'ow 'ee crashed on't floor.' Suddenly she heard footsteps on some stairs she couldn't see. She quickly thrust the bottle into her jacket, crept outside and walked up to Strandgaden.

'Ooh, it's tha' grand and shiny in them bottles in t'store, and the lamps! They're not lit tonigh', mus' be cos is's so early. – Lamps out in t'street! – Grand to see 'ow they pay for it all 'ere down south in town. 'F only I could live in 'ere an' no' a' 'Ellemyr, that'd be summat, sooner 'an ploughin' through bogs an' 'eaps o' stone, an' sloggin' away at sea in wind an' rain.'

She stopped in front of a window which was full of bottles standing in rows on white shelves, with red and blue labels with gilt edges.

In the middle stood a lamp on a brass base, casting a golden glow around.

Oline stood there fixated by the sight. 'Wonner wha's in a' those lovely bo'les – bet it's thick an' sweet an' burnin' strong. – 'F only we lived down in town an' 'ad reg'lar money an' loss of it. Aye, if things in this world 'adn't turned out so wretched, she c'd be wed t'a rich landowner, mebbee t'a prince, oo knows? God bless us!' She laughed softly and shook her head at her own folly, wiped her eyes with the knuckles of one hand and rubbed them dry on her apron. A passer-by barged into her and knocked her off the narrow pavement and down into the gutter, where she lurched sideways, but managed to put down a hand to catch herself, so she finished up squatting down.

''Ave to keep yer wits abou' you 'ere in town,' she muttered, nodding to herself, as she struggled up again. 'It ain't like trottin' abou' in t'field back 'ome. No' a' all!'

She wandered onwards, filled with an agreeable feeling, half tearful and half laughing. She'd just take a little stroll along Strandgaden as far as Smørsalmindingen,* there were so many fine things to look at, then she'd turn round and go down to the boat. By then Jens would be back from the baker's, so it would be a good time. But first she'd better drink up that bit left in the bottle, it wasn't worth keeping.

She turned the corner by Sakritsgaarden, walked down

it a couple of steps, and when she couldn't see anyone she pulled out the bottle, lifted it to her mouth and emptied it.

Was that all there was left? She licked her lips and hammered the cork in with the edge of her clenched fist. Surprising how little there was in that half-pint. How stupid of her, that she hadn't bought a whole bottleful. But there was time to put that right, she had enough money for another half-pint if she got the cheapest sort. How about if she ran along Smørsalmindingen, down to that one-eyed old fogey. Yes, that was it, she'd do that.

She ran along looking to neither right nor left, keeping close to the gutter where she was less likely to be bumped or shoved. Things were looking up, she thought. If she could only have a trip to town every now and then, the world wasn't such a bad place after all, and Sjur Gabriel was a good and hard-working husband, even if he did beat her occasionally, and the good thing about that was that he didn't harbour a grudge. If he'd been angry one night and knocked her about, the next morning it was as if it had never been. And it was a blessing as well that he never talked to her in the daytime, whether he was in a good mood or not. Sjur Gabriel was such a sober and serious man. – If only he'd take a drink now and then, like so many others, – but that was just the way God had made him.

'Aye, aye, God 'ave mercy on us all.'

As she was thinking this, she had reached her destination. She went into the booth, asked for a half-pint of cheap liquor, handed over her last coins and drank the whole lot down in one gulp in the corridor outside. Then she hitched up her skirts, hid the bottle and set off back the same way she had come.

She staggered a little as she walked. Everything she could

see was swimming in a purplish-red fog. She was laughing and talking, with her hands folded under her apron. And the whole time she was thinking that when Sjur Gabriel got back to the boat he mustn't notice that she'd been drinking.

She reached Torvegaarden and turned down it. When she had got halfway along, she stood still for a moment and ran her hands over her headscarf and clothes to make sure everything was in place. Then she walked on, filled with an urge to sing, which she only half stifled. 'And when he got to Norway, he bought himself a dog, he bought himself a dog, he bought himself a dog,' she sang under her breath. It was the next part of the song that Guri had been singing. Suddenly she stopped. Instinctively she took a step back and flattened herself against the wall on the dark side. Yes, there was no doubt about it. It was Sjur Gabriel's tall, broad-shouldered figure with the stooping back and the beard projecting from under his sou'wester she had seen entering the pub where the porter had wanted to dance with her. It was her he was looking for, she knew that quite clearly despite her befuddlement. All her limbs started to shake as she set off quickly past the pub, not daring to look into it, reached the end of the street, turned the corner and was in the Triangle half a minute later. All she could think about was that she had to be sitting in the boat when Sjur Gabriel arrived, in her normal place at the oars with her boat jacket on, waiting for him.

'Where've you bin, Ma?' asked Jens, as she stepped down into the boat and put on her boat jacket.

She did not answer at once.

'Where's your da?' she said shortly afterwards with a tongue that refused to obey her. 'I though' we were off now.'

'We've been ready long since,' said Jens. 'Da' wen' off to

look for you.'

'We'll 'ave to wait till 'ee comes then,' she answered in a thick, stifled voice, and sat down between the two oars she normally rowed.

She sat hunched over with her elbows on her knees and her cheeks in her hands, and moved restlessly, as if small shivers were passing through her. Her jaws moved, and she half-mumbled the song about Rubakken. Then followed a hoarse, clucking laugh and after that a sniffling, as if she was about to cry.

Jens's face took on the look of an old man as he sat there.

After ten minutes had passed Sjur Gabriel arrived. He stepped straight into the boat without saying a word, untied the moorings and sat down to row.

Oline waited until they had passed the many vessels which lay in the inner harbour. Then she pushed out her oars and started to row. But they wouldn't work properly. She couldn't row at all, just sat there chattering and slurring 'Dunno wos' wrong wi' them oars.'

Once they had passed the fortress flagpole, Sjur Gabriel shipped his oars and stood up. Then he grabbed Oline by the scruff of the neck and took her oars from her, one after the other. After that he lifted her up and threw her into the stern of the boat, where he punched her with his big, clenched fists for as long as he had the breath, without heeding where the blows fell.

Jens, who was sitting in the bows, stood up and watched wide-eyed, wailing at the same time: 'Oh, don', Da', oh don', Da'.'

Oline received the blows without making a sound, and then lay there like a lifeless lump the whole way home, half on her stomach and with her face turned up against the side of the boat.

Jens sat down in his mother's place and rowed. He was terrified that his father might have killed his mother, but he didn't even dare to stand up and look at her for fear of provoking his father, who was sitting and rowing slowly and rhythmically with frowning brows, which covered his eyes like a thundercloud, staring far out to sea, as he every now and then projected large clumps of brown spittle out over the gunwales.

4

When they tied up at at the Hellemyr boathouse in the clear moonlight, Sjur Gabriel jumped ashore, reached out for the oars and fishing nets which Jens passed to him, and carried them up into the boathouse. Then he came back for the foodbox and his oilskins, and curtly ordered Jens to get off the boat.

Jens looked at his mother, and then sent his father a beseeching glance, as he involuntarily cocked his head on one side.

'Ged ou', I said,' shouted Sjur Gabriel, shaking his fist at him.

Jens climbed ashore and silently obeyed his father's brusque gesture to help pull the boat up onto the wooden struts. Then Sjur Gabriel locked the boathouse door, made the boat fast and locked the chain with a padlock.

After that he set off up the rough slopes between the large mossy humps of stone and the sparsely tufted patches of grass, with the foodbox in his hand and his oilskins over his arm. Jens followed a little behind, full of an oppressive worry for his mother. She hadn't stirred at all – and she had fallen so remarkably heavily.

Tears ran ceaselessly down his face, which was sweaty from rowing. Every now and then he rubbed his cheeks and wiped his nose with his fingers.

Finally they reached the shack in which they lived. It consisted of a kitchen with a black hearth and a living room with a beamed ceiling and one single window at waist height with tiny panes, some of which were broken and replaced with glued-on rags. In the kitchen there was a small porthole, which could be opened in good weather to give a weak light. In bad weather, when the wind and the rain blew against it, it was completely dark.

Sjur Gabriel lifted the wooden latch and turned round to look for Jens, who was following reluctantly ten or twelve paces behind.

'Ge' yersel' over 'ere!' he shouted angrily.

Jens took longer steps.

'Ma'll freeze to death,' he said, as he came nearer.

''Old yer tongue, lad!' He was seized by the shoulder and thrust in through the doorway.

Like someone used to finding his way in the dark, Sjur Gabriel stepped over the high threshold and into the living room, then went over to the long, narrow table, which had a bench along one wall. He sat down, found a spoon, pulled a small wooden bowl and a wooden trug towards himself and began to eat.

'Come 'ere an' eat!'

Jens sat down beside him, and he also got hold of a spoon and a wooden bowl with some sour milk in it. He reached over to the same trug as his father, dipped his spoon into the milk and swallowed the food with a gulping sound in his throat. The cold porridge, which was so thick and stiff that it was hard to cut through it with the spoon, was difficult to get down this evening. After swallowing a few mouthfuls, he licked the spoon clean, wiped it under his arm and put it back in the table drawer. Then he sat still whilst his father slurped the porridge and milk, and the steady breathing of his sleeping sisters filled the air around him.

A gleam of moonlight came through the window panes. He could make out the outline of his oldest sister's black hair with the red ribbons, down by the stove where she made up a bed on the floor every evening for herself and the youngest.

When Sjur Gabriel had had enough, he cleaned his spoon in the same way as Jens, stood up with a burp which resounded through the room, and began to get undressed.

A moment later he was sitting on the bed, kicking off his shoes.

'Ge' to bed, lad,' he said to Jens, as he heaved his legs up into bed and pulled the woollen blanket over himself.

Jens thought of his mother's empty place behind Father in the bed, and went quietly out to the kitchen, feeling with his hands until he got hold of a ladder which was propped against the edge of an open trapdoor to the attic. He started to climb up it, then stopped and considered.

No, the best thing would be to pretend he was going to bed. Then when he was sure that Father had fallen asleep, he would creep down again in his socks and go and fetch his mother. Then at least she could sit down on the hearth or lie down on the kitchen floor, if she wasn't dead or crippled at least. He hoped she wouldn't wake up and try to get up and fall headfirst into the sea. Oh, it was so shameful and miserable. Just think if the folk from Søndrehellen came by and saw her in the morning yet again. No, he absolutely had to get her into the house.

He reached the top rung of the ladder, knelt down on the edge of the opening and crept into the little attic space, which was so low that it was only in the middle he could stand up. Through a slightly open vent, a faint gleam fell across the floor, where two boys aged seven and nine lay

41

asleep on a layer of straw, with their heads under the rafters and a few woollen blankets over them.

Jens tramped loudly across the floor, undid and dropped his shoes as noisily as he could, pulled off his jacket and stretched out on the straw beside his brothers.

He had hardly lain down before he could hear his father's thunderous snoring from below. At once he was up again, dressed quietly, picked up his shoes and crept cautiously back down the ladder. He hurried over to the door, lifted the latch, listened to make sure that it really was Father's snoring that had reached him, and then he squeezed through the opening as carefully and silently as a thief. Once he was outside he put on his shoes and set off at a run over the flat boggy meadows which lay around the house and outbuildings, and down the slope towards the sea.

It was so far that under normal circumstances it would take over fifteen minutes to get down and almost half an hour to walk back up. But Jens was running so fast that after seven minutes he was standing beside the boat, leaning over his mother, who was still lying in the same position.

'Ma', you gotta wake up now,' he said, shaking her. When she gave no sign of life, he repeated his words more loudly and tugged her arm as hard as he could.

She uttered a hoarse groan and hunched her shoulders as if she wanted to be left in peace.

'Ma', you gotta get up an' come 'ome,' he repeated a couple of times in a voice which was both fearful and insistent.

She tried to raise herself up, but tumbled backwards, turning her head as she did so, so that her face was visible. Then she hastily shielded her eyes with her arm and whimpered pitifully: 'You mun't 'it me any more, Sjur

Gabriel, spare me jus' this once in t'name of Our Lord an' 'is son, Sjur Gabriel.'

'Ma, can ye' no' 'ear i's jus' me,' Jens burst out, and started crying loudly at the same moment.

Oline grabbed hold of the gunwale with one hand and pushed from behind with the other so that she got into a sitting position.

'Well, if it in't our li'l Jens,' she exclaimed in relief, looking around. 'Wha' you bellowin' for?'

Jens just cried more and more loudly.

'Wha's wrong wi' you, lad?' She got to her feet, but staggered sideways so that she had to lean down and support herself on the gunwale a couple of times before she could stand properly. Her teeth were chattering with the cold.

'Where's yer da' got to?' she asked, as she got hold of Jens's shoulder and climbed out of the boat.

'Gone 'ome,' Jens sobbed.

'You be'er go too,' she said anxiously. 'Be off now, or you'll get a beatin'.'

'Da's sleepin' at 'ome.'

'Is'ee?' she asked in disbelief. 'You're lyin'. I'll jus' sit 'ere a while, an' come up later.' She lifted up her skirt from behind and pulled it over her head and shoulders, then settled herself down with her back against the boathouse door.

Then Jens explained how matters stood, and begged her to come straight away.

'My li'l Jens,' she mumbled, her voice catching in her throat, and slowly shook her head. 'So you wanted t' look after yer mis'rable ma'. May God an' 'is son bless you.'

She got up, let her skirt fall down again and set off up the same slopes where Jens and his father had walked an hour or so earlier. To begin with she climbed slowly and unsteadily, bent over as though she had a pain in her chest and couldn't straighten up. Gradually she regained more control of her movements, and finally she was moving quickly and sure-footedly, whilst keeping her body as stiff as a rod. And the whole time she was making a low, moaning noise, like someone in pain who cannot stop themselves.

'Our Jens, our Jens,' she said, after they had climbed up the slopes and were walking along the squelching path through the boggy fields, which gave way under their feet. 'When ye'r a grown man you'll be ashamed of yer ma', so yer'd be'er pray to God and 'is son so 'ee 'as mercy an' teks me afore then.' She wagged her head slowly from side to side as she spoke. 'Yer ma' 'asn' allus been such a wretch of an 'oman,' she went on straight after, 'bu' i's a cruel an' mean world, so i' is; us poor sinners 'as an 'ard time of it.'

''F only Ma' could be'ave when ye'r in town,' said Jens in a pitiful tone.

''S the devil's own problem,' she answered without stopping or turning round.

'Can ye no' tell 'im t'go t'ell, Ma?'

'Many's the time I 'ave done, an' 'ee does it an' all, but then 'ee jus' comes back, 'ee comes back, God 'elp us.' The last words were accompanied by a deep, groaning sigh.

'Bu' ye knows 'ow mad our da' gets,' Jens burst out reproachfully.

'I's jus' so 'eavy inside o' me,' Oline started again, 'so awful 'eavy.' Jens could hear from her voice that she was crying. 'I dunno 'ow it 'appens, but i's as if I'm breakin' in two wi' sorrow an' misery from morn to nigh' an' from nigh' to morn.' She blew her nose, and her voice become more and more tearful. 'Everythin' seems to be weighin' me down, it's all so nasty an''orrid, wha'ever I turn me 'and to. I jus' wish I'd never been sent into this world, an' then when I 'as a li'l drink, i' all becomes so ligh' an' clear an' fine an' grand, the likes of which you never saw. – Then it's all one wi' the Englishman an' the 'ole caboodle.'

'The Englishman, who's 'ee?' asked Jens.

''Ee's the one I wer engaged to when I wer a lass of seventeen, 'ee wanted to marry me an' tek me wiv 'im to Paradise, but then 'ee went an' got drownded, the ninny.'

'Then 'ee were trickin' yer, 'cos Paradise aint 'ere on earth. I's some place off in 'eaven where Adam and Eve was born.'

'Well I dunno, but 'ee said we was goin' to Paradise, an' 'ee 'ad give me money so's I c'd get some nice clothes to tek wi' me!'

They had now reached the hut. Jens hurried to get there before his mother and opened the door cautiously.

'I's not a good idea for 'im to 'ear us,' he whispered. 'Best tek yer shoes off, Ma.'

He leant against the wall and pulled off his shoes. Oline followed his example, and they tiptoed quietly in.

'Are you goin' to get into bed, Ma?'

'I think I'll try. Your da' is an 'eavy sleeper.'

'Mind ou', mind ou',' whispered Jens anxiously, as the door made a creaking sound when Oline opened it.

'I'll close t'door.' He stood in the doorway after Oline had gone in. 'I wanna see tha' i's all all righ'.'

He could make out her silhouette as she crossed over to the bench and unfastened her clothes. Straight after there was a dark shape creeping up into the bed from down at the foot end, and slowly stretching out against the wall. He stood there for a moment listening to the quiet rustling of the straw from the bed, which soon went quiet. His father slept on obliviously, and his mother lay as still as a mouse. Then he shut the door, crept up the attic ladder and lay down on his bed. A moment later he was sleeping like a stone.

5

Sjur Gabriel was at his wits' end. Many a time he had sworn that he would never again take Oline with him on trips to town, but just as often he had had to admit that it was an even worse idea to leave her at home.

For Oline managed to get away anyway.

When she felt the urge to drink, it was impossible to keep her under control. As soon as he had left she would hail a passing boat and offer to row, or to pay with a pail of milk or something else, if they would take her with them. In town she would sell the fish she had caught in secret the night before, and drink her fill with the money.

Often it happened that she stayed in a public bar or wandered around the local area and along Strandgaden for such a long time that it was too late to find a boat returning home. So she had to walk overland, setting off across the stony meadows and the barren rocks – not to mention the fact that it was almost twice as far as the boat trip.

Then she came tottering back to Hellemyr late at night or early in the morning, most often to be beaten by her husband, who was out of bed at sunrise – unless, as occasionally happened, the struggle of the journey had sobered her up or she had lain down in a mountain cleft and slept off the intoxication, so that she could set about her work straight away. Then he made do with spitting and muttering and cursing her at a distance.

At times she got drunk without having been in town. That was when she had taken the chance to travel up the fjord to Salhus with some boat or other which was headed north. In Salhus there was a general store which served beer and spirits. But it was most often difficult to get herself home again from there, so it was not often she resorted to that solution.

In the summer months, when Sjur Gabriel did not go out to fish because he had to be on high alert in order to get their scanty hay harvested, Oline most often had to manage without spirits. Now and then she did get the chance to drink a drop over with Kari Træet, an ancient crone who was pensioned off at the neighbouring farm, but it was extremely difficult to get the chance to steal away to visit, and in any case she was given so little that it had no effect on her. She didn't dare sneak off to town or over to Salhus whilst Sjur Gabriel was on the farm.

But when autumn came and her husband began to go out fishing again, she made up for it and ran off from her home the first chance she got.

If she came back by sea, she was always absolutely dead drunk. Tales were told that on the journey home in strangers' boats she would be bubbling over with good spirits, singing and humming and rattling on so that they had difficulty restraining her. Then when they dropped her off at the Hellemyr boathouse, she would walk off up the hilly path staggering and babbling, laughing and stumbling. She took her time, and sat down often on the stones along the edge of the path. If people came past she would talk to them and walk along with them, regardless of whether they were going in her direction or the opposite one, whilst she rambled on at random, without getting any answer.

Yet the moment she spotted Sjur Gabriel she clammed up instantly. However blind drunk she was, she never forgot her fear of her husband.

Sometimes it happened that she had imbibed so much in town that she fell asleep on the way home and had to be hoisted up on to the boathouse floor, where she lay until Sjur Gabriel or one of the children found her.

Her movements were unpredictable, however. At times she could keep herself in check for six or seven weeks at a time, even during the times when her husband was out regularly. But then suddenly the craze came over her and lasted for weeks, so that she ran off as often as she could manage and drank herself silly, worse than before.

Eventually Sjur Gabriel made his mind up that it was best to take her with him when he went fishing and then into town, when he calculated that she was due to have one of her fits. Then at least they could save what she paid in return for a lift, because no-one could tell him that people were so simple as to take her along for free. When she came along with him there was a chance that he could keep an eye on her after all, although, as he said, she was 'slipp'ry as an eel in 'is fingers'. And then there was also the fact that she was a good help with both rowing and fishing, so long as she was sober.

This was in late autumn. Then winter arrived with darkness and snowstorms, blizzards and all sorts of horrors. It passed with wearisome, back-breaking toil, and the days began to lengthen again.

6

One day in the middle of April Sjur Gabriel was in Strusshamn* with the confirmation boat. Ingeborg, the oldest child, was preparing for confirmation, and once a fortnight she had a class with the parish vicar. Three of the farmers in the local district took turns to row the children there and back in Magne Søndremyren's longboat. He was the wealthiest of the parents; he lent them his boat in return for being excused the rowing.

In recent days Sjur Gabriel had felt his heart grow lighter. It was now ten weeks since Oline had last touched spirits. Such a thing had not happened for four years. Work had gone so easily and smoothly during this time, both at home and elsewhere. Everything had been done at the right time, and he had got further with the spring sowing than the people at Træet.

On the way home he was wondering how much of the potato patch Oline and the boys had managed to get sown. That morning when he had left they had made a good start, and if they had worked hard it would have made a real difference. Oline was such an incredibly fast and efficient worker, despite the fact that she was now pregnant again. Yes, poor thing, she really was a steadfast toiler. If she could only carry on as she had been these past months, he could not have wished for a better wife.

When Sjur Gabriel and Ingeborg came back from Strusshamn in late afternoon and were getting close to home, they could see Jens and Little-Adna standing by the well outside the house, stirring with long sticks. Now and then they jumped in the air and emitted eager shouts of joy or surprise.

'P'raps they're fishin' for toads again!' exclaimed Ingeborg.

'Satan's spawn!' muttered their father, lengthening his stride. It couldn't be that Oline had run off again. He went white in the face, clenched his fist and waved it threateningly in the air. If Oline was at home, how come they were out there muddying up the water instead of working on the potato patch. But he would give them a good hiding, those damned troublemakers.

He started running along the swampy path, making the water splash up around him.

Ingeborg was frightened. Without thinking she ran too, close behind her father, and tried to warn Jens and her sister by swinging the hymn book and catechism, which she was carrying wrapped in a kerchief. She did not dare to shout.

But Jens and Adna were completely absorbed in urging a large toad out of its hiding-place at the edge of the well. Suddenly Jens saw reflected in the well a blue-painted wooden box, a swinging arm and immediately after it his father's furious face; in the same second he dropped his stick and hurtled, barefoot as he was, at full speed past the house, across the meadow, over a rocky slope, straight through the half-finished potato patch, kept going, threw himself over the fence to the neighbour's fallow field and did not stop until he reached a shed filled with stacks of peat. He flew in there, dropped to his hands and knees and peered out.

Little-Adna, who had no idea of the reason for Jens's sudden move, turned her little pointed head with its yellow-brown hair gathered into a knot in her neck, to see what he was doing. At that instant she felt such a violent blow from behind on her ear that she flew to one side like a ball, tumbled in a heap and banged her head on a stone. For a moment she lay there without moving. Then she flailed about with her arms and legs and got up onto her knees. She looked around timidly and put her hand to her head, which was burning and hammering, while she felt something warm running down over her nose. Straight after that she discovered the blood on her bodice, her sleeves, her hands, and on the front of her soaking wet skirt. Then she began to wail loudly and piercingly, without pausing. At a distance you would have thought they were slaughtering pigs one after the other in an endless procession.

Sjur Gabriel just continued on his way without taking any notice of Adna. The older boy Nils was sitting on the stone slab in front of the door carving a willow flute; he kicked him out of the way and with an oath stepped over Magne, the youngest, who was lying on his back in the kitchen playing with a kitten.

When he heard the child's piercing screams he half turned and glanced outside. When he saw the blood streaming down over her, an uneasy expression crossed his face, and he looked uncertain. He scratched behind his ear and turned his head away. Then his glance fell on Oline's bodice and work skirt, which were hanging up beside the hearth on a wooden hook.

'Aye, I might'a known,' he said under his breath, nodding dejectedly.

Then he pitched forwards over the kitchen table, leaning on his elbows, and buried his head in his hands. He uttered a few deep, groaning sighs and muttered a few unintelligible words.

Shortly afterwards the screams from outside ceased, and all was quiet. Like someone afraid of being discovered, he put his face around the edge of the open kitchen door and peered out. Ingeborg was on her knees with her skirt tucked up and a bowl of water in front of her, washing the blood off Little-Adna, who was standing with her arms stretched out stiffly in front of her, whilst her narrow, thin shoulders shook with cramp-like spasms. Ingeborg was pale and her face was puckered as if she was on the point of crying. He heard her talking to her sister in a sympathetic and reassuring voice. Their brothers were watching silently.

'We'd best go in and find summat to wrap round your 'ead,' said Ingeborg, getting up and taking her sister's hand to lead her in.

'No, no,' screamed Little-Adna. 'I don' wanna. Our Da'll 'it me!' She tried to pull away with an expression of utter terror.

Ingeborg bent swiftly down, put an arm around her legs and lifted her up, carrying her towards the cottage door, as she called to Nils to bring the bundle of books.

Little-Adna clung to her sister's neck and turned her head away, wailing: 'Our Da'll 'it me – our Da'll 'it me.'

'No, ee'll not 'it you, sit still now and you'll see, ee' ain't seen you bin 'urt. Wha' were you doin' in the well? You know 'ee can't stand it. Tha's why 'ee were cross.'

Sjur Gabriel went into the living room without closing the door behind him.

Little-Adna peeped after him as Ingeborg put her down on the kitchen floor, and seemed to be reassured when she saw he'd turned his back and was slowly pulling off his homespun jacket.

'Stand 'ere a minute,' said Ingeborg, and searched round the kitchen to find something to bandage the wound.

''Ere's a cloth,' called Sjur Gabriel, taking a cotton kerchief with yellow flowers on it out of a chest with iron hinges, which he had pulled out from under the bed and opened with a key to the padlock. He held out the kerchief without looking, keeping his back turned to the kitchen door.

'Isn' i' too good for tha'?' asked Ingeborg doubtfully, taking the kerchief hesitantly. She knew how much Father valued that pretty cloth.

'Jus' look after i',' said Sjur Gabriel resignedly. 'You be'er wet it a bi' first,' he went on, following her into the kitchen.

Little-Adna grabbed hold of Ingeborg's skirt and stared fearfully at her father.

'Where'd she get 'urt?' he asked, bending over the child.

'There,' answered Ingeborg, pointing at a wound on her forehead, from where the blood was still seeping gently.

'It weren' 'er fault,' he said mildly, stroking her hair. 'Poor li'l Li'l- Adna, it were our Jens I were after.'

Ingeborg folded over the kerchief, dipped it in water and tied it round her sister's head.

'Now it'll soon be be'er, Li'l-Adna,' said her father, who had crouched down beside her and was gently stroking her little wet hand.

'I think you best go to bed, Li'l-Adna. – You c'n sleep in yer Da's bed now.' He spoke in a caressing tone. 'I'll gi' ye a bi' o' that *lefse* we go' from t' vicar's wife.'* He took hold of her under the arms and lifted her up.

'Tek this wet skirt off 'er, Ingebor',' he went on, holding her up in front of him. Then he carried her over to the bed and spread the blanket over her, putting a *lefse* with syrup on it in her hand.

Nils and Magne had come into the living room. They looked longingly at the food box with *lefse* in, which Sjur Gabriel had been carrying when he came in.

'Is it long since yer ma left?' asked Sjur Gabriel, sitting on the bench and changing his trousers.

'Dunno,' they both answered at once.

'Was she 'ome when you 'ad dinner?'

'Aye. She gev us some tea an' all.'

Sjur Gabriel got up and looked over at the bed. Little-Adna had fallen asleep with the *lefse* in her hand and her mouth full of food.

'Look 'ere,' he said, and took the rest from her. 'You two c'n share this bi.'

Ingeborg was busy getting the bedding ready on the floor over by the stove.

'I think the lads c'n move up t't'loft any time,' he said, as he hung up his Sunday clothes over by the stove. 'I's warmed up a treat.'

'We'd best sort out some 'ay come mornin' then,' answered Ingeborg.

7

Oline was expecting to give birth any day.

For the last couple of months she had been sober again. But there were good reasons for that, thought Sjur Gabriel. Partly it was the time of year when he himself was at home the whole time, and partly Oline no doubt felt so heavy and unwell that her normal inventiveness had deserted her. In addition to that, Sjur Gabriel had asked the vicar to admonish her. He had made it clear to her that in her present condition she had extra reason not to transgress. If she did not abstain from her dissolute behaviour, she must be prepared for Our Lord in his wrath to bring her to bed of a crippled child. Such things had been seen before.

His words had scared Oline. She was often in tears during this time, and was constantly haunted by thoughts of death. Sometimes she would sit for ages at a time hunched over by the hearth, rocking her head and staring stiffly in front of her. Apart from that she attended to her household tasks as usual. Food was always ready at the right time, and she worked in the fields as well as she could manage right to the end. She shuffled slowly along, had difficulty in bending down, frequently groaned out loud and hardly ever spoke.

For the last week or so Sjur Gabriel had said it was best she stayed in the house. The corn and the hay were safely gathered in, and the rest of what needed doing he and the kids could manage on their own. She'd better sort out some baby clothes and bedding for the cradle too, so they had something to wrap the child in when it arrived.

Oline took a willow basket and went up to the loft. There she knelt down in front of a chest and pulled out the few little shirts and swaddling clothes she had kept, put them in the basket, added a few cloths and lengths of woollen material on top and carried it all down to the living room, where she sat down to cut, patch and sew, with tears dripping the whole time from the tip of her nose down onto her work. She carried on with this for a few days, then she washed the small garments, as well as what she herself would need for the birth, dried it in the fresh air and smoothed it on a roller with a smoothing board.* Sjur Gabriel carried the cradle down from the loft and put fresh straw in it. Oline made a pillow, which she filled with cut-up rags. Over the straw she spread the undamaged part of a threadbare blanket, and on top of that a piece of cotton drill; then she covered the whole thing with a duvet which she had sewn from an old underskirt and a piece of blue-striped cotton material lined with hemp.

Sjur Gabriel was pleased with this collection, which he examined in secret when Oline was not in the room. If everything had been newly bought and of first-class quality his admiration and satisfaction could not have been greater.

How neat and nimble-fingered Oline was! No-one could match her in that respect. He had always been quite sure of that.

Then one night towards the end of September Oline awoke with back pains and knew that her time had come. She sat up, crept carefully out of bed, threw a skirt around herself and sat down over on the bench, where she moaned quietly, holding her back with both hands. It was pitch black in the room, and Sjur Gabriel's loud snoring completely drowned out her groans. She sat there thinking that she would have to wake him up, but couldn't bring herself to do it. So instead she stood up and walked up and down the floor, wailing and bent double, still holding her back. Then she felt such a violent pang that she sank down onto her hands and knees, where she stayed. When it wore off a little she crawled over to the bed, got hold of it and pulled herself with difficulty to her feet.

'Sjur Gabriel,' she gasped, pulling at his shirt up by his shoulder. 'I reckon it's startin'.'

He was sleeping like a stone.

'Sjur Gabriel,' she repeated more loudly. 'You 'ave to go fetch Lars's Adna.'

He woke up with a hiccupping sound.

'Wha's a ma'er?' he said drowsily. 'You out'a bed?' He sat up bewildered as he realised she was not in bed beside him.

'I'm startin' labour,' she groaned. 'You mus' 'urry.'

She staggered back to the bench and sat down in the same position as before, whilst she wailed louder and louder, and large cold drops of sweat ran down her forehead.

Without saying a word, Sjur Gabriel swung his legs out of bed, grabbed his trousers which were hanging on the bedpost and pulled them on. Then he fumbled with his hands for his shoes on the floor.

'Sh'd I p'raps ligh' a lamp for you?' he asked, when he had buttoned his jacket and was feeling for his cap hanging on the wall.

'No need – oh God the Father and God the S - on, 'ave mercy on me! – Oh God the Father and God the S - on, 'elp us in our 'our of need – ow – ow – ow. – Wha' in t' name of Jesus shall I do? – Aah! – Aah! – Aah!'

Sjur Gabriel could hear her as he ran across the boggy field and turned right, where he joined the track which led from the sea past the Hellemyr land and onwards up to the nearby farms. There was a strong wind from the south with drenching rain blowing straight into his face, and the night was black. But Sjur Gabriel dashed along the bumpy track which wound in and out through the huge heaps of moss-covered stones as sure-footed and easily as if it had been broad daylight.

After about ten minutes he could feel that he was treading on softer ground. 'Mus' be tha' Lars Træet's potato patch,' he thought, and veered a little to the left until he could feel firmer ground beneath his feet.

So he must be getting near the house. Yes, sure enough, he could make out the outline of the long low building with the main door in the middle.

In one bound he was up the two stone slabs which lay one on top of the other to make front steps, and the next second he was hammering with clenched fist on the iron-hinged door, which was divided in the middle.

A furious barking answered him.

He knocked again, and the dog barked as if it had been paid to.

'Skipper! Skipper! Stop yer infernal noise, ye pest! – Come 'ere. Come 'ere!'

Sjur Gabriel recognised Lars Træet's voice.

The dog's barks subsided into a growl, and straight after the top half of the door opened.

'Who's tha'?' demanded a brusque voice.

''Ellemyr folk,' answered Sjur Gabriel breathlessly, as he took off his cap and dashed the water off it.

'Anyone'd think ye were tryin' t'smash t'door down,' said the voice crossly. 'Wha' a dreadful racket in t'middle of t'nigh'.'

'We need your Adna righ' now,' said Sjur Gabriel.

'Our Adna's not 'ome.'

Sjur Gabriel felt as if he was choking. 'Where's she gone?' he asked.

'O'er on Askøy.'

'Wha' time'd they come for 'er?'

'Las' nigh'.'

'Mebbee she'll be back soon?'

'Mebbee. No' easy t'say.'

'Hm, hm,' muttered Sjur Gabriel, wringing his cap between his hands. 'Our Oline were righ' poorly when I se' off. I reckon she were well in labour a'ready.'

'Could well be,' replied the other indifferently. 'Our Adna won' be back afore dayligh', any case,' he added after a while.

Sjur Gabriel asked what time it was.

'Jus' struck twelve,' was the answer.

So it was five hours until it would be daylight, thought Sjur Gabriel. He stood there with his head bowed. The rain pelted against the side of his head and trickled from his hair down over his face. Without thinking he put on his cap and heaved a deep sigh.

'I dunno wha's ter do,' he muttered, as if to himself.

'The's allus ol' Kari, our Adna's mother,' said Lars.

'S'pose there is,' he answered, unsure and hesitant.

'She's nearly as good, I reckon. Our Adna learnt i' all from 'er, leastways.'

'F only she'll come along,' said Sjur Gabriel. 'I'm afeard - - 's awful weather an' all.'

'Depends wha' kind a' mood she's in.'

'Mebbee you c'd ask 'er?'

'I think you best go an' ask yersel',' said Lars, and opened the bottom half-door.

Sjur Gabriel went inside. The dog started up barking again, and Lars silenced it again.

Sjur Gabriel felt his way forward a few steps and got hold of a ladder which he started climbing.

"Er door's jus' up there on t'left,' said Lars after him, as he went back to his bed, taking the dog with him.

A moment later Sjur Gabriel was standing in a small attic room with a sloping roof, in which he could just make out the outline of a window opposite.

'Oo's tha' comin' in?' came a voice from the corner of the room.

Sjur Gabriel didn't know why it should be, but old Kari's voice always reminded him of a weasel which had once hissed at him, baring its teeth.

He explained who he was and why he was there, trying to make his voice soft and persuasive. He knew that Kari would not be well disposed towards him. He had never concealed his feelings whenever he had seen her anywhere near Oline. Once he had even cursed her as an old boozer and threatened to give her a good hiding, when he'd seen her sneaking around Hellemyr not so long ago.

'Huh,' said Kari with a scornful snarl. – 'So now Sjur Gabriel needs our ol' Kari, does 'ee, the ol' boozer - - . Well, well, you never know 'ow things'll turn ou'.'

'True enough,' answered Sjur Gabriel.

'Well, well, pride goes afore a fall, so it do. Aint tha' the truth.' These words were followed by a rattling, almost inaudible laugh.

'When i's summat like this – birthin' pains. She were screamin' really bad, our Oline. – We're all jus' people – .' Sjur Gabriel was stammering in half sentences and wringing his wet cap.

'You didna think o' tha' when you promised a poor ol' worn-out woman a good 'idin', did yer? Nuffin' like tha'. – A fine welcome tha' was.'

'You 'ave ter come, Kari,' pleaded Sjur Gabriel. 'Wha's goin' to 'appen to our Oline? – It'll be the death of 'er, – an' the kid. – Wha'm I ter do when we need 'elp?' He shuffled to and fro, talking in a broken voice.

'Aye, need meks folks 'umble,' said Kari, with another unpleasant laugh.

'I'll pay,' Sjur Gabriel went on. 'As much as you wan'.'

'Best we sort that ou' now. 'Ow much you offerin'?'

''Alf a speciedaler,' said Sjur Gabriel after a moment's hesitation.

'Aye, you reckon you'll ge' off wi' such a scrapin', bu' we'll 'ave none o' tha', laddy.'

'An 'ole one then!' he almost screamed.

'An 'ole,' she repeated, savouring the words as if she had something tasty in her mouth. 'I'll do it for an 'ole. – Ee, Go' bless us poor sinners, comin' 'ere an' draggin' an ol' critter from 'er bed in't pitch dark!'

Sjur Gabriel could hear from the sounds coming from the corner that she had sat up in bed and was getting dressed, talking to herself all the time in her dry scraping voice. It sounded as if she was asking questions and answering them, and every now and then she uttered a: 'Heh, heh, heh'.

Sjur Gabriel didn't know whether she was laughing or hissing.

'Wha' the de'il!' she exclaimed suddenly, rummaging around in her bed so that the straw creaked. 'Them bed bugs musta' eaten me garters. You'll 'ave ter ligh' this bi' o' candle – see 'ere, come over an' I'll pu' i' in yer 'and.'

Sjur Gabriel went closer, reached out his hand and got hold of a stub of candle.

'Open't stove door – there, see – righ' in front o' yer. Yer'll fin' twigs in't 'earth.'

Sjur Gabriel moved over and instinctively put his hand on what he was looking for straight away. He opened the oven door, stirred the peat blocks which were glowing on the underside, blew on them, thrust a twig in and lit the candle with it. Then he went over and handed it to Kari.

She pushed aside a wooden bowl with the remains of some porridge and a pewter beaker, which were standing on the table by the bed, dripped a little wax onto it to fix the candle on when she put it down, and set about searching all around in her bed again for the garters. Sjur Gabriel followed her movements, his eyes gleaming with impatience.

'Never seen the like! 'S like watchin' Satan 'isself!' he muttered.

She looked altogether like a witch, sitting there with her wizened face, its countless wrinkles encrusted with dirt. The loose jowls of her sagging cheeks hung down below her chin, and the outermost tip of her red, dripping nose looked as if it was glued on. Her eyes were almost hidden by her swollen eyelids and the grey eyebrows, which stuck out in two stiff clumps either side of her nose. Her head and ears were wrapped in a black woollen cloth which was wound round her neck and knotted on the crown of her head. The grey worsted shirt hung down baggily over her shrunken breasts, her green bodice was unhooked, and her skirts were bunched up around her hips. Her legs were covered by long socks which were pulled up over her knees, and her feet were stuck into coarse woollen slippers. She was sitting hunched over, because there was not enough room to sit upright.

Finally she found her garters under a couple of carding combs full of tufts of wool which were lying on the table.

She knotted them on, raised herself cautiously from the bed and let her skirts fall down over her legs.

She then stuck her feet into shoes, hooked her bodice together, pulled a large shawl over her head with some difficulty, shuffled on a homespun jacket and took an apron out of a chest, the only piece of furniture in the room apart from the bed, the table and a wooden stool.

And the whole time she was moving her large, sunken mouth and cackling on and off like a magpie before a storm.

'Nasty weather,' she said, glancing at the window against which the rain was lashing.

'You mus' come now, Kari,' said Sjur Gabriel.

She grabbed a skirt which was hanging on the wall, threw it round her head and shoulders and fastened it in front with a safety pin.

'An' you'll gi' me the daler when the birth is done,' she said, squinting over at Sjur Gabriel.

'You c'n be sure o' tha",' he answered, going towards the door.

Kari wasn't worried that he'd cheat her of it anyway. She knew that she was reputed to be a witch who could put the evil eye on animals or people if she wanted to.

'I'm comin' – go on – I'll jus' snuff the ligh' ou".'

Sjur Gabriel did as she said and went backwards down the ladder.

Kari went over to the bed, lifted the pillow and pulled out a bottle, took the cork out and raised it to her lips. Then she thrust it into her bodice under her jacket, blew out the candle and followed Sjur Gabriel.

When they got down the dog began barking again from

the living room. Kari muttered a curse on it, opened the door and went out into the rain and the darkness together with Sjur Gabriel.

He walked first and she followed a couple of paces behind. Neither of them uttered a word on the way.

8

As they got close to the Hellemyr shack they could hear Oline's ear-splitting screams. Through the window Sjur Gabriel could see that the lamp was lit inside. He increased his pace, Kari hobbling after as fast as she could, and a moment later they were in the living room.

Oline was kneeling in front of the bench with her back to the incomers. Her arms were flailing and she was banging her head on the wall. Beside her stood Ingeborg, her arm round her back.

Kari took off her head covering and told Sjur Gabriel to help her lift Oline up off the floor. Then she gestured to him to sit down on the bench and place Oline on his lap. With considerable effort she got Oline into the position she wanted. Sjur Gabriel braced himself against the wall; it took all his strength to hold on to her. She was driven wild by the pain, bit herself on the arm, twisted herself sideways, threw herself backwards and yanked at Sjur Gabriel's hair, as she uttered long-drawn-out howls of misery.

Kari nodded with her witch's nose and muttered that it would not be long now. She knelt down in front of Oline, pushed up her skirts and investigated whether the baby was in the right position. Then she asked Ingeborg for something to place the baby on.

Ingeborg, whose face was swollen with crying, pulled the basket of baby clothes across to her. Kari rummaged in it and found a piece of flannel which she laid across her lap. Then she demanded scissors, some melted tallow and two bowls. She should pour some warm water into one, she told Ingeborg, and get it ready now.

The labour pains came thick and fast. As soon as the pain

wore off, Oline's arms hung down slackly, her eyes closed and her face, streaming with sweat, went deathly pale and sank back on Sjur Gabriel's chest. She seemed to fall into a doze.

But it was only for a moment that she had peace.

Then she began again as before, more and more violently as time passed.

Kari pulled the bottle out of her clothing and asked Ingeborg for a cup. She poured a little of the contents into it and got Oline to drink some. Sjur Gabriel could smell what it was, but he made no objections. He knew that it was thought to be a good idea to give brandy to women in labour.

It did also seem that the drink revived Oline somewhat. She came to her senses, and asked after Lars's Adna. But straight afterwards she clenched her fists and emitted a shriek which was so wild and dreadful that Sjur Gabriel trembled and shook. Several more followed, and they ended finally in a hoarse, inhuman howl.

Sjur Gabriel could tell from Kari's movements that something was happening, and at the same moment he could hear the weak, fretful cry of the newborn. Kari snatched up the scissors and leaned further in towards Oline's body. Then she dropped the scissors, wrapped the piece of flannel around the baby and passed it to Ingeborg, who sat down on a stool with it and covered it with the lower part of her skirt.

Dots of fire were dancing in front of Sjur Gabriel's eyes. He squeezed his eyes shut and felt something warm and wet on his cheeks.

'Praise be to God,' he said in a loud voice, and heaved a deep sigh of relief.

Oline was a lifeless clump hanging in his arms, whilst Kari finished seeing to her.

'Now we'd best get'er to bed,' she then said to Sjur Gabriel, standing up with a great effort. 'I reckon she's dropped off!' she exclaimed, quickly pulling out the bottle again, grabbing the cup and pouring some in. She had to prise open Oline's lips, which were clamped shut, before she could get some brandy into her.

As the last time, it did Oline good. She opened her eyes and looked around dully.

When she realised that the baby had been delivered she folded her hands and burst into tears.

'Thanks be to Our Lord an' 'is Son!' she repeated several times.

Sjur Gabriel picked her up, putting one arm around her shoulders and the other under her knees, and carried her over to the bed.

Kari followed him, pulled off Oline's skirt and wound a long strip of woollen cloth around her stomach, slid a piece of cotton drill folded in half beneath her, pulled up the covers and went over to collect the baby, which was whimpering pitifully.

Sjur Gabriel had been out to collect the warm water, which he poured into the bowl.

Kari dipped the baby into the water, rinsed it, dried it on the piece of material and began to dress it.

'Is i' a girl?' asked Oline from the bed.

'Boy,' answered Sjur Gabriel, even though he seemed not to have looked at the baby at all. 'Big an' 'ealthy.'

'Nother boy – aye, thanks be to Our Lord an' 'is Son for all things!' Oline whispered.

Sjur Gabriel picked up the other bowl, carried it out and

emptied the contents into the fire on the hearth.

Then he came back in with water and scrubbed away a pool of blood on the floor in front of the bench where he had been sitting with Oline.

When the baby was ready it looked like a twelve-shilling loaf wrapped up in a shawl. The tiny red face was framed in a woollen bonnet which was tied under its chin. It cried continuously.

'Now you best eat summat,' said Sjur Gabriel, after Kari had got the baby to start suckling. He had put food out.

'Don' go to any trouble,' said Kari, glancing sideways at the table.*

'You mus''ave a taste o't new-churned bu'er, a' least,' Sjur Gabriel insisted. 'An' 'ere's 'errin' soup. – Ea' now whilst i's warm.'

''S no' needed,' muttered Kari, as she sat down.

Sjur Gabriel had to repeat his invitation several times, and even put the spoon in her hand, before she began to eat.

Ingeborg was standing over by her mother. She could not get enough of watching her new brother.

''Is li'l fingers – 'is li'l nose – 'e's go' nails! I reckon there's 'air unner 'is bonnet!' she exclaimed at regular intervals.

When Kari had eaten she stood up. 'Thanks,' she said, and shook Sjur Gabriel's hand with her stiff, wrinkled fingers.

'Ye'r welcome,' he answered.

Then she held out her hand to Ingeborg and to Oline, although the latter had fallen asleep, said the same to them and received the same reply.

'I'll be on me way then,' she went on, after which she emitted a mixture of a yawn and a burp, and finally said: 'Jesus be praised! Ye c'n 'ear I'm full o' good food.'

Sjur Gabriel was holding something flat in his hand, wrapped up in a black silk kerchief with bright yellow borders. When he unwrapped it, it turned out to be a bank book. After licking his fingers, he extracted from it a few dirty, carefully smoothed-out banknotes.

''Ere you are,' he said to Kari, who had wrapped her skirt round her head and was ready to leave. 'One, two, three, four, five – tha' makes a daler.'

''S righ'," she replied.

'Tek a look a' wha' you got, so's you know I ain't chea'ed you,' he went on, his gaze fixed on the notes.

She brought them up close to her eyes and passed them through her fingers.

'Aye, tha's righ' enough.'

Then she rolled them up and pushed them inside her clothes up by her neck.

'Well, g'day to yer and thanks.'

She gave him her gnarled fingers once more.

'Thanks to you an' all.'

Then she went over to the bed and said goodbye and thanks to Ingeborg. Oline had fallen asleep again, but was woken up unmercifully once more.

'Aye, aye, strange 'ow things turn ou'. Pride goes afore a fall,' she muttered, with an unfriendly sideways glance at Sjur Gabriel, as she limped out of the room.

Four days later Oline was standing in the kitchen, thin and worn, stirring the porridge pot on the hearth. Her cheeks were greyish-blue and hollowed out, her lips dry and yellow. There were blue-black rings around her eyes, which were staring with a haunted expression. In front of her, in a shawl which was knotted around her neck, hung the newborn, suckling her breast. Magne was lying in front of the stove and raking in the ashes, amusing himself by scattering them across the floor. Little-Adna was sitting on the doorstep to the living room, screaming. Ingeborg was out feeding the pig. Jens and Nils had gone fishing with their father.

9

It had been a tough time for the folk at Hellemyr. Oline had suffered with open sores on her legs the whole winter. Kari Træet, to whom Sjur Gabriel had once again had to resort, had uttered spells and invocations, applied various dubious treatments both externally and internally, and tried all kinds of secret witchcraft in order to cure her, but the result was that the sores became worse and worse, and the pain more and more unbearable.

During this time Sjur Gabriel had often found Oline drunk, both when he returned from town and at other times too. He knew that it was Kari who supplied her with brandy, and in addition that Oline had given her the little she owned of silver brooches and finery in return. Yet he dared not give vent to his anger with Kari for fear that she would stop attending to Oline. But finally, when he realised that Oline had stolen money from him in order to reimburse Kari for the brandy, he could control himself no longer. He thrashed Oline until the blood flowed from her nose and mouth, and the next day he threw Kari out and swore that if she turned up again on his land he would bundle her into his basket and throw her overboard in the middle of the fjord.

Kari had left the farm with a dreadful curse on him and everything he owned, and with a threat to get her own back. This gave Sjur Gabriel a new burden to bear. He was continuously tormented by fear of the misfortune which Kari would call down on him and his property. When one of his cows shortly afterwards became so ill that he had to slaughter it, he did not doubt for a second that it was Kari who had caused it. Therefore he was vastly relieved when he heard about a month later that she had toppled down the loft ladder in a drunken state and killed herself instantly.

In recent times Oline had kept to her bed. She could no longer drag herself around on her swollen legs, which were constantly suppurating and bleeding.

The child, which had been born in the autumn, had been named after his father at the christening. Despite her wretchedness Oline continued to suckle him. His cheeks were pale and puffed up, but his body was skinny, and recurring digestive problems made him scream day and night.

In the end Sjur Gabriel had to bring himself to fetch a doctor for Oline. When he saw the state she was in, he held his nose and declared that she must be taken into town immediately and admitted to hospital. If not, her sores would become gangrenous, and her leg would have to be amputated.

'Wha's to become of the li'l one then?' Sjur Gabriel had asked, pointing at the child in the cradle.

The doctor had answered that he should thank God that the kid hadn't snuffed it long ago, with the tainted milk his mother had been feeding him.

With a heavy heart Sjur Gabriel decided to do as the doctor had told him. He borrowed a dung sledge from Lars Træet on which he pulled Oline down to the water, laid her in the bottom of the boat and rowed off with her. Jens and Nils went along too and stayed in the boat with their mother whilst Sjur Gabriel walked to the hospital and negotiated a bed. Half an hour later he came back together with two men carrying a grey-painted coffin-like contraption in a harness over their shoulders. Oline was placed in this and they carried her away.

So Sjur Gabriel had to take charge of the six-month-old baby. He fulfilled his unaccustomed duties tirelessly. At night, when he was most deeply asleep, worn out and exhausted after a day's toil, and was woken by the child's screams, he got up and walked up and down for a long time, rocking the baby in his arms, or he took it into his bed, put a dummy in its mouth and held it to his breast, so that it might think it was with its mother, and settle more easily. When it had messed itself in the cradle, he changed the sheet and washed it with rags and warm water, which he always kept ready on the peat embers in the hearth.

At the start a young lass who had recently given birth to her third illegitimate child came along once a day to suckle Little-Gabriel. But that actually made things more difficult, and Sjur Gabriel was forced to conclude that it was better that she stopped, because he would never get the child weaned if it went on.

From that day onwards his solicitude for the child was redoubled. It went so far that he could hardly tolerate anyone else picking it up. He had become convinced that no-one else could do it as well as he could. He was confirmed in his opinion by the fact that Little-Gabriel seemed to share it. When the child had a screaming fit there was no-one other than its father who could manage it and calm it down. This awareness filled Sjur Gabriel's heart with secret joy and pride, and bound him more and more tightly to the boy.

In the daytime, when he was working in the fields, he was constantly on the alert. Every half hour he had to go home and see whether Little-Gabriel was awake, or investigate what Ingeborg was doing with him. Then he would sit down and feed him, rock him to sleep and set off again with many exhortations to Ingeborg to keep a close eye on the cradle.

At this time Ingeborg was thirteen years old, and she laboured and struggled as best she could. But even though she was well-grown and resourceful for her age, and used to working, she could not really cope with it all. Sjur Gabriel said to himself that they just had to make the best of it. There was far too much for her to manage. When the porridge was lumpy and half raw, he understood that the reason was that she was not strong enough to pound it properly. When it was burnt, he ate it without complaint, and just asked her not to lay such a large fire under the pot next time. He was glad that she was there now that Oline was away, although at the same time he fretted over the fact that she was not in service somewhere, which had been the plan when she was confirmed so early.

He himself toiled like a slave from morn to night, taking care of the work in the fields, milking the cows, churning the butter and mucking out the pig when it got too filthy. It would have been easier if he had been able to sleep at night, but there was small chance of that. He longed for Oline to return home, and recognised more than ever that despite her great weakness she was a hard-working and capable wife.

10

When summer arrived and the hay harvest began, Sjur Gabriel realised he would have to look for a boy to help him during the busiest period, no matter how reluctant and unhappy he felt about it. He sent a message over to Salhus and got hold of a good-for-nothing day labourer called Aslak, who called himself a 'champion 'aymaker'. Sjur Gabriel didn't like the lad, but since no-one else was available he decided to make the best of it. However, he was cautious enough to engage him just for a week to start with. They agreed that he would get 12 shillings a day and free board.

Even on the first day Sjur Gabriel could see that Aslak was lazy and sloppy. He comforted himself with the thought that he wasn't considering marrying the lad, but told himself at the same time that these six days would be more than enough to drive him demented, if Aslak carried on as he had begun.

One night after work, on the third day after his arrival, Aslak had sauntered over to the neighbouring farm, where there were a couple of girls he fancied getting to know. He had spent a couple of hours there, danced a *Halling* in the haystore and been treated to a pot of ale.* On the way back he took a short cut across the open land next to Sjur Gabriel's meadow, and in his befuddled state he forgot to close the gate behind him.

During the night all the cows – not just Sjur Gabriel's own but also those belonging to his neighbour, as well as some untethered horses – had wandered into the meadow and eaten all the grass they could find on the large, flat marshy ground next to the house.

Sjur Gabriel had had a restless night, as the child had had stomachache. Towards morning he had quietened down, and eventually fallen asleep. At 3 o'clock Sjur Gabriel got up to wake the lad, who was sleeping in the hayloft, and set him to work.

It was a still, misty morning with a leaden sky and stripes of ochre in the east.

The moment Sjur Gabriel lifted the latch and opened the door, he saw the terrible sight of the devastation wreaked by the cows. He went wild with fury. With a bellow he seized hold of a haypole and rushed out on bare feet across the meadow, still sodden with the night's dew, and towards the grazing cows, which fled to all sides. A few, which had eaten so much that they couldn't manage any more, were lying in the middle of the grass with their legs drawn up beneath them, gazing dully at Sjur Gabriel as if the whole thing was nothing to do with them, until they were struck by the haypole, which fell whistling across their backs. Then they finally realised that something was wrong, lumbered to their feet and galloped off with their tails in the air. The horses were more unruly, but Sjur Gabriel ran at them like a berserker. In the end he managed to clear the field and get the gate closed. He stood for a moment staring at the ravaged meadow, grinding his teeth and fuming with rage. Suddenly he started to weep. He sobbed as bitterly as a child whose heart is broken, with a hiccupping sound in his throat. He did not shed many tears. It cost him too much effort to produce them, and the ones which did emerge did not run down his cheeks, but flooded into his eyes, which looked as if they were swimming in water. After a while he stopped crying and set off at a run down towards the hayloft, kicked open the door which was fastened on the inside by a wooden peg, leapt a few rungs up the ladder which was leaning against the beam, swung himself up, and got hold of a mass of wiry, matted hair, which he tugged at with all his might, pulling a head and a chest covered by a sacking shirt out from under a woollen blanket. An anguished howl pierced the air, two arms waved violently, and a couple of legs in rough homespun underpants kicked out. Sjur Gabriel let go of the hair, grabbed hold of both arms and held onto the wrists with one hand, threw himself onto his knees on the chest of the prostrate figure and began to punch him resoundingly. The howls redoubled, but Sjur Gabriel did not let go. He kneed him, kicked him in the ribs, and headbutted him time after time. Aslak roared and begged and struggled violently to escape. Bit by bit he inched forwards to the edge of the loft. Sjur Gabriel, who was still on top of him, was pulled along with him. He saw and felt nothing until they both of them fell over the edge. With a crash they landed on the barn floor. Sjur Gabriel managed to put his hands out and landed on all fours. The lad landed on his back. He stopped yelling. He just moaned quietly and did not move.

Sjur Gabriel stood up. He had banged his knees and all the punching had made his knuckles bleed. Otherwise he was in one piece. Without looking round, he went into the living room. As he drew near to the cradle where Little-Gabriel was lying, the child opened his eyes, smiled at him in happy recognition and reached his little arms up towards him.

Sjur Gabriel started, and then felt a sudden wave of gladness and peace washing over him. That innocent child had recognised him and smiled at him. It was the first time anything like that had happened to him. Before he knew it he was on his knees by the cradle, bending down over the little face and kissing it. The child started playing with his beard and laughed out loud as it was tickled under its nose. Sjur Gabriel lifted the boy out of the cradle, wrapped him in his covers and started walking up and down with him in his arms. He could not put him down or get enough of looking at him. Little-Gabriel had recognised him and stretched out his arms to him! Had you ever seen anything like it! Now the whole farm and all his property could be left to Our Lord's whims, if only he could keep this Little-Gabriel, this utterly marvellous lad, whose like had never been seen in this world. This was his child, his own flesh and blood, his dearest possession. He carried on walking up and down, rocking the child in his arms, long after it had fallen asleep. Eventually he laid it carefully back in the cradle, covered it and went to bed himself. His limbs were all bruised and aching. He felt as if his legs could no longer carry him. He had to have an hour's sleep before he was in a fit state to begin the day's work.

11

The events of that morning cost Sjur Gabriel more than the grass which had been lost. Aslak had sustained a broken rib in the fall, and had also suffered other injuries. Sjur Gabriel had to send him to hospital and agree to pay for him for six weeks. In addition he had to pay a fine which the sheriff imposed for a violent attack on a sleeping man. Sjur Gabriel's complaints about the loss Aslak had caused him were dismissed. The lad denied that he had left the gate open, and Sjur Gabriel had no witnesses.

All this upset Sjur Gabriel deeply. The day after Aslak had been carted off, he sat down in the evening in the living room with his savings book open in front of him and brooded over all his misfortunes. How could a poor man get by in this world when he was persecuted like this by God and man? He counted and counted, working out the sums he would have to spend before Oline came home again. She had now been in the hospital for three months at 16 shillings a day. That made 12 speciedalers and 32 shillings. And the last time he had heard from the hospital, the message was that she would be there for another month. That made an extra 4 speciedalers. Then there was this business with Aslak. That would come to 5 speciedalers and 4 shillings. On top of that he reckoned that this year he would have to buy hay for at least 4 speciedalers to replace what had been ruined. That made 25 speciedalers and 36 shillings in all, that might just as well have been thrown into the sea.

Sjur Gabriel dragged his fingers to and fro through his coarse, greying mop of hair and his stiff stubbly beard, his loud sighs wheezing through his body. This hard-earned money, these dalers which he had scraped together shilling by shilling, ever since he was an apprentice! How he had laboured and struggled and sweated in order to earn them, and scrimped and saved, barely even allowing himself to buy some chewing tobacco. And he had often said to himself that he had done really well to manage to put by 39 speciedalers and 72 shillings in his savings account. He had been proud of it. And it had given him the strength and the courage to keep working away. Toiling and digging and striving and scraping it together. It was as if this savings book had kept him going in the darkest and heaviest hours, reminding him what sort of a fellow he was, even though he didn't have a better wife. For it said in the book of sermons that he who has a good wife shall increase his goods. But he had increased them anyway, even though he didn't have a good wife, but on the contrary one who drank and wasted his substance and was now costing money in hospital.

Oh, why should things turn out this way with these savings of his! He raised his arm, waved it up and down and then let his clenched fist fall onto the table with an almost soundless thump. Oh, God our Father in Heaven on High, how had things come to this!

He had started to draw on the money for the burial of the first child. Since then he had buried three more, and each time he had plundered his savings. But now things were as bad as this – it was enough to lay him in his grave.

But then it must be because God had not blessed him and his undertakings. And in that case, what was the point? Even if he toiled until his fingernails bled, it would simply turn out the same if Our Lord was against him. And he understood now that Our Lord was against him, because he had been a slave of mammon and boasted about his savings book and his industriousness. That was why things had turned out this way. Pride goes before a fall, Kari Træet had said. He was learning the truth of that now.

He closed his bank book, placed his elbows on the table and rested his bearded chin in his hands, so that the corners of his mouth were pulled sharply upwards.

Pride goes before a fall, that was what the vicar had said from the pulpit as well, when he was in church last spring, and then after that they had sung about working and planning being in vain if God does not build the house. He muttered the verse of a hymn as well as he could with his mouth clamped between his hands:

In vain we rise in early dawn
And toil with heavy labour.
Our effort cannot bring reward
Without God's grace and favour.
Each soul must strive with sweat and toil
His bread and meat to savour.
But if Our Lord won't bless the work
*It loses all its flavour.**

But how was a poor man to behave, in that case? He who slaved and strove in order to provide for himself and his family was committing a sin, and he who didn't give a fig was also committing a sin.

Yet there were some people who profited from their labours. Just look at Magne over at Søndrehellen. They had been farm labourers together – equally poor the pair of them, and now Magne was a big shot with new buildings and eight cows and two horses and everything spick and span. And Magne had more children than him and had buried just as many. That was crystal clear proof that it was Our Lord's blessing that made the difference. But how could God be so cruel as to treat people so differently? The vicar said that he was a father to all of us. An earthly father would not treat his children like that, even if they had sinned and been disobedient.

And he was no worse than others.

Worse than others –

It was as if someone suddenly grabbed him by the scruff of the neck and pointed into the air, and he could clearly see himself standing in a barn at daybreak, digging a hole in the earthen floor with a spade. It was a great many years ago. But he *had* stood there, and he *had* dug that hole. And beside him had stood a barefoot lass in her underskirt and blouse, trembling and freezing with chattering teeth and holding something in her hands wrapped up in a ragged apron. And when he reckoned that the hole was deep enough he had taken what she was holding in her hands without looking at her, and knelt down and thrust it into the hole. But then the apron had fallen open and he had seen the elbow of a tiny child's arm. Then he had gone berserk and had shovelled spadeful after spadeful down into the hole at furious speed, and hammered the mound with the flat of his spade with all his strength in order to flatten it. And when the hole was filled he had strewn manure over it and trodden it flat so that no-one would see anything.

He sat there unmoving, staring ahead with eyes wide and beads of sweat on his brow. He could see all the details of the event with a terrible clarity. He heard his own voice saying to the lass: "F you ever say anythin', I'll kill yer." He saw himself returning to the lads' room on stockinged feet, creeping into bed and cautiously pulling the woollen blanket over himself, in order not to wake the other lad, Rasmes. And how he snored as the others got up, and pretended he was sleeping so deeply that it was difficult to rouse himself. And after that, the terror that had come over him every time he had to walk past the barn in the evening. He had also been plagued by a gnawing conscience in the immediate aftermath. But then, when he had left that village and found work many miles away, it was as if it had blown away completely. Now and then it did happen that he dreamed about it, and woke up dripping with sweat and had to get up and light a candle and chew some tobacco in order to fall asleep again. But in later years it had happened less and less. What did it mean, that just this evening, as he was sitting there thinking of other things entirely, this old, long-forgotten event should pop up and overwhelm him like a nightmare? Was it Our Lord, who wanted to remind him of his past sin and make him understand that He had not forgotten it? Was that why He tormented him with adversity and vexations on all sides? But how could a God up there in Heaven, who had his hands full with everything else, bear a grudge for such a long time and take revenge on a poor creature like him, who had striven and toiled and been an honest man all his days and never done anything wrong apart from that one single time! And he had repented and begged God for forgiveness. For many years afterwards he had put money in the collecting box for the poor and needy every single Sunday he was in church. Could it be that Our Lord was so unyielding and merciless? In the Bible it said that if your sins were as red as blood, they would become as white as snow. That word he had believed and trusted in. But now it looked as if all his calculations were wrong.

He straightened up, leant back against the wall behind the bench and thrust his hands into his trouser pockets.

But if that was how things stood, there was nothing more for him to do in this world. What was he to do, how was he to get along if Almighty God was persecuting him? In that case the best thing would be to hang himself or to sink to the bottom of the sea. Yes, that would perhaps be preferable. Then he could call in at Salhus, buy a bottle of liquor of the sort that cost an ort for a pint, gulp down as much of it as he could and then tie a stone around his waist and let himself sink. Then surely Our Lord on high would have to be content and recognise that he had atoned enough …

But then he would be sent to Hell afterwards …

Aye, that must be what Our Lord wanted, since He could not see His way to forgiving him. So he would be tormented for all eternity for the sake of that one sin. Well – if that was how it was, then so it would have to be. No-one could avoid his destiny. He would end up in Hell anyway. If he decided to take his own life, at least he would escape the remainder of his misery here in this world.

And now, since he had had to use up his savings, he had nothing more to look forward to … Nothing more to look forward to …

He blinked as he looked around the low-ceilinged room, through whose windows the evening summer sun cast a dim light. His glance passed over the heads of the children on the bed on the floor over in the corner, along the floor and up to the table with the half-empty porridge bowls, and took in the marriage bed and the cradle where Little-Gabriel was lying. There they stopped. Their blank expression was transformed, and the corners of his mouth trembled. Little-

Gabriel, yes, that was true, he had him to look forward to. Since Our Lord had given him that boy, He could not have abandoned him after all. No, Little-Gabriel he could not leave. For as long as that boy lived, he too would have to live. It didn't matter what happened to his savings. Little-Gabriel was the best thing he owned anyway. That was the wonderful thing about that boy. If he now had fifty shiny dalers on one side of the scales, and Little-Gabriel sitting on the other, and Our Lord came along and said that he had to choose between the two, then in God's name he would reach out with both hands for the one Little-Gabriel was sitting on, and let the other fall, even if it was straight into the fire. Yes, that was how it was. No possible doubt or confusion about that matter.

'Aye – aye,' he uttered with a deep sigh, folding his hands across his jacket. ''F only Our Lord dunna tek 'im from me, I'll b'lieve 'ee's gonna forgive me, a'er all.'

He raised his eyes heavenwards and went on in a fervent voice, which kept breaking into falsetto as he spoke: 'I mus' tek upon me all me werries an' sorrows an' bear 'em like a cross an' a scourge fer all me sins, an' 'ope tha' when I die Our Lord'll think I've bin punished enough, an' tha' 'ee'll let me in a' leas' to't forecourt of't Kingdom of 'eaven.'

And without pausing for breath he launched into a subdued hymn tune, dwelling on the notes for so long that he ran out of breath, then being forced to break off and gulp in some air before continuing:

O Lord, turn not thy face from me,*
Who lie in woeful state,
Lamenting all my sinful life
Before thy mercy-gate.

A gate which opens wide to those
That do lament their sin;
Shut not that gate against me, Lord,
But let me enter in.

And call me not to strict account
How I have sojourned here …

O Lord, turn not thy face from me,

no, he'd already sung that –

A gate which opens wide to those

he'd sung that line too. – Oh well, that would have to do, he couldn't remember any more.

After that he felt calmer. He went out of the living room, climbed up the ladder to the attic, put the savings book back at the bottom of the chest and locked it with a solid key which was hanging on a string around his neck, against his skin. Then he went down again, undressed and got into bed, muttering all the while through his teeth: 'Aye – aye, God 'ave mercy on us all, aye – aye, on us all, aye!'

12

Sjur Gabriel had not been asleep long before Little-Gabriel began to scream. He heard it in his sleep, but could not bring himself to wake up. He struggled and fought, but it was as if a weight was lying on his breast and his eyes, paralysing all his limbs. Finally he drew breath and let out a shout. Then he sat up in bed and began to hush and rock the baby. But it made no difference. The child just screamed more and more loudly. So he got up and gave him a dummy. No, he just spat it out and twisted his head away. He held a cup of watery milk to his mouth. No, he wouldn't drink either. Then he looked to see if the boy needed changing, put dry cloths under him and rocked him again. But nothing helped. He picked him up, wrapped him in blankets and walked up and down the floor with him, rocking him to and fro and chattering comfortingly: 'Hush – hush – hush. Wha's wrong now wi' our Li'l-Gabriel? Is 'is li'l tummy upset? – Hush – hush – hush – is our l'il lad so poorly? 'as 'ee got tummyache?' – He could hear the little stomach rumbling and churning, as the child twisted and turned in his arms. After a while he became calmer. He laid the boy down in the cradle, fetched some water, changed the cloths under him again and washed him, while nattering away: 'There, there, now our Li'l-Gabriel's feelin' be'er. Now – 'ee's got rid o' all tha' nasty stuff, now our Li'l-Gabriel's grand again.'

He covered the child and rocked him again. But it was not long before he began to complain once more. Suddenly he started rolling his eyes and pressing the back of his head into the pillow, as a sort of choking, snarling noise could be heard through his clenched lips. Beads of sweat broke out on his face, and his body stiffened. Sjur Gabriel was beside himself. He splashed some water onto his face, but to no avail. Then he picked up a bottle of a mixture which smelt so acrid that it made him sneeze – something Oline had used on her leg – and waved it under the boy's nostrils. No effect at all. He had no idea what to do, picked Little-Gabriel up and put him down again, wringing his hands in despair. After a while the symptoms abated. The eyelids closed, and the unnatural stiffness disappeared, whilst the child gave short, moaning sobs. Then he lay still and drew heavy, staccato breaths as if worn out by the exertion.

Sjur Gabriel felt an inexpressible relief and offered up a silent prayer of thanks to God. He sat down on a stool, rocking gently and hushing the child. But a couple of minutes later he jumped up and bent over the cradle, scared by the same snarling sound. Was it starting again? No, surely Our Lord would not have the heart to do it. That poor innocent child, who had done nothing wrong! - - But yes, he did have the heart to do it, and it came back, worse than before. All he could see of the eyes was the distended, bloodshot, gleaming whites. The face was blue and dripping with sweat, the mouth was foaming, and the body was as stiff as a board and icy cold, the little hands clenched tight.

Sjur Gabriel tore at his hair, fell to his knees and cried aloud that God must come to his aid. He turned away in anguish to avoid looking at that dreadful sight, but the next moment his eyes were drawn back again. What in the name of Jesus and all God's holy angels could he do. Oh, how stern and cruel God could be!

'In Jesu' name, jus' tek 'im , tek 'im!' he cried out loud, standing still by the cradle after walking around the room as if in delirium. 'Tek 'im, jus' don' torture 'im!'

Little-Gabriel was still lying as before. He had now stopped making any noise at all. Whitish foam was bubbling from his lips down over his chin. Now and then the little body with its chest thrust out was shaken by a tremor that looked as if it would break the child's bones.

Oh, so stiff, so horribly stiff! He felt the child's limbs to see if he could bend them. But no, they were like frozen fish on a winter's day. Frozen! – Suddenly he had an idea. What if he tried to put him into warm water – everything thawed in warm water. – Warm water would soften his limbs. In one bound he was across the room and got Ingeborg out of bed. She must light a fire under the largest pot. He would run and fetch water from the well.

Ingeborg threw on her clothes, half stupefied with sleep. Her father yelled to her to hurry up; Little-Gabriel was dying.

When Ingeborg saw the child in the cradle, she began sobbing and hurried out to the kitchen. Her father had already gone for water. He dashed like a boy in bare feet to and from the well and got the pot filled in less than a minute. Ingeborg broke the peat slabs over her knee, whilst the tears dripped onto them. Straight after the tongues of flame were licking round the sides of the pot. Her father added kindling, and picked up a piece of plank which he had bought to repair the living room floor with, broke it in half and cut one half into firewood with his sheath knife; he threw them into the hearth and said to Ingeborg: "ere, keep goin', burn up everythin' you c'n find, jus' ge' tha' wa'er 'ot fast!'

When he came back into the living room the attack was ebbing away. Little-Gabriel was grizzling in a low, moaning voice. His eyes had returned to their normal appearance and were blinking and closing, his limbs had relaxed into softness and his breast was heaving with deep breaths.

Sjur Gabriel bent over the cradle, his hands gripped together behind his knees. His eyes were shining with hope and fear, his lips compressed in his pinched mouth. He was so tense with anticipation that he hardly dared to breathe.

'There, 'ee's restin' now, Jesu be praised!' he muttered. ''Ee'll be sleepin' soon. God 'elp you, poor li'l angel!'

He straightened up slowly, passed a hand over his eyes, folded his hands and held them out in front of him. He stood there without moving with his head on one side and an expression of devoted gratitude, watching Little-Gabriel, who was dozing as his body shook now and then with violent tremors.

'The wa'er's on the boil,' came a fearful voice from the doorway. Sjur Gabriel turned his head and saw Ingeborg, who had opened the door soundlessly and was now standing with one foot on the threshold and her hand on the latch, her face blackened with soot and tears.

''Ush,' said her father, raising one hand in warning. ''Ee's sleepin'. You c'n go back to bed.'

There was a mildness in his voice which Ingeborg was not used to, and which moved her so that she started to cry again. She came into the room, quietly pushed the door to and moved to stand a couple of paces from the cradle.

'Com' 'ere,' said Sjur Gabriel, moving aside a little. 'Look 'ow good an' quiet 'ee's sleepin'.'

'You ge' some sleep, Da'. I'll sit an' rock our Li'l-Gabriel,' she said.

'I dun' feel like goin' a' bed. – Soon be time t' wek up.'

He looked round the room. The faint glow of the summer night had given way to the growing light of dawn.

'Look, look!' called Ingeborg. ''Ee's startin' over! Oh, ee's startin' over, ee's startin' over!'

'God 'elp us – God 'elp us!' groaned Sjur Gabriel. 'You mus' be quiet, li'l Ingebor", he said with tears in his voice. 'Tha' won' mek it be'er.'

He stroked the back of her head several times with a fumbling helpless gesture. 'Our Li'l- Gabriel's scared, 'ee's scared when you yell. - - Oh God 'elp us – God 'elp us!'

The fit got worse and worse. The child's breast wrenched and cracked, as it heaved and fought for air. The eyes rolled more wildly than before. The pupils vanished beneath the corners of the eyelids, where they stayed fixed with a lifeless stare. The head bored backwards, the chest arched upwards. The growling sound from the throat, the blue-black colour, the dripping sweat, the yellowish foam – all of it started up again. And then the dreadful stiffness, the icy cold of the limbs, the tiny fingers so tightly clenched that the nails were blue-black.

Ingeborg leant over the cradle and kissed the little hands.

"Ee's frozen – 'ee'll freeze t'death!' she shouted, breathing on the hands to warm them.

'Frozen - ! Warm wa'er!' it struck Sjur Gabriel again like a bolt of lightning. And leaning forwards, he ran with long strides out to the kitchen, shouting to Ingeborg that she should stay by the cradle. He seized a tub, pulled it over to the hearth, took a bucket and poured the boiling water into it. He noticed that it was leaking, but he didn't care about that. At desperate speed he fetched water from the well, poured it into the hot water, put his foot into it to feel if it was the right temperature, and then lifted the tub and carried it in, putting it down on the living room floor.

Little-Gabriel lay as before. Ingeborg had fallen to her

knees next to the cradle.

When her father arrived, she stood up and looked at the tub in wordless fright.

Sjur Gabriel was white in the face. His mouth was open, and his tongue was sticking out between his teeth.

He tore the covers off the cradle and quickly lifted the woollen cap off Little-Gabriel's head. Then he untied the ribbon at the neck of the nightclothes the child was wearing.* But it was impossible for Sjur Gabriel's shaking hands to loosen the clothes from the stiff limbs. Without further thought he picked up the seemingly lifeless body, knelt down by the tub and lowered it into the water, with his arms under the neck and the knees. After a few seconds, life returned to the eyes. The pupils slowly slid back into place. For a moment the eyes were fixed on his father's face. Sjur Gabriel felt it was as if they were smiling at him, – and then the eyelids closed heavily, opened again and closed several times. At the same time he could feel the back giving way and relaxing; the fingers unclenched and the little arms sank down loosely at the sides. Then the child began to whimper and moan, and that sound was like heavenly music to Sjur Gabriel's tormented senses. For he knew that it meant that the fit had passed.

'Did y'ever see the like!' he said to Ingeborg in a voice that was laughing and crying all at once. 'In't tha' jus' like some sort o'miracle? I nivver seen summat like tha' in all my days! T'lad's gone so soft, soft as new-churned bu'er in all 'is li'l limbs.' He gently removed his arm from under the knees so that Ingeborg could see that the legs sank down, and took hold of one arm and moved it up and down.

''Ave you seen the like in all yer born days, lass?'

He laughed with joy and shook his head.

'No, no, no – I'd nivver a' b'lieved it possible, nivver a' b'lieved it!'

Ingeborg had stopped crying. She was overcome by amazement at what was happening.

''S over now, 's all over,' said Sjur Gabriel almost cheerfully. 'When 'ee starts breathin' like tha', I know 'ee'll be sleepin' soon.'

He was silent for a moment, listening to the child's short, staccato breaths, which were occasionally punctuated by deep sighs. The small head slid tiredly to one side and came to rest on his father's arm. There were still beads of sweat around his mouth and on his forehead, but the complexion looked normal, if a little wan.

'You be'er go an' sleep fer a bit, you Ingebor', or you'll be all washed ou' in t' mornin',' said Sjur Gabriel, when he had laid Little-Gabriel in his cradle after taking off his clothes and drying him on Ingeborg's threadbare skirt, which she had taken off to give him.

Ingeborg was standing at the foot of the cradle, holding her skirt as a shield in front of her naked legs.

'F only 'ee don't start over,' she whispered.

'I reckon not. 'Ee's sleepin' so deep an' peaceful. Not like afore, when 'ee 'ad that shiverin' in 'is li'l body. – You c'n go an' sleep.'

Ingeborg went over to the mattress, let her skirt fall onto the floor and crept quietly under the covers.

Sjur Gabriel was filled with reverent gratitude. He did not doubt for a moment that it was God who had inspired him with the thought of the warm water. Now he could face anything that was to come. God had forgiven him his youthful sin and wished him only well. He listened to Little-Gabriel's calm, regular breathing and joyfully watched the little face, which had begun to regain colour as he slept and looked so blessedly healthy that you would think nothing at all had been wrong with the lad.

Then he got up from the stool he was sitting on, went over to the cupboard which was built into the high foot end of the double bed and took from it Kingo's large hymn book with brass clasps.* He sat back down in the same place, opened the book and started reading hymn after hymn, singing slowly under his breath. After a while his eyelids grew heavy with sleep and his hands holding the book fell into his lap. But he fought against it, forced his eyes open again and read on:

Jesus dies and earth is trembling,
O my heart, learn righteous fear
Die then, all my wicked grumbling!
Die and get thee far from here!
God and Man has died for me
Since my Adam ate the tree
Bringing all men – all men – condemnation
But now Christ has won – has won – salvation.

Jesus, I Thy death am grieving – grieving
For I caused Thy passion deep
Yet Thy death - - -

No, he could not carry on. His head sank back and rested on the side of the bed, and his fingers released their hold on the book, which slid between his knees, down the side of his leg, and came to rest on the floor. Sjur Gabriel slept with half-open mouth and his arms dangling loosely.

13

Sjur Gabriel was in town to pick up Oline and bring her home. When he rang the bell at the door of the hospital he was shown into the office, where he paid what was outstanding of the cost of the treatment. Then he went out to the front hall and waited while they sent for Oline, who had been sitting ready all day with her bundle of clothes in her hand. When Sjur Gabriel saw her coming, it struck him that she had grown even smaller, and that her hands were exactly like his mother's, when as a lad he had seen her dead body.

'Well – 'ow' is it wi' you?' he asked when the porter had let them out and they were standing in the street.

'Me leg's all 'ealed up,' she replied. 'They give me ointment in a paper te' rub on i'.'

'I sh'd 'ope so. T' money's bin runnin' ou' like sand. – Awful long time it's taken an' all. – Sixteen dalers an' thirty-two shillin'.'

'Aye, tha's a lo' o' money,' said Oline humbly.

''S all goin' t'same way. We'll finish up on't parish, me an' the kids.'

'You munna 'ave such 'orrible thoughts,' muttered Oline.

Sjur Gabriel made no answer, but walked on with his hands behind his back, striding ahead. Oline followed at his heels.

When they had reached the corner of the square and the Triangle, he came to a stop.

'I'm jus' gonna buy some fish-'ooks,' he said to Oline. 'Go down to t' boat, an' I'll be there straight.' With that he left her.

Oline carried on walking slowly. Suddenly it felt as if she

had lead weights on her legs. A couple of times she stood still and seemed to consider. Then she went slowly on. In this way she reached the Triangle. She went over to the railings, leaned over and caught sight of the boat, where Jens was sitting with his back to her. All at once she was seized by a deep depression. She saw in her mind's eye the cabin back home with its low, dark living room and the black hearth, where she would have to rake and root about day in, day out, the same thing over and over again. The swampy pasture outside, the pigsty and barn and the hard labour inside and out – it all filled her with a corrosive, consuming distaste. She turned round, glanced around to check and then walked quickly, almost running, back across the Triangle, and turned left into Torvegaarden, where she went into the inn and got hold of Guri, to whom she sold one of the items of clothing she had in her bundle, borrowed a bottle and bought some brandy. When she had left the taproom and was standing drinking behind the stairs, she heard someone come in, open the taproom door and ask after her. She recognised Sjur Gabriel's voice and was so frightened that she trembled from head to foot. When he had left she came out of her hiding place, went over to the entrance door and peeped out. She saw him walking up along Torvegaarden. Then she hurried out, crept downhill, keeping close to the house walls, and straight after was back in the boat.

When Sjur Gabriel arrived a little later, he looked sombre and careworn. Without saying a word he unmoored the boat and sat down at the oars. Oline rowed strongly and regularly, and kept going all the way home. Sjur Gabriel had to admit to himself that whatever it was she had drunk, it had not made her incapable.

A week later Sjur Gabriel was returning home from the fields after his day's work. He was carrying his spade over his shoulder like a rifle, and in his hand he had a bucket which was full of potato tops for the pig. Jens and Nils followed, each holding a spade which they dragged along the ground behind them.

'Is Ma' back ye'?' asked Jens as they came into the kitchen.

Ingeborg, who was ladling out the evening gruel, answered in the negative.

'I jus' 'ope Ma' 'ain't got lost,' said Jens, looking apprehensively at his father.

''Old yer tongue!' answered Sjur Gabriel, as he went into the living room and picked up Little-Gabriel.

Later that evening, when the children had gone to bed and Little-Gabriel had fallen asleep, Sjur Gabriel was sitting on the bench over by the table cutting tobacco for his clay pipe. He was talking quietly to himself, occasionally shaking his head.

How could Oline fall back into her old ways the moment she had got out of hospital, after he had spent so much money on her – it was too bad of her. He'd believed she would have come to her senses by now. You'd have thought she'd had time enough, all those weeks she'd been lying there and just costing money. One hundred and twenty-two days at sixteen shillings a day – that was a great deal of money for a poor farmer. But nothing had any effect on her. God knows what it was that drove her; she just carried on as if she was a dumb creature and not a human being with a living soul in her body.

Sjur Gabriel grabbed his cap and wandered outside. He could not settle. It was the second day Oline had been gone. Yesterday, whilst he was having his after-dinner nap, she had taken off. She had never been away from home for such a long time before.

As if at random he strolled into the cow barn and the haystore, stood there for a while looking around, drifted out again, peered into the peat shed and even opened the door to the pigsty a crack. Then he set off down to the sea.

During the day the weather had worsened. Now it was blowing a full storm. The sea spray was crashing over the mooring posts and was tossed high into the air.

No Oline to be seen.

Slowly and with head bent Sjur Gabriel walked back up. There must be something wrong. In his mind's eye he saw Oline's body floating with the tide somewhere, face down as she had been that evening in the boat two years previously, when he had thrown her into the stern. Just like that she was lying. Or broken on a rocky slope, having fallen from one of the cliffs over at Sandvig mountain. Face down, just like in the boat.

Aye, doubtless it was not for nothing that Skipper from Træet had been standing there in the sunset a few days ago, howling so dreadfully with its nose turned up towards the windows of the Hellemyr cabin, and was not to be driven away by threats or kind words. Oline had shaken her head, and he could see that she was thinking like him. Someone at the farm was marked for death.

He sighed deeply as he walked along.

It was true that Oline had been sinfully fond of the drink, worse and worse with each passing year – and he was only human, after all. But despite that – perhaps he had been too heavy-handed when he beat her. – One thing was certain: if she returned home this time, she would not hear a word from him, even if she was so drunk that she could neither walk nor see.

'I'll nivver 'it 'er no more – I swear to God,' he mumbled, when he was back at the cabin once more and lifting the latch on the door.

Next morning at around eleven o'clock, as he was coming back from an outlying field with a basket of peat on his back, he saw Oline approaching the hut. She was walking with small, stiff steps, with her head turned to one side and her hands thrust under her apron right up by the waistband. Silently, like a gliding shadow, she slid past him and into the kitchen.

Sjur Gabriel felt rage boiling up inside him. Unconsciously he clenched his fists at her. But then he remembered his promise from the previous evening and made do with spitting and muttering: 'Devil tek i'!'

He followed her into the kitchen and emptied the peat onto the earthen floor.

'Where you bin?'

Oline looked wretched. Her face was puce and her lower lip hung down, trembling.

'Went ter Salhus,' she answered, laying kindling under the pot.

'Wha' you doin' there?'

'Buyin' salt.'

'Fer two days?'

'It blew up bad,' – she pushed some twigs in between the peat blocks. 'We cou'nt se' off' – she bent down and blew on the fire – 'til i' were after nine.'

Sjur Gabriel followed her movements with eyes blazing.

'Damn' soak!' he snarled, grabbed the basket so hard that it gave a loud creak, slung it on his back and stomped out of the kitchen.

Oline had clapped both hands to her face with an expression of fear, and now stood half turned away, with her back bent and her shoulders hunched in order to receive the blows she expected. When she heard the kitchen door slam she peeped up and could hardly believe her eyes. But at once it became clear that Sjur Gabriel had left without beating her. She was so overcome by this unexpected event that she simply sat down on the low hearth, covered her face with her stiff, grey-striped worsted apron and cried, shaking all over.

After a while she got up, put one foot up on the hearth and began to stir the oat flour into the boiling water in the pot. Her hands were trembling badly, and she spilt some flour every time she took a handful from the wooden box hanging on the chimney wall. Her head was spinning and her temples throbbing. Her throat was burning, and her heart seemed to move all the time in her chest.

'We din' think we'd see yer any more, our Ma,' she suddenly heard someone say in a mocking tone. She turned her head and saw Ingeborg standing in the middle of the kitchen with her hands on her hips and her mouth set in a twisted grimace.

Oline made no answer, but carried on pounding the gruel feebly and without strength.

'Le' me!' Ingeborg exclaimed. "F I 'ave ter do all the rest, I'll ge' this done an' all.' She took the stirring stick from her mother.

'Ge' off wi' yer!' Oline commanded, trying to take the stick back.

'You ain't up ter workin', Ma. – Go an' lie down an' sleep i' off afore our Da' comes back.'

'You tryin' ter teach yer Ma, ye' wicked lass!'

Before Ingeborg knew what was happening, she was seized around the waist and flung across the kitchen floor. 'S'pose you think yer wretch of a Ma's so weak an' poorly you c'n treat 'er 'ow you like. You jus' watch ou'!' Oline raised her arm and threatened her. 'Them kids as don' respec' their parents, they belong ter't devil.'

'An' wha' about them parents as drink theirselves silly an' be'ave like pigs?'

Before she had even finished speaking she felt a resounding slap on her cheek.

'Yer'd think parents like tha''d think twice,' she continued, undaunted.

'Now yer'd be'er give up afore ye drive me mad,' Oline said with her teeth chattering.

Ingeborg tossed her head and left the kitchen. Straight away she put her head round the door again and said in a voice which was shaking with scorn: 'Be'er no' 'ave 'erringbones in't porridge like las' time yer'd bin off in't town. Our Da'll be proper put ou'.'

'In't name of Our Lord an''is Son!' groaned Oline, clasping her hands together and holding them out in front of her. She stood like that for a few minutes, hunched over with her head bowed. Her half-closed eyes stared down into the hearth with a helpless expression, and her mouth was pursed, sucking in her cheeks. After a while she pulled herself together, finished stirring the gruel, lifted the pot from the fire and carried it in to the table.

14

The years passed, and the people at Hellemyr struggled on in the sweat of their brows, from winter to spring and from summer to autumn. Oline drank, and Sjur Gabriel toiled, as his hair grew grey and his back became more and more bent. Jens and Ingeborg had gone into service in different places. Little-Adna and Nils inherited their places in the daily activities. Otherwise there was no noticeable change.

This went on until Little-Gabriel was six years old.

When Sjur Gabriel returned home from fishing or a trip to town, Little-Gabriel would come running towards him. If it happened that his father couldn't see him at once, Sjur Gabriel was beset by a sudden fear, so that he hardly dared to ask where the boy was. Then when Little-Gabriel appeared, he would cling on to his father's leg until he was lifted up onto his shoulders and made to turn somersaults over his head.

In summer, whenever it was at all possible, Sjur Gabriel took the boy with him into the fields. They would set off hand in hand, Little-Gabriel with a small rake over his shoulder which his father had made for him. Then when he had raked some hay together and made a little stack, his father would praise him, saying he was 'a t'rrific worker'. Or he would let him help to distribute the hay when it was taken down off the drying fences and spread out to dry. Sjur Gabriel went to great lengths to ensure that the boy didn't realise that he had to do it all again afterwards.

At harvest time he stood beside his father with his little wooden scythe, believing that he was scything grass, breathing hard and labouring away, asking his father the whole time whether he was doing it right.

With his little wheelbarrow he wheeled home peat from the outlying field and wool in the autumn, when the sheep had been sheared, always next to his father. On the journey to church on Sundays he stood in front of him and pushed the oar in order to help with the rowing. Or if the weather was too unstable he sat on the floor of the boat between Sjur Gabriel's legs, asking questions and chattering away, getting a nod or a single word as an answer.

Nils and Magne would be rowing for real, silent and serious. In the stern sat Little-Adna and Oline, if she had come too, something which happened less and less often as time passed. Sjur Gabriel was embarrassed at being seen with her, and the children no less so. They well knew that the whole of the village was aware of her shame. Many a time Sjur Gabriel had a hard battle to fight with himself in that regard. He felt that a stone was added to his conscience when he didn't take her along to God's house. If anyone needed to come there, there was no doubt that Oline did, and no-one could know whether or not one fine day she might be struck by the word of God and turned away from her sins. Oline herself said nothing. She preferred to stay away.

In church Little-Gabriel would sit on his father's lap, and most often he would be asleep with his head comfortably resting on his father's Sunday jacket.

He sat on his father's lap at mealtimes too. Sjur Gabriel fed him and ate his own meal at the same time, a spoonful each.

'Now our Da' – now Lil'Gabriel,' the boy would say, making sure the whole time that it was done properly. When Sjur Gabriel teased him by taking two spoonfuls at once, the boy would pull his beard and shout: 'Will ye be'ave, our Da'!' – the expression Oline used when she drunkenly reprimanded the children. At that Sjur Gabriel pretended to be frightened, and hastily made up for it, chuckling to himself.

What his mother sought in liquor, his father had found in Little-Gabriel. It was him he yearned for, it was him he looked forward to seeing. However downhearted and careworn he might be, the sight of Little-Gabriel always made his heart lighter and his mood softer. This fair, curly-haired boy with his big head and his thin body was what gave his toil and his struggles meaning and brightened his wretched existence. And not only his, but also Oline's and his siblings'. They used him as a shield, as an interpreter and a negotiator between themselves and Sjur Gabriel. And it never failed. If Little-Gabriel was not nearby at the critical moment, they felt wholly and utterly helpless.

15

Sjur Gabriel was standing over by the pigsty with a fisherman from Salhus, who was haggling over the price of two of his new piglets. He was holding Little-Gabriel by the hand; the lad had a green woollen shawl wrapped around his neck several times, crossed over his breast and tied behind his back. The evenings were bitterly cold and raw despite the light and sunny days of May, and Little-Gabriel had had a hoarse throat since the night before.

The fisherman from Salhus was not completely sober. He thought that Sjur Gabriel's price was too high, so he grabbed hold of him, half in jest and half in irritation, shook him by the shoulders and jabbed him with his knee.

At once Little-Gabriel flew at the fisherman, shoved him and pummelled him with clenched fists on the part of his legs he could reach.

Sjur Gabriel had to pull him away by force from the laughing and staggering peasant. Then the little boy began to cry, hiding his face in his father's coat-tails. Sjur Gabriel was alarmed by the uncanny noise issuing from the lad's throat. It sounded hollow and hoarse like someone blowing a rusty trumpet. He had never heard such a grating hoarseness.

He picked up the lad and carried him into the living room. He realised that he was not going to agree a sale on this occasion.

The air in there was heavy with a grey mist, and there was a sour smell of damp peat. He had asked Little-Adna to light the stove so that it would not be too cold for Little-Gabriel. But the wind was blowing down the chimney and driving smoke and particles of ash out of the damper. The first thing Sjur Gabriel did was to lift the burning peat bricks out into the hearth. Then he fed Little-Gabriel and put him to bed in his own bed.

That night Sjur Gabriel dreamt that he was cranking a pump which would not produce water. He pumped with all his might, but the pump just whistled and groaned. There was a person hidden inside it who was wailing with a noise which terrified him. Finally he woke up. Oh, that heaving and grating – where could it be coming from? – Oh no, it was Little-Gabriel's throat, which was making the sounds as he slept. It sounded absolutely dreadful, but it was only a cold after all. Why it should pierce his heart in such a way, that little bit of hoarseness - - . Anyway, if it wasn't better in the morning, it would perhaps be best to rub his chest with some warm candlewax.

Suddenly Little-Gabriel threw his arms wide. There was a sound from his throat as if he was choking. He jerked upright into a sitting position, tugged at the woollen scarf round his throat and screamed that he wanted it off.

His father tried to calm him down. But the lad moaned and twisted, waving his right arm about as if he was trying to fend something off. It was as if he was not fully conscious, but fighting with something invisible which was tormenting him.

In the end he quietened down, let himself be laid back down on his pillow and fell asleep.

Sjur Gabriel glanced at Oline, who was lying on the other side with her face close to the wall, sleeping like a log. What kind of a mother's heart could she have, sleeping through it all, thought Sjur Gabriel, as he lay down again. But he could not sleep. He lay there listening to the rusty, grating groans which issued regularly from the boy's throat. After a while it seemed to him that it sounded like the clanging of the church bell, ringing for a funeral.

The next day Little-Gabriel was not allowed to accompany his father to the fields.

When Sjur Gabriel returned home for his afternoon meal,* the lad stumbled over to him, lifting his arms and saying: 'Li'l-Gabriel tired, wanna go t' bed.'

During the afternoon he got worse. He lay on his back without moving. The sound in his throat had changed to a dry, sharp rattle. Suddenly he burst out in a long, staccato scream, and then lay still as before.

Little-Adna was so frightened that she rushed from the room and ran off to find her father.

It took about twenty minutes for her to get back with Sjur Gabriel. They had run the whole way and were quite out of breath when they reached the house.

When Sjur Gabriel entered the living room and saw the lad in the bed, it was as if he had been punched in the chest. He staggered backwards, and his face went deathly pale. His knees shook, and he tottered like a drunken man. He could hardly recognise Little-Gabriel, these two or three hours had changed him so much. Those flabby features, that rattle that sounded like the cry of a bird, the dimmed eyes, the sharp, narrow nose and then that tortured look of endurance – oh, how it all bore in upon him in a flash, and how it pierced his soul!

Like a sleepwalker he walked over to the bed and bent over the lad.

"Ow's our Li'l-Gabriel doin' then?' he murmured with trembling lips.

As he spoke, a hot tear fell onto Little-Gabriel's forehead. He opened his eyes to his father, looked at him for a moment with an expression so full of love and helplessness that Sjur Gabriel felt as if his soul was melting and flowing out of him.

Little-Gabriel tried to raise his arm. Twice it fell back down again. But eventually he managed to lift it, took hold of his father's hand with his tiny, burning fingers, put it to his lips and kissed it.

Sjur Gabriel sank down on one knee, hid his face against the bedpost and knelt there for a moment without a sound.

Then he stood up again and bent over the lad once more. At that moment Little-Gabriel had a fit like the one which had terrified Little-Adna so much that she had run for her father. This time it was more severe and lasted longer. Sjur Gabriel held him and moaned softly. He thought the lad was about to give up the ghost.

When it was over, Sjur Gabriel dashed over and tore his sea jacket from the wall. 'I mus' go t'town an' fetch doctor,' he said. 'Come on, lads!'

Nils and Magne, who had come in from the fields, were standing at the foot of the bed watching their brother with scared faces. They ran towards the door, saying 'We mus' ge' changed!'

'No time fer tha'!' shouted Sjur Gabriel.

The lads grabbed their caps and hurried after their father, who was running at full speed down to the sea.

16

By the time Sjur Gabriel reached town it was 7 o'clock in the evening. He moored the boat at Skuteviksbryggen,* because the district doctor he was looking for lived on Sandvigsveien. During the whole trip he had not uttered a word, but rowed with such force that the water frothed around the bow. Nils and Magne had also done their utmost. When they shipped the oars the sweat was dripping from all three.

Sjur Gabriel was unlucky. The district doctor was away, and the one he was referred to down on Øvregaden was out for dinner. From there he went to a third, who lived on the town square. Not at home. The fourth he sought was out visiting a patient. The fifth was old and tired and not strong enough to set out on a boat so late in the evening. And everywhere they asked him why he had not gone to the man whose responsibility it was, Dr Pedersen in Sandvigen.

Sjur Gabriel could have howled in despair. He had a gnawing pain in his chest, and the whole time it was as if he could hear Little-Gabriel's rattling breaths. His throat burned and ached, and he felt as if his tongue was covered in sand.

When he arrived at the sixth place down in Veiten, he was shown into a back room where he could see in front of him the back of a man who was sitting bent over a table and writing, his head framed between two lighted candles. It seemed to Sjur Gabriel that it lasted an eternity before he straightened up, half turned in his chair and asked what the matter was.

Sjur Gabriel explained his errand.

'Hmm,' said the doctor without putting down his pen. 'It's a long way. And it's almost 9 o'clock.'

'I'll give yer a speciedaler,' said Sjur Gabriel, who had remained standing by the door.

'A speciedaler – well, my good man, that is hardly sufficient for such an onerous journey in an open boat – '

'I'll give yer two, 'f only y'll come righ' away.'

'Why don't you go to Pedersen – the district doctor in Sandvigen? – He's the one who's in charge of that district.'

So Sjur Gabriel explained that Pedersen was away, and that this was the sixth place he'd been directed to. Finally he said: 'You c'n 'ave two speciedalers 'n seventy-two shillin' – tha's all I've got – s'long as you come straigh'.'

The doctor put down his pen and stood up.

'I suppose I shall have to – if that's how things stand – . Terrible time to choose – . Where've you moored the boat?'

'Skuteviken.'

'Heaven preserve me – in Skuteviken! I've never heard anything like it! Why on earth not tie up in the Triangle, if you expect decent folk to come along? – Tramping all the way out to Skuteviken – '

While he was uttering these sentences at intervals, muttering under his breath, he was exchanging his slippers for boots and pulling on an overcoat.

'A horrible sound in his throat, he says – difficulty breathing – .' He pulled out a drawer, took something out of it and put it in his pocket. Then he pocketed a bottle of medicine too, seized his hat and said to Sjur Gabriel that it would be best to open the front door before he put out the candles.

Shortly afterwards they were in the street.

It was a lovely evening. The sky was clear, and the approaching dusk had not yet conquered the diminishing daylight. They set off in silence. Sjur Gabriel went first with his long strides, almost running. He turned round every other second to check on the doctor. The latter had difficulty keeping up. He called out that he couldn't go that fast.

'You 'ave t'come quick!' replied Sjur Gabriel, without slowing down.

When they reached the boat they found Nils and Magne asleep, one curled up on a thwart with his head in his arms and the other lying in the stern. Sjur Gabriel shouted to them to get to the oars, and a minute later they had cast off and were on the way home.

Sjur Gabriel pulled on the oars with the strength of a giant. Each time the doctor in the stern struck a light to light his pipe, he could see that the face in front of him was dark red, and his eyes were bloodshot and gleaming like tawny embers.

He began to ask for more details about the child's illness, how long it had been going on, and what the symptoms were.

'Sounds as if it could be the croup,'* he said, after Sjur Gabriel had answered him, and he thought to himself: 'That kid is done for.'

'He's no' coughin',' said Sjur Gabriel.

'No, they don't cough with the croup,' answered the doctor.

'S'pose it's dangerous, tha' illness?' Sjur Gabriel then asked, his voice breaking.

'Aye, it's a devil of a sickness!' the doctor exclaimed.

Sjur Gabriel was silent for a couple of minutes. 'D'you

not think you c'n 'elp our lad?' The words emerged with an effort from his dry lips.

'We'll see, my good man – we'll see whether blood-letting can do anything.'

From then on no words were exchanged between them. In silence Sjur Gabriel pulled in to the Hellemyr landing, ordered Nils to make the boat fast to the mooring posts and hurried up the hill. The doctor, who had understood from Sjur Gabriel's answers in the boat that the situation was critical, made great efforts not to delay him. When they were ten-twelve steps from the cabin, a peculiar cry met their ears.

'What on earth – ? Do the cocks crow at this time round here, or what is that?' asked the doctor, taken aback. Sjur Gabriel walked on without answering him. He felt a great knot in his chest, and his throat constricted so that he felt he would choke, while blackness swam before his eyes.

In the open kitchen door stood Little-Adna, crying. She stood aside for her father and the doctor without saying anything.

Inside the living room Oline was sitting, rocking her upper body to and fro and picking at her apron. On the table there burnt a wax candle stuck into the neck of a bottle. The doctor picked up the candle, went over to the bed and observed the child, who was now lying still and breathing heavily, whilst his chest heaved. He passed the light to Sjur Gabriel and asked him to hold it so that he could see, and then began to feel the child's wrists and feet, finally pulling one eyelid up to look at the pupil.

'There's nothing to be done,' he said softly, as he straightened up. At that moment the same cockcrow as before erupted from Little-Gabriel's rasping throat, wilder, sharper and more long-drawn-out than before, a heart-rending sound of suffering and misery. Oline clasped her hands over her head. The doctor bent over Little-Gabriel.

'Can ye no' 'elp our lad?' asked Sjur Gabriel, who was standing stiff as a statue with the candle in his outstretched hand.

'Here no man can help,' answered the doctor darkly. 'It will soon be over.'

Sjur Gabriel passed the candle to Oline.

'Has he been shrieking like this for long?' asked the doctor.

'A couple'a hours,' Oline guessed. 'Bu' i's go' worse an' worse.'

Sjur Gabriel bent over the boy, whose breathing was growing weaker and weaker. Suddenly Little-Gabriel reached out his arms, caught his father round the neck, looked at him with a look of recognition and deathly fear, and as the scream broke from him once more, he pressed his heels down and thrust his chest high into the air, twisted from side to side and then fell back with his eyes closed. His face was ashen and bathed in sweat, with blue patches beneath his eyes, his mouth was open and foam bubbled copiously from his lips. He lay still a while, hardly breathing, then his eyes opened wide, the pupils flickering restlessly. He drew a long, whistling sigh, his face muscles twitched as if in cramp, and his whole body was shaken by a spasm. Then he stretched out his limbs and lay still.

The doctor placed his thumbs on his eyelids and pulled them down, then closed his mouth.

'It is over,' he said, moving away from the bed.

Sjur Gabriel folded his hands, held them above his head and said in a loud voice: 'Praise be to God!' – the same words as had escaped his lips on the night when he heard Little-Gabriel's first weak cry. At that moment his only thought was that the boy had been released from his dreadful suffering, and relief flooded through all his senses.

17

The doctor had gone. He had refused payment. Oline and Nils were ferrying him back. Little-Adna and Magne had cried themselves to sleep, and Sjur Gabriel sat by the bed watching Little-Gabriel, frequently wiping away a blueish liquid which kept seeping from his mouth. He had washed the child's hands and face in warm water, put a clean shirt on him and folded his hands across his breast.

So the Lord had taken his boy from him after all.

Now surely he must be avenged, that stern, cruel God up there.

He visited sinners like a devouring fire, it was written somewhere.

So the whole thing had been wrong. All his calculations were a mistake and a failure. The fact was that God never forgave, he just punished, punished, punished.

'Verily, thou shalt not escape until thou hast paid every last farthing,' he had also read somewhere.

Now the last farthing was paid. Now there was no more to give.

His own life? – Oh, how welcome Our Lord was to take that! It would be the greatest boon which could be granted to him in this world from now on. Then he would find Little-Gabriel again.

But what if he was turned away? – What if Our Lord would not recognise him, but banished him to Hell, amongst the damned?

Oh no, he could not do that, because now he had been avenged, now the debt was paid, paid down to the last, the dearest farthing. He sat there looking at the child and following his train of thought. It occurred to him dully that after Little-Gabriel had been buried he would travel alone over to Salhus, buy a bottle of brandy, row out to the middle of the fjord where it was deepest, tie himself to a large, heavy boulder, empty the bottle in one draught and then let himself fall over the side of the boat. He didn't make a definite decision about it, but the thought of it had a soothing effect on him.

As he sat there, something remarkable happened to him. He was no longer aware that Little-Gabriel was dead, but it seemed to him as if it was that summer night nearly seven years ago when the boy had had cramps, and he had saved him by bathing him in warm water. Now he was lying there dozing, and would soon be having another fit, and then he would carry in the tub of warm water and lower him into it fully clothed, and so it would pass and the lad would be well again. The warm water was standing ready out on the hearth. The tub was stored upside down beneath the kitchen table, and as soon as the lad began to move he would run out to get it. It was this he was waiting for hour after hour, with his eyes fixed immovably on Little-Gabriel's face.

The candle burned down and went out. But he didn't notice it. The day had dawned long ago, but he was still sitting in the same position when Oline and Nils returned from town.

Oline walked over to the bed and stood looking down on Little-Gabriel. Suddenly she clapped her hands to her face, bent over and burst into tears, saying: 'Now I've bin punished for me sinful life!'

It was only then that Sjur Gabriel was released from his hallucinatory state. He looked around the room, ran his hand through his hair and remembered everything. The same day that Little-Gabriel had been buried, Sjur Gabriel travelled to Salhus. When he returned home late at night, he walked away from the boat without tying it up. Staggering and singing hymns, he walked up the hills with a half-full bottle of brandy under his arm. Every now and then he stood still and took a drink from it. In the morning Oline found him snoring on the floor in the kitchen, with his head on the hearth.

From that day on both husband and wife at Hellemyr drank.

Notes

Chapter 1

a few ort: before 1875, when the modern krone was introduced, the monetary system in Norway consisted of speciedaler, ort and skilling. There were 24 skilling in one ort, and 4 ort in one speciedaler. When the modern system took over, one speciedaler was converted into 4 kroner.

narrow alleys leading down to the quay: i.e. 'Torvegaarden', which the author has annotated as ' the many narrow alleys in Bergen which slope down from Strandgaden to the harbour, and end at the seawall and the boat steps. Here can be found living quarters, warehouses, shops and inns'.

rye cakes: i.e. 'strilekaker', small cakes made with rye flour which were especially popular with the local farmers.

the Triangle: a jetty on wooden posts in Bergen harbour, where fish were brought ashore and sold.

Stril: a derogatory term for fishermen from communities north-west of Bergen.

a wooden box: wooden boxes with lids and handles were often used for carrying food.

Chapter 2

where Rubakken lives: this is not a recorded local song, although 'Rubakken' exists as a surname in Norway. A 'stabbur' is a storehouse for grain, raised up on rocks or pillars to keep rodents out.

an 'ole three ort and twelve shillin': see note to Chapter 1. The price Oline finally sells the breastpiece for, 12 shillings, is only half an ort and little more than Sjur Gabriel got for the fish.

a Halling leap: 'Halling' is a folk dance during which the men perform wheeling leaps, sometimes touching the roof rafters with their feet.

Chapter 3

Smørsalmindingen: 'Almindinger' (nowadays 'almenninger') in Bergen are the wide sloping avenues, often with planted areas, which in many places lead from the higher streets down towards the lower ones. They have houses on both sides, which from a distance look as if they are built on terraces (author's note). The word 'allmenn' means 'common', i.e. they are common ground.

Chapter 6

Strusshamn: a village on Askøy, a small island a few kilometres west of Bergen. It was formerly known as Strudshavn.

lefse: a traditional soft flatbread made from potatoes and flour.

Chapter 7

a smoothing board: before the advent of irons and ironing boards, material was smoothed while damp by being rolled round a wooden roller and pressed by a flat board of carved wood.

Chapter 8

Don' go to any trouble: it was the custom to provide good food for an important visitor, and for the visitor to display reluctance to eat.

Chapter 10

Halling: see note to Chapter 2.

Chapter 11

In vain we rise ... : a translation of a German hymn by the Reformation author Lazarus Spengler (1479-1534). This is the second verse of a hymn that begins 'Forgjæves er Arbeid' og Konst' (In Vain is Working and Scheming).

O Lord, turn not thy face from me: I have not been able to find a source for the Norwegian hymn, so I have substituted a similar English one (from *Hymns Ancient and Modern*, no. 93).

Chapter 12

the nightclothes the child was wearing: Skram calls the outfit a 'Stril', which she explains is an all-in-one garment like a modern sleepsuit.

Kingo's large hymn book: Thomas Kingo (1634-1703) was a Danish bishop and poet, published a hymn book in 1699 which is still used. The hymn 'Jesus dør, og Jorden ryster' is one of Kingo's, here in a translation by Mark DeGarmeaux.

Chapter 15

his afternoon meal: i.e. 'non', one of the main meals of the day which would be eaten around 3pm.

Chapter 16

Skuteviksbryggen: the oldest preserved wharf in Bergen, formerly called *Skudevigsbryggen*.

the croup: a respiratory infection common in babies and young children. Before vaccination it was frequently caused by diphtheria and was often fatal.

Two Friends

1

One afternoon in the early 1850s a peasant woman came walking unsteadily up Ladegaardsbakken in Bergen.*

She was so small and spindly that from a distance you would think she was a child. It was only when you got nearer that you discovered she was an old woman. Her back was bent from the hips, leaning forwards at an angle. Her red nose was stuck on her flat, sallow face like a swollen lump. Her lower lip hung down on her chin, seemingly too heavy to be hoisted up into its natural place. In the middle of her lower jaw were two long narrow teeth which had grown crookedly to either side, leaving a gap in between. No other teeth could be seen. There were no eyebrows over the small red eyes, which gleamed beadily like worn copper coins.

When she reached the top of the hill she stood still and wiped the drops of sweat from her nose with her thumb and forefinger. The sun was shining directly into her face. She screwed up her eyes and turned her head to one side.

Ahead of her lay Sandvigsvejen, which led onwards into town, with its deep sandy wheel ruts and many bumps and hollows. To the right the open grassland with the long, tarred rope manufacturers shelved downwards towards the boathouses. Over their red rooftops, beyond the shimmering white waves, you could make out the point of Nordnes with the fortress, where the flag moved occasionally in the lazy breeze. To the left the rocky scree with its masses of raspberry bushes and clumps of long grass sloped upwards towards the mountain. A river bed with a trickle of water in it wound its way deep down between boulders of many different sizes. Further away towards the town you could glimpse under a whitish, steamy layer of fog the grey stone wall and white and black burial crosses of the cemetery of the Church of the Holy Cross.

After pausing for a moment the woman shuffled onwards. She was drunk, and was weaving about from one side of the road to the other. Now and then she stumbled, but saved herself from falling over by flailing her arms and shifting the weight of her upper body.

The few people she met stopped walking and turned to watch her. This part of the road was fairly empty. It was not until she had passed the cemetery, where the main road narrowed between the cabins and cottages which stretched down towards Stølen with open spaces in between for drying and bleaching washing, that there were more people around.*

'Madam Tosspot! Hey up, 'ere's Madam Tosspot!' There came a sudden shout from a few barefoot children, who were playing 'The Farmer Wants a Wife' outside the labourers' lodging house, whose yellow façade towered up on the left with its many small windows, at some distance from the other houses on top of the hill.* ''Ooray for Madam Tosspot!' And they set off running gleefully after the old woman.

At that sound it was as if youngsters sprouted from the earth. In a moment the few who had been playing had turned into a whole crowd. Giggling and hallooing, they followed on the woman's heels.

Madam Tosspot rambled on without any change of expression on her stiff, apathetic face. Only when they pulled at her jacket tails or tapped on her scarf-covered head did she suddenly turn round and hiss at them like a cat. At that they were scared and leapt backwards a few paces, but as soon as they saw her back they began to run after her as before.

'There's Tippler Tom an' all! Look ou', now we'll 'ave some fun!' called one of the larger boys in a grating falsetto, pointing down towards the corner of Skudevigen.

All eyes turned in the direction indicated, and in the next moment the air was rent with piercing screams of joy from a multitude of children's voices.

A parade of male and female tramps, big and small, was coming towards them. At their head a drunken porter was forging ahead with wild hops and expansive arm gestures, as if he was fighting his way through a swarm of people. Now and then he stood still to address the crowd, who clapped their hands, laughed and made a commotion.

It was not long before the two processions came so close to each other that they were bound to collide. Madam Tosspot, who was rambling onwards as before, didn't seem to hear or see them. A sudden push in the back sent her tumbling straight into the arms of the porter, who was just then turning round to walk on, after stopping for a moment to say something to his companions which provoked a storm of laughter.

Tippler Tom threw his arms around Madam Tosspot and bent over her with a wide astonished grin, exclaiming: 'Wha's this? – Is tha' you, Ma Oline?'

'They're kissin', Tippler Tom an' Madam Tosspot's kissin'!' came a shout from the onlookers. ''S i' time ter call the banns? 'S a luvly couple!'

Tippler Tom stopped hugging Oline and fumbled for her hand.

"Ow abou' we tek a stroll, our ma,' he said affectionately. 'You an' me tergether, Oline. Le's 'ave yer 'and.'

Oline held out her hand with a hoarse grunt. Then they wandered off hand in hand, staggering far to one side and then to the other, sometimes moving forwards and sometimes backwards, occasionally right round in a circle.

Tippler Tom's heavy bloated body looked even larger beside Oline's skinny little figure. On one side of his big, bulging head sat the remains of a panama hat. The brim was almost completely detached from the crown, which had large gaping holes in it. A grey knitted jerkin was pulled down over his threadbare trousers with their loose, hanging seat. A porter's rope dangled from his shoulder down over the bent and crooked back.

They made their way along the rutted Stølegade with its low houses of varying shapes and sizes, all with pointed gables. On one side the row of houses was squeezed up against Mount Fløyen just behind them, and was partly built up on its slopes. Some of the house fronts stood on granite walls which were ten to twelve feet high, with steps set sideways to the house or projecting out into the street, whilst others were at ground level. From the kitchens at the back you could walk out into the tiny backyards, where the green mountainside formed a solid wall.

When they had walked for a while, Tippler Tom stopped and stuck two stumpy fingers down into his waistcoat pocket.

'I think I still go' four shillin', he said. "F you've go' summat t'add to it, Oline, we c'n 'ave some fun this evenin'!'

'They're mekin' a couple, they're settin' up 'ouse! 'Ooray for Tippler Tom an' Madam Tosspot!' the bystanders shrieked, nudging Oline and pulling at Tippler Tom's porter's rope in their excitement.

Oline lunged half-heartedly at those closest to her, and

stuck out her unnaturally long tongue.

'Tek no notice of them good fer-nothin's – pah!' Tippler Tom spat into the midst of the flock. 'Give us yer arm, li'l Oline, an' i'll be easier!'

Oline did as he said. She was walking as if in a daze, staring straight ahead of her, regardless of whether they were going east or west.

'You need cheerin' up, Oline,' said Tippler Tom in an affectionately reproachful tone. 'We'll 'ave ter drop in somewhere an' 'ave a refreshin' drink.'

'I ain't go' no money,' answered Oline.

'In't this where yer daugh'er lives?' Tippler Tom said suddenly, stopping in the gutter.

'Aye, there.' Oline pointed across the street at a long, brown, single-storey house with four sets of windows, two on either side of the front door, and with attic gable windows set into its red roof.

'Tom, Tom the Tippler man,
'ee can' tuck 'is own shirt in,
'is Da' were a lord!'

the chorus went up. The porter joined in:

'Tom, Tom the Tippler man,
'ee 'ad a luvly wife.
She kept 'er shift in the oven
an' a sweet'eart back in 'er room!'

'I'll teach yer, yer pack o' rascals!' – He was overcome by a sudden fit of rage. He swung his rope and ran with his arm raised at the mob, which scattered and fled, only to return straight after.

'Come on, li'l Oline,' said Tippler Tom, turning to her. 'Le's go an' pay our respec's to Madam Tønnesen. Isn' tha' wha' she's called, yer daugh'er?'

'Reckon she is, since 'er 'usband's called Tønnis.'

Tippler Tom dragged Oline with him across the street, and then they clambered up some steep steps with side panels of solid wood decorated with two rows of S-shaped peepholes. They kept stumbling, and the enterprise looked hazardous, but they made it safely to the top, where they reached a narrow covered veranda, which ran along the front of the house and was edged with two-foot-high panels matching the ones on the steps.

''Ere!' yelled Tippler Tom, turning towards the flock below as he placed his large blue paws on the edge of the railings. 'Now Tippler Tom's in't pulpit, so now you'll 'ear wha' a fine preacher 'ee is.'

''Ooray for Tippler Tom the preacherman! 'Ooray, 'ooray' 'ooray!'

'Beloved fellow sinners,' began Tippler Tom, baring his head, where his grey hair was matted together in a solid mass, 'unless you become as children or drunkards you will never be admitted to the kingdom of 'eaven. P'raps you don' believe i', yer frog'eads? Consider the birds of the air – tha's 'ow i' is wi' me an' all. Soon as they le' me ou' o't work'ouse, they go' work all lined up fer me. – They daren' do owt else – they're afeard o' wha' I'll say, tee hee' – he screwed up his eyes and laughed hoarsely. 'These damn' new-fangled ideas, this 'ard labour rubbish, tha's jus' invented as a cross an' a trial for God's critters. – Bu' they'll nivver ge' the be'er o' me. – Beat tha', said the devil, as he stood in the pulpit' – he thumped the railings, threw back his shoulders and emitted a howl of laughter.

"Eavens preserve us, 'ee's tha' cocky these days,' exclaimed a maidservant who was standing amongst the onlookers with a basket on her arm. 'Ever since they said in't paper tha' Tippler Tom were Bergen's wittiest tramp, 'ee thinks 'ee c'n rampage abou' jus' as 'ee likes.'

'Aye, i's turrible wha' our Lord 'as ter pu' up wi'', lisped a toothless old woman with a yellow-edged scarf wrapped around her head like a turban, a short patched underskirt and her feet in a pair of cut-down men's boots. She raised her dull eyes heavenwards and shook her head. "Ee's bin actin' up like tha' for thir'y years now, I reckon, an' still Our Lord 'as the patience ter spare 'im.'

Oline had sat down on the veranda without more ado, tucked her knees up under her chin and wrapped her arms around them.

'Wha's 'appened ter Madam Tosspot?' some were shouting, standing on tiptoe to try and get a glimpse of her. 'Madam Tosspot mus' be the sexton. You fergo' t' say Amen, Madam!'

At that moment the door behind Tippler Tom opened, and a mannish-looking woman with a bibbed apron, dangling earrings and a tulle cap with silken ribbons over her shiny brown fringe came into view.

'May I ask what is the meaning of this?' she asked in a loud voice, her flaming cheeks turning pale as she caught sight of Oline.

Tippler Tom turned round.

'Migh' I ask 'f i's no' Madam Tønnesen I 'ave the honour to haddress?' he said, attempting to adopt a deferential stance.

'I'll give you honour, you drunken pig! Jus' mek yersel'

scarce, be off wi' yer righ' now! – Run down to't docks an' ask Tønnesen to com''ome as quick as 'ee can!' The last sentence was shouted in through the half-open front door.

'Well, an' you such a decent 'oman, usin' tha' kinda language! You should know be'er an' tha', Madam,' Tippler Tom admonished her.

'Get yersel' down off my steps, you work'ouse drunkard, or I'll put the skids under you!' Madam Tønnesen grabbed his shoulder with her large, bony hand.

Tippler Tom wrested himself free.

'Tek yer 'ands off me when I'm spreadin' the word!' he yelled. ''S true, I've become a vicar, le' me tell you. – This 'ere's my flock!' He pointed down at the street. 'Ho ho, Madam! Ask 'em 'f I'm no' as good at preachin' as t'vicar they laid to rest las' week.'

''Ee is, 'ee is!' howled the onlookers in chorus.

'There, you can 'ear for yersel', Madam.'

Madam Tønnesen stood there indecisively. Her nostrils flared and her mouth opened, even though she kept pressing her lips together.

'Won' one of yer go fetch a copper?' she suddenly shouted over the railings.

'No, we won', not us!' they bellowed back at her.

'You ain't talking abou' fetchin' t'polis, Madam?' Tippler Tom put his hands on his hips and shook his head at her. 'Surely you in't goin' to be such an unnasheral daugh'er as t' go an' fetch …'

'See 'ere, jus' keep yer peace, Tom, an' be off wi' yer.'

Madam Tønnesen, her arms shaking, had stuck her hand in her pocket and fished out a coin, which she placed in the porter's palm, closing his fingers over it.

''S jus' wha' I said, I knew yer'd see sense 'f you wus 'andled proper,' said Tippler Tom triumphantly.

'Well then, be off wi' yer,' said Madam Tønnesen placatingly. ''S no' very nice, all this 'ubbub right by me windows.'

''Course, 'course, I'm off now. – 'Bye, Madam, 'bye to yer,' he bowed repeatedly, his voice smooth and unctuous. 'Ta' fer now, an' come again soon. – I'll do tha', wi' many thanks.' He turned and staggered down the steps, taking no notice of Oline, who had remained sitting in the same position, seemingly paying no attention to what was going on. Her listless eyes seemed unable to fix on anything, and her jaw moved up and down as if she were chewing or talking to herself.

'Off you go, you an' all, wi' yer sidekick,' continued Madam Tønnesen through gritted teeth, as she bent down and got hold of her mother's shoulders from behind. Then she put her knee against Oline's back and propelled her towards the edge of the steps, as Oline loosened her arms from hugging her knees and waved them about wildly. She moved her head up and down, forward and back, trying to discover what it was that was pushing her along. Suddenly she threw her head on one side and bored her two long teeth into the hand on her shoulder.

Madam Tønnesen pulled her hand away with a jerk and shook it up and down. Then she gave Oline a final shove with her knee, making her slide over the edge of the steps. Halfway down she turned head over heels, and finished up down on the pavement in a sitting position.

'Wow! Madam Tosspot's bashed 'er backside! She's come down 'eadfirst!' screamed the jubilant onlookers.

'Whassa', you pushin' yer own ol' Ma down t'steps?' called out Tippler Tom. 'You sh'd be ashamed o' yersel', yer unnasheral *Stril*!* 'Ave you ever seen the like – down t'steps!'

Madam Tønnesen had watched her mother's descent with her shoulders raised and hands clasped in fright. However, when she saw her start to crawl around on all fours straight after, making an attempt to get to her feet, she realised that no harm had been done. She went inside hastily, shutting the door behind her.

When Oline had regained her feet, she bent down and picked up a sharp stone and hurled it towards one of the windows of her daughter's house. It went straight through the glass.

'Come on, le's go up again – she's no' gonna' ge' away wi' this,' Tippler Tom declared, taking hold of Oline's hand and placing his foot on the bottom step.

At that moment a stocky man in white work trousers, a shiny hat and a blue denim overshirt with arms rolled up pushed his way through the crowd. He smelled of stockfish; his hands were red and damp from herring brine, and there were large wet patches on his clothes.

''Ey up, i's Tønnesen! Tippler Tom be'er look ou'! Shove over, 'ee's terrible strong!' came from the onlookers, who moved out of the way of the approaching man.

'Where d'you think you're goin', you damned sot,' said Tønnesen, taking Tippler Tom by the scruff of the neck and dragging him down from the steps; he gave him an almighty push, so that he tumbled into the middle of the street, pulling Oline with him.

''Scuse us, Mister Foreman,' began Tippler Tom, when he had pulled himself together a little. 'I was jus' accomp'nyin' yer mother-in-law up to 'er daugh'er.'

'You jus' shut yer filthy mouth an' shift yersel' ou' of 'ere, else I'll gi' yer summat to think abou', you ol' soak!' He went up to Tippler Tom and shook his fist under his nose.

'Well tha's a nice way ter greet yer nearest an' dearest! An' you ain't no more'n a dockworker a'er all, Mister Foreman!'

'Shove off!' Tønnesen bellowed. ''F you mek me real mad, I'll bea' yer flat as a shillin' – You got tha', you pisspot?' With that he placed the palms of both hands on Tippler Tom's back and shoved him down the street, which sloped steeply downwards at this point.

'Jus' gi' me time, gi' me time, Mister Foreman sir, I'm goin', aren' I?' – 'S tha' a way ter trea' a feller Chrishan?' yelped Tippler Tom, as he descended the street at a forced trot, still holding on to Oline's hand.

Tønnesen remained standing at the top of the hill, watching them until they turned the corner of Stølen by Smedesmugalmindingen.* All at once the crowd around him had disappeared. The whole swarm had followed after Tippler Tom and Oline.

Down on Almindingen at the corner of Øvregaden Tippler Tom suddenly stopped and laid a finger on his nose with a profound expression. ''Ow many skirts you wearin' today, li'l Oline?'

'Two,' answered Oline, as if talking in her sleep.

'Ye should 'ave neither silver nor gold in yer belt, an' no more 'an one kirtle, which bein' interpreted means skirt,' intoned Tippler Tom in a sermonizing voice. 'Tek off t' bottom skirt, li'l 'oman,' and he laid his hand on her shoulder and bent down to look into her face, 'then we'll go an' sell i' ter Madam Davisen in Påtholle, so's you c'n add a couple'a shillin' an' all.'*

Oline didn't seem to understand. She stood there rocking on uncertain legs, staring helplessly ahead.

'We'll not 'ave enough else, silly,' he went on, shaking her crossly. 'You din' think I were goin' ter fund refreshments all on me own, did yer?'

'No, tha's no' likely, is i'?' mumbled Oline uncomprehendingly.

'Well then, tek off yer underskirt an' don' 'ang abou', he ordered brusquely. 'You gonna' say no, you sozzled ol' fish?' He grabbed her black worsted overskirt with both hands and hoisted it up over her head.

'Did yer see tha'? Now there'll be fun, Tippler Tom's undressin' 'er!' the people around them cried delightedly.

'Come on, ge' tha' underskirt off, else yer'll 'ave me ter deal wi', said Tom threateningly.

Oline fumbled at her waist with gnarled fingers, and managed to undo the hooks, letting the threadbare green baize skirt slide down over her legs.

A fifteen-year-old boy in grey trousers held up by braces over his shoulders with a grey woollen shirt underneath came walking up Øvregaden. He was humming a popular song, marking the beats by stamping his wooden clogs on the sharp cobbles; when the melody demanded it he took a few dance steps. On his head sat a cap with a stiff peak shading his eyes, and under his arm he carried a bundle.

When he caught sight of the crowd up by Smedesmugalmindingen, he stretched out his neck with a look of curiosity in his wide-open eyes, and set off running towards it.

At that moment the knot of people began to move. The circle opened up, and he could see Tippler Tom with something in his hand which he was dragging along the street, and with Oline on his arm, lurching towards him. With a jerk the boy came to a sudden halt. His head sank forwards as if his neck had been broken. His fingers groped irresolutely down his trousers, and he turned round slowly. All at once his back hunched and his whole body seemed to shrink. It looked as if he wanted to leave, but couldn't move. He stared down as if paralysed at one of his clogs which had fallen off his foot. He could hear the crowd approaching. In a moment it would knock him over if he didn't move. He stole a glance to each side. Just next to him on the left was Bødkersmuget. Suddenly he bent down, snatched up the clog, took a couple of long unsteady strides over the gutter and the narrow pavement and reached the alley, starting to climb up its steep stone steps.

'Come along wi' us, Sivert! Tippler Tom an' Madam Tosspot's goin' t' Pâtholle ter sell 'er skirt for booze!' a boy's voice called after him.

He pretended not to have heard.

'I's 'is gran – yer know, i's 'is gran,' said a voice straight after. And then: "Ee's ashamed, 'ee don't want no-one ter see 'im.'

Once Sivert was sure that they had all gone past he sank down on one of the stone steps halfway along the alley and buried his face in his hands. A silent scream of pain and hatred convulsed him. The shame gnawed at his heart and burned in his temples. Almighty God! To have to endure this time after time, time after time. Such consuming ridicule and mockery – and his grandfather was just the same. There was not a boy in the whole world who was worse off than him. And how could he expect to get on in the world? People would be afraid to get involved with a rabble like that. All at once he became aware that there was someone on the steps behind him. Quickly he put his hand down on the stone surface and let himself slide in a sitting position all the way down the steps. When he had reached the bottom he stood up, slipped round the corner of the alley and ran like a thief down Øvregaden. At the bend by the German Church he stood still, looking back. No, there was no-one to see, the street was so winding; but he fancied he could hear an echo from them. Oh, if only it was not a sin to kill! He could get hold of her and drown her down by Kvarven,* or push her over the edge somewhere up on Sandvigsfjældet, where she passed by on her way to and from town. His grandfather too, although he was more bearable. At least he didn't wander around making a street spectacle of himself.

2

Down in Dræggen, halfway between the German Church and the dock area, lay a small house.* It looked old and crooked. The grey paint was badly weathered by sun and rain; only here and there could you see remnants of it in long, blistered strips. The front had two low windows with tiny panes; then there was the front door, and another window which was higher up and even smaller than the two others. Up above in the middle was a small pointed gable with a shutter standing open.

The front door opened directly into the kitchen. There stood a stout woman of medium height, washing up cups and plates, which she was stacking upside down in a trough. She was dressed in a skirt and jacket, and had a cloth cap on her head, decorated with zigzag braid and fastened under her chin with a starched bow. Both her hands and her broad face were covered in masses of brown freckles. Her nose was short and shapely, her mouth small and curved with very thin lips. Of her eyes you could make out only two narrow slits, as the rest was hidden beneath heavy, strangely hooded eyelids. On her feet she had felt slippers which were trodden down at the back.

The door opened with a squeak of its hinges, and the woman turned her head to see who was entering.

'Oh, it's you, Sivert, – I thought it were Father,' she said, carrying on with her work.

The boy went into the living room beside the kitchen without answering.

When the woman had finished washing up, she sprinkled coffee from a cone of paper into a kettle which was standing on a trivet over the fire in the hearth.

'Mus' be time fer food then,' she said to herself, as she picked up a large loaf of dark bread and a knife and started cutting slices off it on the kitchen table.

 Shortly afterwards the door opened again, and a man in sackcloth working clothes came in to the kitchen. He hung his dented woven hat on a wooden peg and wiped the sweat from his forehead with his sleeve.* Then he went over to the hearth and took off his clogs.

'Yer Da's in town again today,' began his wife. She was standing with her back to her husband, spreading butter and *gammelost* on the slices of bread.*

'Aye, so I've 'eard,' answered her husband, sighing as he sat down by the kitchen table, which was so high that only the tip of one slipper reached the floor. He took one of the bread slices and began to eat.

'Can ye no' talk to 'im an' tell 'im to stay 'ome?' his wife went on in a sulky voice. ''Ee allus use' to. 'S turrible 'avin' 'im botherin' us afore we know where we are, 'im an' all. Seems ter me we've more'n enough wi' yer Ma.'

'I reckon tha'll stop any'ow, soon enough. 'Ee's on 'is las' legs …' the rest of his speech was incomprehensible. His mouth was too full of food.

'Wha'?' said his wife. 'Yer can't ea' an' talk a't same time. – 'Ere's coffee.' – She passed him a steaming bowl which she had poured out on the hearth. 'Will I bring yer food in't other room, Jens?'

'No, I'll jus' 'ave it 'ere.' He took the bowl and drank from it. 'I've ter go down an' check on Da, so I'll 'ave to 'urry …' Again his words were muffled by the chewing.

'A fine lot o' good tha'll be. I'd no' bother 'f it were me,' huffed his wife.

''F only you'd known our Da like 'ee use' ter be, Marthe.

Sjur Gabriel Hellemyren were t'most 'ard-workin' an' straight-up feller on …' – he took a bite – 'two legs,' he finished off in a thick voice.

"'S all t' more shameful 'ee's the way 'ee is, then,' interjected Martha.

"Ee 'ad such a no-good wife, poor chap. 'Ow c'n a man mek ends mee …' Now he had no more time, but put the coffee bowl to his lips.

"Ow many wives ain't got no-good 'usbands,' said Marthe, tossing her head.

'An' then our li'l lad died for 'im. – 'S enough ter break yer 'eart …' he got no further for a mouthful of food.

"Ow many don't 'ave ter put up wi' losin' kids?' Marthe was buttering one slice after another and putting them on a pile. "Ain't we lost four of ours, an' yer don' see any of us goin' off 't rails! Tha's jus' summat yer've made up as an excuse.'

'People in glass 'ouses, puff puff,' – Jens was lighting his clay pipe – 'shouldn', puff puff, throw stones!' With that he shoved his feet into his clogs, grabbed his hat and hurried out.

When Marthe had finished buttering bread, she swept the crumbs on the table together with her hand, down into her apron. Then she opened a door beside the hearth and threw the crumbs into a small fenced-in backyard.

"Ere, chick-chick,' she called. 'Well, I think they've gone ter roost already.' She peered into a woodshed, where some hens were asleep on a perch up under the roof. 'Aye, they 'ave an' all, tha's awful early fer town chickens. Oh well, they c'n 'ave it in 't mornin'. – Time enough.'

She closed the door and wiped her fingers on a damp teatowel, then changed her apron and went into the living room, where she sat down by the window to knit.

Over on the bench in the corner sat Sivert, leaning against the wall and staring into space, lost in thought.

On the table between the windows lay the bundle he'd been carrying under his arm when he came in.

'Tha's nowt t'leave lyin' on't dinin' table, our Sivert,' said Marthe, pointing at the bundle. 'Yer dir'y apron covered in wax. Tek it ou' to't kitchen.'

On his mother's words Sivert got up, picked up the bundle from the table and carried it out. Then he came in again and sat down as before.

'Wha's wrong wi' yer this evenin', Sivert? Yer look ou' o' sorts.'

'Nowt' – he answered with a little twitch.

'You don' want yer food either. Wha's up wi' yer?'

Sivert twitched again, and a tremor passed over his face.

'Yer granpa's bin 'ere again today – drunk, o'course,' she then announced in a tone of voice as if she was speaking to herself, which she frequently did.

'They're a sorry couple, yer Da's parents,' she went on shortly after, and then carried on talking in short bursts, knitting and shaking her head. 'I jus' 'ope you kids'll tek warnin' an' not be'ave like tha' when ye're grown up.

'Both jus' as bad. – Yer nivver saw owt like it. Nay, my parents was different – they migh'a bin poor, bu' they was decent. – Anyone 'oo knew' em 'ad respec' for' em.

'Spick an' span, an' tha's 'ow Ma kept us too. – An' the livin' room, shinin' it were, floors so clean you c'd ea' yer dinner off 'em – wi' flowers in't windows like 'ere, an' starched curtains like ours – even if Da's workshop was in't livin' room an' all. Tha' rich ol' Thor Monsen was 'is best friend – they 'eld prayer meetin's together.'

144

'Was 'ee a preacher-man, your Da?' asked Sivert.

'Not 'xacly a preacher-man, bu' 'ee was righ' God-fearin', Ma an' all. – An' ye'll ge' nowhere wi'out tha' in this world. I don' reckon yer Da's parents were tha' fussed wi' bein' Chrishans. Tha's a' t'bottom o'it all.'

She was silent for a minute or two, then she lowered her knitting and looked across at Sivert.

'Wha's up wi' yer tonigh', lad, ain't you 'ungry or wha'?'

'No.'

'Bu' you mus' be 'ungry. I'll go get you a drop o' coffee.' She got up and left the room.

Once Sivert was alone, he suddenly began to snivel. His face muscles quivered, and he grimaced in anguish. Then he threw himself face down on the table and cried so hard that he shook.

"Eavens preserve us!' Marthe was standing beside him with her hands full of food and coffee. "As your Master bin beatin' you?'

The boy just sobbed.

"Ave you ruined t'candle moulds? Look a'me, Sivert lad. You've no' lost yer place?'

'No Ma, I ain't,' Sivert stuttered.

'But wha' is it, then, child?'

'It's Gran!' he suddenly shouted with a hysterical sob. 'She were 'angin' onter Tippler Tom's arm. – They were goin' t'Pátholle t'sell 'er skirt.'

'Tsk, tsk, aye, it's a dreafful thing fer a granchil' to 'ave ter see,' Marthe burst out indignantly.

'There was an 'ole crowd followin' 'er,' Sivert went on. – 'They yelled a' me.'

'Aye, tha's jus' like them good-fer-nothin's! But there's no 'elp you cryin', Sivert lad, tha' won't change owt.'

'It brings shame on us,' sobbed Sivert.

'Not on you, lad. Wha' c'n you do abou' it? No decent folk'll blame you kids for it.'

'No, bu' even so –' Sivert groaned.

'Come on, dry yer eyes and come an' eat.' Marthe put the slices of bread and the coffee cup down on the table.

''Ere comes yer Aunt Ingeborg,' she peered out through the window. 'Ain't she lookin' puffed up, – she be'aves as if she were a lady, ever since she took to wearin' capes, don' she jus'. – Lor', don' tell us she's comin' 'ere? She is an' all! Wha's up now, wha's she makin' a fuss abou' this time?' Marthe sat down and picked up her knitting.

Sivert had quickly straightened up and dried his eyes on his shirt sleeve. Now he got up for his food and coffee and hurried back to the divan.

Straight after that there came a knock, and before Marthe could say 'Come in' the door opened and Madam Tønnesen stood in the room.

'In't Jens 'ome yet?' she asked, looking round.

''Ee's bin an' gone,' was the answer.

'Aye, I c'n tell by the smell!' said Madam Tønnesen. 'Tobacco stink an' 'erring stink! Why don' you open a window in this lovely weather?'

'We ain't got such fine noses down 'ere in Dræggen as you lot up in Stølen,' replied Marthe in a dry, sarcastic tone. 'Bu' when it comes to 'baccy stink an' 'errin' stink, I sh'd think Pitter Tøn'esen's wife'd be well acquainted wi' them smells.'

'Well jus' you stop a minnit! Tønnesen changes 'is clothes out in't kitchen afore 'ee comes in, an' 'ee always smokes long pipes an' much dearer 'baccy. Anyways, a foreman don't get 'is 'ands mucky like a labourer.'

'Ain't you the lucky one!' said Marthe, wrinkling her nose

with an audible sniff.

'Aye, thank the Lord, I can' complain.' Madam Tønnesen tossed her head so that her long earrings dangled.

'Won' yer sit down?' asked Marthe after a moment.

'I c'n stand all righ'.'

'Worried yer migh' mess up yer finery?' Marthe looked askance at her colourful fringed shawl, which hung so far down that its point reached the hem of her dress.

'No need to poke fun, Marthe lass, 's easy to see ye'r jus' jealous.'

'Jealous!' Marthe laughed scornfully.

'Well, why else'd yer be so worried abou' my clothes? I can''elp it if you 'aven't the money to wear a cape.'

'You'd no' catch me mekin' such a spec'le o' missel', Marthe shifted in her seat and clattered her knitting needles. "S enough if one of us in this 'ere family puts on airs.'

'They'll be sour, said t'fox ...'

Madam Tønnesen was interrupted by the door opening to admit Jens.

'You ou' an' abou'?' he said in a voice which did not express any particular pleasure at seeing his sister. He went across and sat down beside Sivert, who was eating with his bowl of coffee in one hand and his bread slices on the bench between his knees.

'Aye, I came t'ask yer 'ow long you gonna let this carry on wi' Ma,' began Madam Tønnesen with an indignant expression. 'She were over at mine again today wi' Tippler Tom. – A great one she is – fallin' down drunk both o'em o' course.' She stopped suddenly as if she was choking on her own words.

Jens leaned forwards with his arms on his knees and clapped his hands together slowly. 'Hm, hm,' he said sadly.

'It ain't no good sayin' hm, hm,' Madam Tønnesen imitated him. 'Any fool c'n do tha'.'

'Wha' d'you expec' Jens ter do, then?' Marthe asked aggressively.

'Oh, tha's righ'! Jus' you tek 'is side. – You'd do be'er ter mek 'im do summat, you're s'pose ter be 'is wife.'

''S jus' a cross you 'ave ter bear, Ingebor', like the rest of us,' said Jens with a deep sigh.

'Cross indeed! Wha' kinda ol' wives' tattle is tha'. Today she picked up a stone an' chucked it righ' through our window. I sh'd think she'll be settin' fire to t'ouse righ' this minnit. I'd be 'appy if she did, then she'd get 'ersel' arrested at any rate.'

'Saints preserve us! Sayin' such things abou' yer own ma!' exclaimed Marthe.

'Aye, tha's a cruel way ter talk, Ingebor',' said Jens indignantly. 'Anyways, i's yer own fault – 'f you be'aved a bi' kindlier ter our Ma, poor wretch, I sh'd expec' she'd leave yer windows alone.'

'Own fault, be'aved kindlier – well you're a great 'elp!' Madam Tønnesen was blazing red, and her earrings were positively dancing. When she got cross she always reverted to the peasant dialect which she and Jens had otherwise discarded. – 'I c'd 'ave tol' missel' tha' afore I came. – Ever since you wus a lad yer've played along'a Ma an' smarmed up t'er. 'F i' weren' fer you, praps she'd a bin a be'er person.'

'Ye're worse 'n a ra'lesnake,' Marthe announced with heavy emphasis on each syllable, ''cos a ra'lesnake, 'ee ra'les a' least, afore 'ee strike, bu' tha's more 'an you do.' Marthe had got to her feet, thrown her knitting down on the table and immediately grasped it again with shaking hands.

'Tek no notice o' 'er, Marthe,' said Jens soothingly. 'You know 'ow she is.'

'Why can' she leave us alone then? Wha's she wan' wi' us?' Marthe was almost in tears.

'I nivver ask''er 'ere,' said Jens.

Madam Tønnesen stood with her head thrown back, surveying the upper panels on the walls.

'Hee, hee,' she laughed. 'I'm jus' standin' 'ere thinkin' wha' mean folks y'are.'

'I come from decent folks, I'll 'ave you know.' Marthe let her hand fall heavily on the table as she stretched out her neck and turned her head from side to side. 'My Da' was a shoemaker and 'im an' Ma was born in town, an' they kep' company wi' rich Mons Thorsen an' 'is folks, an' 'ad both t'vicar an' t'store owner to their funeral. Tha's more 'an wha' yours'll 'ave.'

"Ush, 'ush, Marthe.' Jens had moved from his place on the bench and laid his hand on her shoulder. 'You 'eard wha' I said, tek no notice of 'er. 'F you've only come 'ere t'stir things up,' – he turned to his sister – 'I'll ask yer t'leave again.'

'I came 'ere t'talk to yer about Ma, but all I ge' is insults!' She was fiddling with her shawl pin with her chubby fingers, which looked even fatter in her mauve string gloves, sliding it constantly to and fro. 'But I'm tellin' you, 'f you don' do summat abou' getting' 'er locked up in't work'ouse, I'll tell Tønnesen to set abou' it.'

'Aye, you c'n set away for me,' Jens grunted. "Ow often do I 'ave ter tell yer, they won' accep' anyone in't work'ouse wha' doesn' come from town distric'?'

'Tha's no' true! I know there's country folks in there, 'cos I asked abou' it. You jus''ave to submi' an application.'

'Bu' wha's the point?' Marthe broke in. 'In six month she'd be ou' again, so we're no further forrard. – Tha's the most time they'll 'ave 'em in there.'

'They c'n stay there if we pay reg'lar,' said Madam Tønnesen.

'I' meks no difference, Ingebor',' Jens replied harshly. 'I tell yer once an' for all, I'll nivver agree ter bring such shame over our Ma.'

'Bring shame!' Madam Tønnesen raised her eyes heavenwards. 'You reckon there ain't enough of tha' ter start wi'? I s'pose it brings honour to all of us, seein' 'er runnin' abou' t'street wi' Tippler Tom.'

'Aye, tha's righ' enough,' muttered Sivert from over on the bench. For once he agreed with his aunt.

''S anyone talkin' ter you?' snarled Jens across to him. 'Jus' you 'old yer tongue.'

'Nay Sivert lad, 's no good talkin' sense to yer Da, 'ee's allus bin like tha',' said Ingeborg acidly.

'I'll 'ave nowt ter do wi' it!' shouted Jens. ''F Pitter Tønnesen goes to t'authorities, I'll go too, mek no mistake. As long as God lets 'er carry on the way she do, 'ee must 'ave some purpose wi' it.'

'I'm not so sure abou' tha', Jens,' said Marthe, without lifting her eyes from the knitting she was busily working at. 'Wha' abou' lunatics, folks 'ave ter do summat abou' them.'

'Oh, lunatics, lunatics' – Jens obviously didn't know what to answer. 'I'm no' talkin' to yer any more. There's no reasonin' wi' crazy women.' He took his clay pipe out of his pocket and began to fill it.

'Will yer listen to tha'! Will yer listen, 'f 'ee can' find an answer, 'ee says we're crazy.' Ingeborg looked triumphant.

'Well, she'll no' be taken to't work'ouse as long as I'm alive, no ma'er 'ow much fuss you mek.' Jens had gone over to the table and was thumping it with the knuckles of his right hand. 'She mebbee mis'rable an' weak, bu' we're all 'uman, an' a ma's a ma a'er all. An' tha's an end of i." He gave a decisive thump and went out to the woodshed, where he began splitting logs.

Shortly afterwards Ingeborg left the house. She went out with a scornful: 'Thanks for 'avin' me,' to which the answer came from her sister-in-law, who did not look up from her knitting: 'Bye an' thanks for visitin."

' – Wha' you moonin' abou' for, Sivert?' A couple of minutes had gone by, during which nothing else could be heard but the clattering of the steel needles. ''Ave you gone a-woolgatherin'?'

'Can' yer leave me in peace? Wha' 'arm am I doin'?' answered Sivert in a whining voice.

'You c'n jus' go an' put t'cups down, lad. You'll be droppin' 'em on't floor, you're 'alf asleep!'

Sivert got up and took the coffee cups out.

'I'm gonna go to sea!' He had come in again and was standing in front of his mother, looking challengingly at her.

'Well, 'ave you 'eard the like.' Her hands sank down into her lap with the knitting. 'You don' mean tha'?'

'Why no'? Olai was 'ired on a brig, an' t'same shipowners're sendin' ou' a big bark in a few months.'

'Wha' kinda nonsense is tha', lad? Wha' put tha' in yer 'ead? 'F yer Da 'ears o'tha', I reckon 'ee'll tan yer 'ide.'

'Wha's i' gotta do wi' 'im? Weren' I confirmed two year since, may I ask?'

'An' now, jus' as ye're 'prenticed to t'candlemaker an' earnin' a few shillin' a week as well as lunch an' dinner?'

'I'll get much more at sea.'

'You jus' be'er forget all abou' it. 'S tha' a steady job for a lad o' fifteen? Don't you remember 'ow 'ard it was for yer Da to get tha' place in Hollændergaten?'*

'D'I ask fer tha', praps? I said then I wanted ter go to sea.'

'Aye, you've nivver known wha' you want. – Firs' you was an errand boy, then you was 'prenticed to a fishin''ookmaker, then you wanted ter be a clockmaker. I really though' you'd settled to summat now.'

'I'm no' stayin' 'ere in town! I can' bear it!' shouted Sivert passionately. 'I nivver know when I'll bump into Gran on't street. 'F you don' le' me go to sea, I'll be doin' some 'arm to 'er – or else to missel'!' He shook his clenched fist, his face red with fury.

'Jus' you stop yer noise, lad!' His mother slapped his arm aside. 'You need t'learn ter button yer own pants afore mekin' such a fuss abou' tha'.'

'I don' care, 'f you don' le' me go, I'll run away! I'm tellin' you!'

'I'll give you runnin' away!' She threw down her knitting and stood up, raising her arm threateningly. Sivert was over by the door in one leap.

'I'll do i', I'll do i'!' he yelled. The next moment he was out on the street.

'Wha' a monkey,' muttered Marthe, peering at him through the window. 'But p'raps i's no' such a bad idea a'er all, you c'n mek a good livin' - . We'll 'ave ter see wha' Jens says to i'. Ah, 'ere comes Trine – 's too bad 'ow late they mek that lass stay on. – An' she's only an 'ousemaid!* God knows where Nils an' Simen 'ave got to? Aye, them kids, them kids – they're allus a worry - . It'll be dark any minute an' all.'

3

The bark *Two Friends* stood out to sea with double-reefed topsails.* It was the middle of February. At the time they left port, the weather was fine with a southerly wind and reasonably calm seas. Towards evening the wind freshened and moved to the west. During the night it intensified to gale force, and they were steering directly into it. The captain had to haul in one sail after the other. Now, the next morning, the sea had become stormy, with head sea and beam sea crashing into each other. It was foggy, and the captain had decided to steer a course north of the Shetlands.

On the edge of the main hatch, with his arm around the stern of a dinghy which was leaning against the hatch waiting for repairs, sat Sivert, dozing with his mouth open and green in the face. In one hand, which was hanging down slackly, he was holding a boot, in the other a brush. Both items bore clear traces of his seasickness.

The first mate was walking forrard on the deck, and stopped by the hatch where Sivert was sitting.

'Saints in Heaven preserve us if that isn't the worst landlubber I've seen in all my born days,' he exclaimed, stopping to spit.

"Ee does nowt but sleep an' puke,' said the cook, coming out of the galley with a canvas bucket of water he'd been washing potatoes in. 'Best thing is to sluice 'im down a bit.' With that he emptied the bucket over Sivert's head.

Sivert uttered a shriek and started up with a bewildered expression. At the same moment he lurched over to leeward, followed by the boot and brush, which he had dropped in his fright.

'That's a fine mess you've made o' my boots!' shouted the first mate. 'Jus' you ge''em dry an' shiny this minute, else I'll tan yer 'ide, ye' wastrel!'

'Bu' wha' 'm I ter do?' wailed Sivert, who had been slung back against the hatch as he squatted by the movements of the ship, and had caught hold of the boot again. ''S no' possible ter stand up when i's rollin' like this!'

'Eejit!' said the first mate, with a kick to his backside. 'Wha' you doin' goin' ter sea? Did anyone ask yer to?'

'Yer migh' well say tha', mate,' exclaimed the cook. 'An' they expec' food an' wages an' all. We sh'd get paid for takin' pigs like tha' onboard ship.'

'Jus' mek yerssel' scarce,' said the first mate to Sivert, who was on his knees being sick, clinging to the corner of the hatch. ''Ere, 'and 'em over!' He grabbed the boot from Sivert. 'You best find summat else to puke on, my boots is too good for tha'!'

''Ere, cook,' the first mate went on, throwing the boots into the galley, 'see if yer c'n mek these into a pair o' boots again.'

'You jus' be'er scrub this lot clean, pigface,' ordered the cook a little later, as Sivert sat on the hatch holding his head in both hands.

'I'm jus' so turrible dizzy,' complained Sivert.

'Well, yer poor critter, so ye'r dizzy, are ye? Well, 's a shame ye forgo' to 'ire someone ter wait on yer!'

Sivert stood up, green in the face, and staggered over to a canvas bucket which was hanging on the galley door. Then he tied a rope to it, crawled up onto the spar to leeward and tossed the bucket overboard. As he reached out over the hammock netting to haul it up, his cap blew off his head.

'Me cap! I lost me cap!' he yelled, looking round at the

cook in despair.

'You best jump in after it then!' bellowed the cook from the galley door. 'Quick, quick, afore we leave i' be'ind!'

Sivert looked helplessly out to sea. He couldn't see his cap anywhere.

'After it, after it!' the cook went on. He leapt over to Sivert, grabbed him by the legs and hoisted him up.

Sivert clung on to the net, dumb with terror.

The door to the companionway opened and the captain came out on deck. He was a stocky, short-legged figure with a red, weatherbeaten face. The skin around his short, stumpy nose with its flattened tip was stretched tight. His small brown eyes were deepset and deeply furrowed; both they and his eyebrows seemed set at an angle, as if they had been forced upwards by staring at wind and weather. Hair and beard were black and bushy, his forehead a mass of fleshy folds, and his lips were thick. He was wearing a pea jacket buttoned up to the top, and had a purple woollen scarf wound several times around his neck. On his head sat a cap of grey duffel cloth with no brim, and his trouser legs were pushed down into his high seaboots, which were folded over at the top. He was walking aft to talk to the helmsman.

'Over ye go after yer cap!' repeated the cook, who was having fun pretending he was going to toss Sivert into the sea.

'Help! Help!' screamed Sivert. 'The bucket! I lost the bucket!'

'Butterfingers!' exclaimed the cook, letting go of Sivert's legs. ''F you nivver got a beatin' afore, you'll ge' one now.' He caught hold of a rope end and set about beating Sivert, who shrieked wildly.

'Wha' the devil's all this about?' The captain came forrard hurriedly. 'I thought for all the world it was the pig being slaughtered.'

''Ee dropped the galley bucket in't sea, capt'n, the best new-painted bucket.'

'Did 'ee, by Christ! I'll gi'ye summat to howl about, I'll learn yer to haul up water to leeward, you scoundrel!' The captain seized the rope end from the cook and belted Sivert until the lad lay writhing on the deck.

'Out o' my sight,' the captain commanded when he'd finished, 'an' don't show yourself again till you've learnt to stand on your own legs and keep your vittles down.'

Sivert went aft. He was staggering about on the heaving deck as if he was drunk, and holding on to anything within reach. He was crying out loud from the pain.

On deck towards the stern was the wheelhouse. In the middle was an area which was open at the front; that housed the ship's wheel, with room for the helmsman. On either side of the opening, which was constructed like a house of cards, was a room which extended so far out on both sides that there was only the width of a man between the outer walls and the sides of the ship. Here were the cabin doors. At the front of the rooms beside the opening sat a small window which was covered on the inside by a curtain made of gathered cotton fabric.

'You'll 'ave ter stop leakin' like tha', stupid,' said the bosun, who was standing at the wheel under the roof of the cockpit as Sivert approached. 'Even if they knock you silly twice a day, you mustn't let the tears come, lad. The more you cry, the more beatings you'll get.'

Sivert could hear from the way he spoke that the bosun was trying to help him. It was the first glimpse of kindness he had come across on board. He looked at the man in surprise and stopped crying immediately.

'It's true what I'm tellin' you, sonny,' the bosun nodded. 'You're much too old for blubbin' anyway. This is somethin' else than sittin' at 'ome be'ind yer mum's skirts, you know.'

'Why're they treatin' me so bad, then?' burst out Sivert, gnashing his teeth in resentment.

'It's no worse for you than for anyone on their first trip, perticular wi' you bein' so seasick an' all. Jus' you wait till you finish throwin' up, then you'll see it gets be'er. An' then you 'ave to learn to fight.'

'Fight, who with?'

'With everyone,' explained the bosun. 'Ye'll nivver get any respec' at sea 'f you canna fight. First thing you 'ave to do when you're on your feet is thrash the cook.'

'What's our course?' shouted the captain. He had been in the bow and was now coming aft.

'Nor'west to north, capt'n!'

'The devil we are, with the sails flappin' like that.'

At the sound of the captain's voice Sivert had hurriedly ducked around the corner of the wheelhouse and escaped into the starboard cabin where he and the second mate had their berths. The first mate slept in the port-side cabin.

Sivert climbed over the chest in front of the lower berth, where the second mate was asleep and snoring, and up into the upper berth, where he stretched out his bruised and aching limbs on the rock-hard eelgrass mattress.

Oh, how he wished he had not come to sea. It gnawed at the roots of his heart to think of how good everything had been at home. And all that he had thrown away, of his own free will and against his parents' wishes, only to end up enduring something as terrible as what he was experiencing now. He was cold and wet and filthy, and then this unbearable nausea. Oh, oh, oh – here it came again. If only he could make it out onto deck in time, so he didn't get anything on the second mate's chest, otherwise there would be another thrashing. He stumbled down from his bunk and onto the deck, leaned out over the railing and let it come. Oh, oh, oh, there was no way out, he would finish up by puking up his stomach and guts as well. If only he was sitting at home with Mother, eating bread with butter and *gammelost* – ugh, he couldn't bear to think of food – but sitting on the edge of his bed in the corner in peace and quiet, lying down at night and sleeping safe and sound the whole night long. Oh, what misery he had brought upon himself.

When he was lying on his mattress again with his face in the pillow and his knees braced against the side of the bunk for support, he fell asleep and dreamed that he was in church, and that the organ was playing a fearfully melancholy tune. Then the bell in the belfry began to ring, and at the same moment the door to the pulpit was wrenched open; the vicar was standing in the doorway shouting something, as an ice-cold blast blew through the church.

Sivert forced his eyes open and sat up. There stood the first mate in the cabin doorway, rousing people for dinner. The organ he had heard was the moaning of the wind, and the ringing the sound of the ship's bell chiming eight bells. So it must be dinner time, and he should have been down in the mess setting the table.

'Second mate, you'd best mek 'aste an' get food on't table. That there corpse ain't gonna move. – Capt'n's cursin' an' blindin'.' As he spoke, the first mate slammed the door and disappeared.

The second mate rolled out of the lower bunk onto his chest and pulled on his trousers, yawning fit to dislocate his jaws.

'Devil take such carrion,' he said a moment later, standing up and pulling on a tunic over his jersey. 'When you gonna pull yersel' tergether an' start earnin' yer keep, yer lazy good-fer-nothin'?'

Sivert lay with his eyes closed, pretending to be asleep.

Half an hour later the door was opened again, and as he lay in the bunk the bosun passed him a biscuit and a bowl of steaming pea soup, with a chunk of meat floating in it.

"'Ere, get that down you, lad.'

'Don' want any,' answered Sivert with a grimace.

'No nonsense, lad! This is the only way to put you right.'

Sivert sat up and reluctantly accepted the bowl.

'You finish it up, every last drop, or you'll get a thrashin'.' The bosun shook his tarred fist at him.

Once Sivert began to eat, it went down more easily than he had expected. When the bowl was empty, he wedged it between his pillow and the wall and began gnawing at the biscuit. Before he had finished it he fell asleep.

When he awoke it was dark. He felt better than he had done since coming onboard, and he lay there wondering how late in the evening it was. Then he wriggled forwards and looked down into the lower bunk to see whether the second mate was there. But it was too dark to see. He crept down onto the chest, stretched his hand over the bunk and felt around. No, it was empty. So it couldn't be eight bells yet, because the second mate was due to have a free watch to sleep between eight and twelve. At that moment the clock struck six bells, and straight after that he heard the shout to turn out.

So it would be best to turn out and go down to the mess and get ready to serve, thought Sivert.

When he came out on deck there was a moment when the wind seemed to take his breath away. There was a greyish light in the sky and large black piles of clouds were racing past the mast tops. There was a smattering of rain, and the sea looked like a mass of moving hills which were crowding in from all sides. The ship was listing so heavily that the leeward bulwarks were almost trailing in the water.

'Ready to go about,' roared the captain, who was standing to windward amidships, peering up into the whirling storm.

'Aye aye capt'n, ready to go about!' came the answer from the bows.

'Hard over!' he yelled, turning to look aft.

Sivert stumbled over to the hood which was pulled right across the steps down to the forecastle, and opened the door, struggling with all his strength to stop it being torn out of his hands. Then he bent double, banging his forehead against the side of the companionway regardless, and crawled backwards down the steps, after managing to close the door behind him with a struggle.

'All hands to po-osts!' he heard the captain thunder, lengthening the last word so that it split into two.

In the small rectangular forecabin, in which the mast cut straight through the oilcloth-covered table, there hung a metal lamp, swaying and smoking. Sivert took a pewter teapot out of a cupboard and shook tea into it from a metal box. The door to the inner cabin was open, and Sivert peeped in. On the small leather-covered sofa lay some rolled-up sea charts. The floor was running with water, which seemed to be seeping through down by the floor from the port store cupboard. In the cabin to starboard the captain's bunk was not made up.

'Blimey, what a mess,' muttered Sivert. 'An' capt'n boasted 'is cabin was allus to be shipshape as a dolls' 'ouse. 'S easy ter see t'cabin boy's bin abed.'

He climbed up on deck with the teapot in his hand. He was amazed to see that it seemed to have grown lighter. He glanced up at the sky to see whether it might be moonlight.

'Come about!' bellowed the captain, putting his hands to his mouth like a loudhailer and trumpeting the words out.

'Ye'd think 'e'd split hissel' in two, hollerin' like tha!' thought Sivert, as he fought his way into the galley and poured water into the teapot from a pan of boiling water, after which he put the teapot on the stove to mash.

'Wha's tha', tha's no place ter put t'pot,' scolded the cook, coming into the galley. 'Tha'll slide off an' break.' He cuffed Sivert and moved the teapot so that it was standing securely.

'Seems tha's a bit calmer now,' said Sivert in an effort to placate him. 'Weather mus' be gettin' be'er.'

'Eejit,' the cook spat. 'We're comin' abou'. Jus' wait, yer'll soon be pukin' again.'

Sivert looked out on deck.

'Yo ho heave ho!' sang the bosun, as he stood with two others hauling on the forestay, which he then made fast to a belaying pin.

'Well, 'ow's things wi' you then?' he asked a little later, as he caught sight of Sivert.

'I'm not seasick any more, no' even dizzy,' answered Sivert.

'Pass us t'coffeepot,' said a deckhand, coming over to the galley door.

'Don' you mean t'teapot?' replied Sivert.

'D'you drink tea slops in't mornin' an' all down in't cabin?' returned the deckhand, as he went off with the teapot.

''Ee's 'avin' a little joke, 'ee is,' said Sivert to the cook. 'Ee says it's mornin'.'

'Are you right in't 'ead, or what?' asked the cook, putting his hands on his hips. 'In't tha' stockfish back there soakin' this mornin', an' ain't it on Fridays we 'ave fish? I think you puked up wha' little brains you 'ad to start with, or are you pullin' me leg?'

Sivert ran along the deck. 'C'n you tell me wha' day it is today?' he asked the bosun.

'Tha's Friday, lad, wha' d'you think it is?'

'I's not mornin', is it?'

'Course it's mornin'. – You've slept t' clock round.'

Sivert was already gone. 'Oh, Jesus,' he muttered, 'tha's mornin', an' 'ere's me makin' tea instead o' coffee. Lord 'ave mercy on me.'

Quick as a flash he tipped the tea out into the sea and filled the teapot with coffee from the forecastle, which he carried aft, where the first mate and captain were already waiting.

'So you gonna oblige us wi' some coffee after all,' growled the first mate.

'Wha's this, you lout?' the captain exploded. 'Can't you think of anythin' else but spoilin' our teapot wi' coffee?'

'I picked up t'wrong one, capt'n, it were so dark I couldn' see wha' I were doin'.'

'I'll give you dark,' answered the captain, boxing his ears.

At that moment the ship heeled over violently. Inside the cupboard the crockery began to slide about, then the door flew open and a plate rolled out onto the floor and smashed, followed by a pewter jug.

'You spawn of Satan, you didn't shut the cupboard door,' roared the captain, jumping up and grabbing Sivert by the back of the collar; he shook him so hard that his head jerked up and down whilst his face turned red.

'You're stranglin' me, capt'n!' squeaked Sivert hoarsely.

The captain released his hold on his shirt collar, got hold of him by the scruff of the neck and pushed his face right down to the ground, where syrup had run out of the pewter jug.

'Now you c'n lick up that syrup you spilt,' he said, rubbing Sivert's nose on the floor, after which he gave him a push with his knee which tumbled him over.

When Sivert got up and revealed his smeared face, the captain and the first mate burst out laughing. Sivert wiped his face with his shirt sleeve, put the syrup jug back in its place and closed the cupboard door. Then he collected up the pieces of the smashed plate.

'How much have you smashed since you came onboard?' asked the captain.

'Two mugs,' answered Sivert.

'Not more! Tha's a smooth lie,' was the scornful reply.

'What about those two side plates then?' said the first mate.

'Tha' weren't me. They fell off t'table when it rolled,' Sivert defended himself.

'Aye, 'f you can't be arsed to put fiddles on't tables, you layabout.'*

'Tha' were back when we set sail, I didn' even know there were such a thing as fiddles.'

'All that gets broken back 'ere, it's you that broke it,' said the captain harshly. 'Understood?'

'Understood!' he yelled more loudly, when Sivert said

163

nothing.

'Yes, capt'n,' muttered Sivert.

'Every last fragment,' continued the captain. 'It's all your fault. Two mugs, two side plates and one dinner plate so far then. There'll not be much left of your wages. We'll buy new ones in Kingston, and there mugs cost half a speciedaler apiece and side plates two ort, just so's you know. It's all the same to me what you spend your money on.'

Sivert stood staring at the shattered plate with a helpless expression.

'How many knives and spoons have you tossed overboard with the washing-up water?' the captain went on.

'None,' replied Sivert gloomily.

'Is that right! Oh well, whatever takes your fancy.'

The captain stood up. 'When we get a day of calm weather we'll do an inventory of what's in the pantry. Then we'll see what's missing.' With that the captain went into the inner cabin and filled his pipe.

4

One afternoon a week or so later, when the captain had had his afternoon nap, Sivert was set to cleaning the cabins. It was the first day since they had set sail that the weather was reasonably fair. The wind was still against them, but it had gradually abated considerably, and the captain was hoping that it would die away by evening and then switch to the north.

He was in a terrible mood. It was now eighteen days since the pilot had left the ship in the archipelago, and he had still not managed to put Scotland behind him; for the whole of the last week he had been unable to measure the meridian, but had to make do with the log and compass and every now and then with taking a sounding.

Sivert was finished with scrubbing the floors and dusting in the cabins. Now he was sitting on the main hatch polishing the lamps, whilst he hummed a snatch of a popular song. On his head he had a canvas cap which the bosun had made for him to replace the one which was lost overboard.

He had now got over his seasickness completely, and was beginning to feel content onboard. He had also learned to fit in better, and got into trouble less frequently than at the start. What he was set to do, he carried out promptly and precisely, and came running like the wind with his cap in his hand when the captain or one of the mates summoned him.

When he had finished the lamps he went down into the cabins and hung the smallest one in the captain's quarters. With the other he climbed up on the table, over which he had spread a piece of canvas, and hung it in its place up by the skylight, which was ajar. Then he jumped down and looked round. Yes, now everywhere looked really clean and shining, not a speck to be seen anywhere. The portraits over the sofa of the captain's wife and children were so bright that they gleamed. – But then he noticed that he had forgotten the mirror over the bench under the windows in the rear of the cabin. He fetched a cloth from the forecabin and began to rub the mirror. Then he put his head on one side to see if it was clean and stopped still to look at his reflection, as he stroked around his mouth to feel if his sprouting beard had grown at all. It was dreadful how dirty he was, black in the face, his shirt stiff with dirt and seawater, and his hair so wild and bushy that it was enough for three people. Once he got to Jamaica he would go ashore and have a haircut and a shave; he could ask the bosun to show him where to go. Then he would buy a piece of soap and wash himself in fresh water. Would his hands ever return to their proper colour? He lifted them up and studied them back and front.

'A clunkin' fist,' he said under his breath, clenching his large, powerful hand with its strong joints and thick fingers. 'Tha'll be good fer splittin' t'cook's 'ead open.' He bared his teeth and made a growling noise as he waved his fist to and fro in front of the mirror, his knuckles touching the glass.

'You standin' there admirin' yoursel', you loafer?' came a sudden voice from the half-open skylight above him.

Sivert was so startled by this unexpected address that he jumped quickly to one side, without noticing that the door to the foodstore had been pushed open at the same moment and something had been pushed through it on the floor. The next moment his foot had landed in a sawn-off keg which had butter in it.

'You startin' yer foolin' again, are ye?' went on the voice.

'You've been OK the last coupl'a days, – that's too much for ye, I s'pose!'

Sivert looked up and spotted the captain standing bent over, looking down through the open skylight.

'I were jus' rubbin' t' mirror, capt'n,' he called out unabashed, leaning forwards so that the captain couldn't see where his foot was. 'You sh'd see 'ow clean an' shiny it all is down 'ere, capt'n.'

'Aye, you've always got a ready answer!' said the captain, moving away from the skylight.

Sivert balanced on one foot, hopping, whilst he took off his butter-smeared boot and wiped off as much of the butter as possible with his index finger, throwing it with a flick of his wrist back into the keg.

As he was busy with this, the door to the foodstore opened again and the second mate shoved a sack of biscuits through the opening with his hands and feet.

'T'devil tan yer miserable 'ide!' he burst out in horror. 'What 'ave you done wi' tha' bu'er, yer filthy swine!'

'There were summat as frighted me so bad, I saw flames afore me eyes, mister mate, – an' then it were jus' like I were struck blind.'

'Aye, yer'll be struck blind sure enough!'

''S true!' Sivert assured him. 'I were polishin' t'mirror, an' then it appeared, an' then I leapt out'o't'way, an' tha's 'ow I trod in't bu'er.'

'What appeared, yer wretch?'

'A ghost,' said Sivert energetically. 'Tha' came driftin' down from t'skyligh' or wha'ever it were, I saw i' clear as day in't mirror, bu' when I turned round it were gone.'

'Aye, tha's a likely story,' said the second mate, trying to look indifferent.

'Story!' Sivert stuck his finger in his mouth, leaned his head back and solemnly drew a cross on his throat. 'You gonna b'lieve me now?'

'Wha'd it look like then?' asked the mate.

'It were dressed in grey,' began Sivert glibly, 'an' a jacket wi' shiny buttons righ' up t't neck, an' a white beard righ' down t't chest, an' its hair an' hands was streamin' water, an' it 'ad a streak o' blood on one temple.'

'Yer fibbin'!' the mate broke in, with a fearful look on his face.

'Fibbin', am I? Oh well, I'll not tell ye any more then,' said Sivert, offended.

'Go on, tell us, what 'appened?'

'It looked tha' miserable,' Sivert continued, 'jus' as if it weren't at peace, an' then it raised its 'and to its 'ead, like this,' Sivert slowly lifted up his arm ' – as if it were in torment, an' then it turned its eyes up so's you c'd see t'whites, an' sighed, an' then it were gone.'

'Din' yer see any more?'

'No' a trace.'

'Nor 'ear nowt?'

'Jus' a sigh.'

'Tha' mus' mean summat,' the mate asserted with a shudder. 'Bloody 'ell.'

'Aye, tha's wha' I think an' all,' remarked Sivert with a voice that sounded as if his teeth were chattering.

'But what'm I to do wi' this bu'er?' The mate bent down over the keg. 'You'll be for it with t'capt'n.'

'We c'n scrape off the muck from me boot wi' a knife,' suggested Sivert, 'an' then we'll mix in some flour or add some lard so's it weighs the same. Folks'll not notice.'

'Aye, ye're not short of ideas,' replied the mate, as he

picked up the keg and took it back into the storeroom.

A little while later Sivert asked the captain for permission to wash some of his clothes.

'Wash yersel' to hell,' answered the captain.

Sivert collected his dirty washing, filled a bucket with seawater which he warmed in the galley, and sat down on the main hatch to wash, with the bucket between his legs.

A little later the cook came along with a vat of hot water, which he put down next to Sivert.

'Don't you go stealin' my water while I go an' get soap,' he said, thrusting a bundle of shirts and socks down into the vat, 'or you c'n go to't devil.'

The captain was walking up and down the deck, swearing and spitting. The weather was getting rougher again, and contrary to his expectations the wind had not veered to the north. Every now and then he snorted loudly, kicked the deck, tore his cap from his head and hurled it to the ground. When he had put it on his head again, he clenched his fist and shook it at the sky. Suddenly he came rushing over to Sivert.

'What's all this? You're not usin' the meat vat to wash your filthy shirt-tails in?' he yelled in a voice shaking with rage.

Sivert, who was sitting at his bucket, didn't think this was addressed to him and carried on washing without pausing.

'And what kind of water is that you're using?' went on the captain. 'Stick your finger in it and taste it, sailmaker.'

A young chap with fair curly hair and a canvas tunic over his homespun jerkin, who was sitting on the other side of the hatch patching a sail, stretched across the hatch on his stomach, dipped his long finger in the water and put it in his mouth.

'That's fresh water, capt'n,' he said.

'Didn't I know it! The saints preserve us from such a pack of thieves!' Sivert received a violent clip around the ear. 'You'll bloody well get nothing but seawater to drink from now on, using fresh water for washing.'

'Tha's no' my water, capt'n!' howled Sivert. 'It's cook's – I'm washin' in seawater, let sailmaker try this one!'

At that moment the cook came along. He denied that the water was his, and Sivert got a beating.

'Ye'll get it back, capt'n, jus' you wait, jus' you wait, tha's a crime to beat someone for summat they ain't done!' yelled Sivert furiously as the captain hit him. Suddenly he twisted out of his grasp, ran over to the shrouds and climbed like a cat all the way up the rigging to the mast top.

The captain stepped back in surprise, then turned round at once and ran back, lifted the vat in the air, sprang up onto the port spar and tipped both water and clothes into the sea. 'That'll learn him to tell lies,' he said triumphantly.

The cook jumped as he saw the captain upending the vat into the sea, and he raised his arms involuntarily; then he stopped himself and gave a forced laugh. 'Serve 'im right, the scoundrel.'

But now it was the cook's turn to feel the heat. The captain discovered that he had used a new and expensive copper cooking pot.

There was an almighty fuss. The captain demanded to examine all the cooking pots, and the cook, grumbling and reluctant, had to get them all out for inspection. As the examination proceeded, the captain's wrath increased. There was something wrong with every piece. One of the casseroles was missing one handle, another had a deep dent in the side, on a third the bottom was almost burnt through, none of them were properly cleaned and some of the rims were covered in rust.

The captain bellowed and cursed and screamed, so that the veins in his forehead stood out red.

'Are you tryin' to poison the whole crew?' he shouted finally. 'Don'cha know that rust is poison through and through, you jailbird?'

'Aye, it don't surprise me tha' 'ee wrecks the pans,' remarked a sailor, who was sitting on an upturned bucket nearby splicing a rope. 'Every single day we get food that's burnt and black, capt'n, an' t' meat soup's so salty it makes yer sweat.'

'Why don't you beat 'im senseless, then?' snorted the captain. 'If I were crew, I'd not put up wi' such a poltroon of a cook. You 'ave my permission.'

'An' tha' fresh water weren't Sivert's, capt'n,' said the sailmaker. 'It was t'cook's, like the lad said.'

'You listen to me, cook,' the captain stood close up to him, speaking right into his face with his thick red lips. 'This'll cost ye a pretty penny when you 'ave to pay for what you ruined.'

'So what the devil are you gettin' upset for when I'm payin' for it anyway?' said the cook defiantly.

The captain looked as if he was about to split in two with rage. He uttered a neighing sound, as his eyes searched in all directions. Suddenly he leapt down into the galley, yanked open the oven door, and seized a piece of wood which was ablaze at one end; swinging it over his head, he set off at a run after the cook, who fled aft.

It turned into a chase around the whole ship.

'Help, help! Capt'n's lost 'is wits, grab 'im!' hollered the cook, tearing round the deck and leaping over anything which stood in his way.

The others stopped what they were doing to watch. Some of them laughed and hallooed, one of them shook his head deprecatingly.

'Now t'cook's gettin' a taste of 'is own medicine! Hurrah! Hurrah!' called out Sivert from up on the mast.

Finally the cook jumped up on the poop and climbed on all fours out onto the jib boom, where he tried to hide behind the flying jib.

The captain stood still below the poop and hurled the glowing, smoking log after him. It whistled past the cook's ear and fell into the water with a hiss. Then the captain turned and strode off down into his cabin. He was breathing hard, and his knees were shaking.

'The Lord protect us from such sinful uproar,' exclaimed the helmsman, a grey-bearded sailor with his hands covered in tattoos, as the second mate came over to examine the compass. 'I've been at sea for nearly thirty years, and I've never seen a captain chasin' folk wi' burnin' brands afore.'

'It's 'avin' the wind against us as does it,' answered the mate. 'T'capt'n soon gets stir crazy in a contrary wind. It were like that on't last trip an' all.'

'Aye, I'll not sail again on this vessel, I'd sooner take hire on a slave ship,' muttered the helmsman.

'Well, if I'd known what I know now,' said the mate, nodding mysteriously, 'I'd nivver 'ave set foot aboard *Two Friends*. T'ship's doomed, that she is.'*

Soon after Sivert crept down from the mast and started washing again.

''Ow many shirts d'ye think ye've earned today, cook?' he asked, as the cook appeared by the galley.

'You'll pay me for those shirts, you can cross yer 'eart an' 'ope to die!' yelled the cook.

Suddenly the cook started to go berserk.* He uttered a howl, kicked the pots, swung the frying pan over his head, lifted the chopping block high into the air and slammed it with all his might down on the deck again. Then he grabbed a rope end and attacked the main hatch with it like a madman, whilst emitting a stream of oaths and curses, mixed with a stifled sobbing sound. He cursed the captain's and the crew's limbs and entrails, the rigging and the galley, the cooking pans and the supplies, the whole ship, and every nail and every rivet of it. After a while he dropped the rope, pulled out a belaying pin and started hammering on a water butt with it, all the time carrying on shouting and cursing. Sivert watched, not knowing whether to laugh or cry. The crew were enjoying it, at the same time as pretending they were trying to calm him down. The helmsman leaned over to look, making the sails quiver. Then the second mate came running, and asked the cook what he thought he was doing. The cook's ravings simply got worse and worse.

'I'll go fetch the capt'n,' said the mate, walking aft.

At that threat the cook dropped the belaying pin, stuck his hands in his trouser pockets and wandered forrards, continuing to curse but in a more subdued voice. Then all at once fury seemed to overwhelm him again. He bent his knees until he was almost crouching down, then leapt in the air with a prolonged bellow, and crashed down again with a thump of his boots.

When the second mate returned with the captain he ordered that the cook be restrained, and with a great deal of commotion and difficulty they finally managed to overpower him. While this was going on Sivert danced round them with a gleeful face, gesturing frantically.

Whenever he could get close enough he pulled the cook's hair or pinched his ears. Once they had bound his hands they heaved him into the paint store beside the galley and shut the door.

In the meantime the wind had got up more and more. The sky was full of a thick, pale grey fog, pierced here and there by strips of dirty yellow metallic light, which made the air heavy and threatening.

5

That night Sivert was woken by a resounding crash, and for a moment he thought it was a cannon from the fort back home, which always sounded as if someone was shooting directly under the windows.

Straight after that the bunk heaved upright beneath him, so that it was almost as if he was standing up. Then it felt like someone pushing from behind, lifting his upper body from the mattress so that he banged his head on the roof of the bunk. He grabbed hold of the side with both hands, and was tossed to and fro so violently that his shoulder joints cracked; then suddenly the bunk turned into a steep hill, so that his legs were straight up in the air – after which the whole thing began again.

The walls of the cabin were creaking and cracking. Outside the wind was howling and roaring, and the sea was crashing against the sides of the ship as if trying to break everything to pieces. And everywhere was a sound of booming, as if enormous dogs were thumping the boards with their tails.

Sivert was surprised that he couldn't hear any tumult of the crew on deck. Were they not doing anything to save themselves and the ship? Or did they know that it would all be in vain, and were they just waiting calmly for the end?

He was sweating with fear. Oh, to think of dying like this - - the ship breaking up - - filling with water - - sinking - - being torn apart - - launching the boats - - him holding tight to a plank - - clinging to the keel - - clinging to the keel - -

He sat bolt upright in his bunk, staring into the darkness, and held on with all his strength in order not to be thrown out or knock himself out on the cabin wall. Every time a bump made him jerk upwards, he gasped for breath and couldn't think straight.

Suddenly he heard a new sound in the tumult outside, like the hissing of a thousand tongues borne onwards by a thundering waterfall. It came nearer and nearer, it was over him and under him, everywhere all at once, until it struck with a crash just above him, and at the same moment he felt water seeping through from above. He felt his head to make sure his skull had not been smashed in. His blood was rushing and singing in his ears, and it felt as if his eardrums were about to burst.

'Did that break through the deckhouse roof over there?' he heard the captain's voice outside.

'Aye, it sprung a leak all right, capt'n,' came the answer.

'Is that you at the wheel, Sølvfest?'

'Aye aye, capt'n.'

'I think we'd better lash everything on board fast right now, it's blowing up worse and worse,' said the captain.

The sound of normal human voices had a reassuring effect on Sivert for a few moments. He lay back on his pillow and tried to force himself to think that there was no danger; but straight after he was sitting bolt upright again. Then he tried lying on his stomach and sticking his fingers in his ears, but that didn't help. In the end he started crying with fear, and suddenly he shouted out: 'O God, our Father which is in Heaven, forgive us our sins and have mercy on us!' He had been so delighted when the cook had his hands bound – oh, oh, oh, this was the punishment for his malice – love thine enemy, love thine enemy. He began to rattle off some incoherent passages of catechism which he vaguely remembered from his confirmation classes. 'Put aside lying and speak the truth, put aside lying and speak the truth,' he repeated several times. That story about the ghost - - why had he made that up? – Oh no, he was nearly thrown out of the bunk onto his head. A man dressed in grey, a long thin beard – . What if it were to appear before him now? His hair stood on end and he screwed his eyes shut in terror – but had to open them again straight after to stare around him, not daring to breathe. No, thank God, nothing to see, not yet, and not yet, and not yet either; he carried on opening and shutting his eyes as he lay there being shaken about, squeezing them so tightly shut that they smarted and burned. Not the tiniest trace of a ghost – but next time - - when he least expected it – standing there before him, ugh, ugh – dressed in grey, motionless, death's head – . For Heaven's sake, what was he to do with himself - - glowing eyes – a raised hand, just like Satan in that picture in his prayer book back home, the temptation in the wilderness – . Oh, what booming and rumbling – . Weather to be wrecked by – to be wrecked, to be wrecked – no ship could endure that – . That lie, that ghost – need to confess it – yes, need to confess, then he won't think of it any more, think of it any more – gladly fall to his knees – gladly let them trample on him - - .

The door opened and he saw the shape of someone coming in.

'Is that you, mister mate?' he asked in a pitiful voice.

He got a growl in answer.

'I want to confess to you, that it was …'

Something was pulled down off the wall, and the door opened and then closed again.

So that was it, that chance was gone. Oh well, it was not his fault. Our Lord ransacked your heart and inner organs

- - the thought was as good as the deed – as good as the deed. – What was that? A gleaming eye next to his bunk – . Now it was gone again, no, no – it was nothing.

Sivert could not bear it in there any longer. He clambered out of his bunk, put some clothes on and went out on deck.

The wind was blowing so hard that he crouched down automatically and held fast to the wall of the deckhouse, struggling to draw breath. Sea and sky had become one, and everywhere was driving spray. The ship was being tossed about like a ball between the high waves. Every time it had fought its way up to the top of a crest, it twisted and shook as if in convulsions, after which it plummeted to a depth which made Sivert dizzy, boring its nose into the foaming waves and burying its bow beneath the oncoming torrent. Then it lay there, lurching from side to side and dipping the tops of its masts in the water, until it rose up again like an animal facing an attack, plunging its stern deep in the water as if about to somersault backwards. And the wind was hooting and raging. The rigging was whistling and singing. The ropes were clanging against the deck and the masts, and there was a rattling of chains and iron fittings. It sounded like the howling of dogs, the bellowing of oxen, the shrieking of owls, the moaning and groaning of spirits.

Rrrrip, rrrrip, came a sound, followed by some short smacks, mixed with a peculiar snarling and growling.

'Rouse the watch to make fast! All hands on deck!' shouted the captain's voice a little way off.

Sivert crawled on all fours over to the helmsman.

'What was it that ripped, Sølvfest?' he asked.

'Aye, it'll all rip soon, the whole caboodle,' answered Sølvfest.

'D'you think we're goin' to sink, Sølvfest?'

'Course we'll sink. Jus' you get back to yer berth. Wha' you doin' on deck anyway?'

At that moment a wave broke over the wheelhouse. Part of the wall of water hit Sivert from the side and propelled him over to leeward, where he threw himself down flat and clung to a waterbutt. The next second he was on his feet and running with a yell over to the lifeboat, which was lying keel up on the rear hatch cover. Frantic with fear, he began pulling at the ropes, screaming: 'Come an' 'elp launch the boat!'

'Have you gone crazy, lad!' Sivert was grabbed by the scruff of the neck by the captain. 'Jus' get a grip on yersel', else I'll heave you overboard!' And with a mighty shove he was thrust aft.

The whole crew had now turned out on deck. The captain yelled out his orders. Sivert could not understand how he could make his voice heard through all the commotion, but as the darkness gradually looked less black, he could make out that he was holding a megaphone to his mouth. The crew repeated the orders. Their calls sounded like hoarse bellows, but it seemed to Sivert that there was something almost cheery in the sound. There was a heaving and a straining, a running and a stamping, a bustling racket on all sides. As he had done earlier when he heard human voices from his berth through the noise of the storm, he felt reassured. The indefatigable steadiness of these experienced old salts did him good. How courageous and carefree they were. He felt suddenly moved. His eyes filled with tears, and he felt a kind of love for them. Surely God could not allow all these hard-working men to perish? No, it was impossible. Most of them had families to provide for, and the others were too young and unprepared for death.

He didn't want to think about himself, for he deserved no better; but the others, the others, surely God would spare them. 'The Lord shall send his angels to watch over you, and they will follow you in all your ways,' he found himself repeating mechanically over and over again.

'Sound the pump, first mate!' shouted the captain.

If he now comes and says: 'Tight as a drum, capt'n', that means all will be well, thought Sivert, and if he says 'Five inches of water', then we're in great danger but we'll come through anyway, and if he says: 'A foot and a half of water, capt'n', then we'll founder but be rescued by another vessel; but if he says: 'Three foot of water' …

'Tight as a drum, capt'n!' said a voice suddenly just next to Sivert.

He jumped, and almost shouted: 'Hurrah!' – but instead he turned to the helmsman and said: 'She's a sturdy ship, this one.'

'Lower the topsail and cut the remnants!' shouted the captain. 'Then secure the bolt-ropes!'

Sivert looked over towards the foremast, where he could make out some long rags hanging down and blowing, flapping wildly as if in anger. Now he understood that ripping sound that had made him believe that the ship was splintering. The topsail had split from the bolt-rope, despite the fact that it had been furled. That showed how wild the weather was. But never mind, he was not afraid, not a scrap, he'd show them what he was made of! All at once he felt full of daring. He spat on his hands and yelled: 'Secure the bolt-ropes! Aye aye, capt'n,' lurched across the heaving deck, caught hold of the backstay and climbed up the shroud, swung out along the yard by his arms, found the foot-rope with his feet and started working on the remnants of the shredded sail, doing his best to copy the movements of the man next to him, as he glimpsed them in the dawning light. It was the first time he had helped to secure a sail, and he had no idea how to do it, but he worked it out instinctively and was soon able to pull his weight.

The captain, who had seen him climbing up, went closer and squinted up into the rigging after him. 'I reckon he's lost his wits from fright,' he muttered. But shortly after he called up: 'That's it, Sivert! You're not so 'opeless after all!'

The storm lasted three full days, with varying wind force. But Sivert was no longer afraid. From the moment he had heard the words: 'Tight as a drum, capt'n', all his fear seemed to have vanished. With courage came self-confidence. He grew cheerful and swaggering, with a feeling of being more in his element the more fiercely the wind blew. This was just the life for him. To join in with everything, heave and haul with shanties and halloos, feel his boots full of seawater and have not a dry stitch on his body, leap out of his bunk with a merry shout in answer to the wake-up call, turn in during the day and out during the night – now he really understood the appeal of life at sea.

Since that night he had been assigned watches onboard, just like the rest of the crew. The very next morning he had asked the captain's permission to do so, and he had agreed with a growl which was half scornful and half appreciative.

These events had at a stroke lifted Sivert from the dregs onboard to become the equal of all the others. Now he had shown that he could hold his own, and that earned him respect. Even the cook treated him more carefully.

The captain was still in a dreadful mood. He swore repeatedly that the Devil had escaped from Hell in order to cause all the mischief which only Satan himself could dream up.

On the very first day of the storm the cook had announced that it wasn't going to be possible for him to serve any hot food. The flames blew out and the contents of the pans splashed out onto the walls of the galley. So they had to make do with bread and butter and a small piece of cheese which the captain shared out to the crew every day from his private store. Every now and then they might get a mug of tea or coffee, which the cook managed to produce with a great effort. The crew were indignant about having to go without, and accused the cook of being a layabout who was using the 'bit of a gale' as an excuse for lazing about. Sivert speculated now and then about a method of boiling up a pan of porridge, if nothing else, but abandoned the idea again, until the second day of the storm, when he heard the captain saying to some of the crew who were grumbling about the lack of cooked food: 'You should be ashamed! Do we get any more in the captain's quarters? Just look at Sivert, he's the smartest of the whole shebang.'

At these words Sivert's heart swelled, and from that moment on he could no longer stop thinking about how to make some porridge. The next morning, while the cook was still asleep, he went into the galley and studied it thoughtfully. All of a sudden an idea came to him. Quick as a flash he was down in the rope store and picked out an iron rod. He carried it up to the galley, where he made it fast to a spike on each wall so that it hung horizontally across the top of the oven. Then he threaded a thin line through the handles of the largest cooking pot and lashed it tightly to the middle of the iron rod, so that it could follow the rolling of the ship without spilling too much of the contents. Then he half filled it with water, stirred in the groats and lit the hob under it. He was almost choked by the smoke which billowed up and out in all directions, and he had to keep going out on deck to rub his eyes and take a breath, but he didn't give up. When it was nearly dinnertime he could announce fore and aft that porridge with syrup would be served, steaming hot and not the slightest bit burnt.

This achievement made him very popular. Sivert was praised both in the captain's quarters and in the forecastle, and the cook was showered with taunts and scorn. He claimed that Sivert had done it out of pure malice, and promised him a thrashing as soon as they reached calmer waters. But Sivert just spat on his fists and asked the cook if he was ready for his coffin.

On the afternoon of the fourth day the storm began to ease off. During the evening the wind dropped, and that night they had a freshening breeze with a following wind and a starry sky with a new moon.

During the following days the crew were set to repairing the damage caused by the storm. Soon the ship was in good shape again, and things returned to normal.

Sivert carried on taking his watches, and still had plenty of time to carry out his other duties. All in all it became more and more evident that he was a quick and hard-working lad, and the captain thought to himself that he had been lucky with his cabin boy this time.

Thirty-three days after they set sail they passed Madeira, and twelve days after that they picked up the easterly trade wind. –

Sivert was standing aft with his arms folded, leaning against the wall of the wheelhouse and staring out over the wake, where small waves, shiny as steel and with broad, silvery stripes of phosphorescence, glided calmly along. The gentle breeze felt cool on his cheeks. The moonlight lit up the sea in white; the ship's rigging cast a wavering shadow on the rippling surface. From the forecastle there came the sound of singing, accompanied by a harmonica. Sivert thought that sailing with the trade wind was like being in paradise. Never had he seen such a blue and cloudless sky. Warm sun during the day, and at night stars like big shiny coins. And then the peace and quiet onboard. No lurching, no reefing, no change from one day to the next. All sails hoisted, the deck sparkling clean, the brass like a mirror, the crew in linen trousers with open-necked shirts, canvas caps and bare feet, even the cook who was as white as a baker's apprentice, no outbursts from the captain, ravenous appetites, undisturbed sleep when not on watch, no more brawls, just utter wellbeing.

And the best thing of all was that they were drawing nearer and nearer to that amazing land where the people were black and they had monkeys the size of errand boys.

6

Back home in Bergen, Marthe was out in the back yard with rolled-up sleeves in front of a washing tub standing on a half-barrel, washing clothes. In order to protect herself from the baking afternoon sun she had wound a towel around her head, which covered her forehead and hung down her back like a scarf. The sweat was beading on her freckled face, as she rubbed at the clothes with her broad, stubby-fingered hands, their skin wrinkled by the hot soapy water. Hens were scratching around her, squabbling over some potato peel. Each time they were splashed by the water from the tub they darted away with an offended cackling.

Suddenly it seemed to Marthe that she could hear someone moving in the kitchen. She cocked her head to one side and could see through the open door an old, stooping peasant, who was standing in the middle of the kitchen talking to himself. He looked dirty and unkempt. His white hair and beard hung down in clumps over his neck and chest. His britches had holes in them both above and below the scraps of leather they had been patched with, and his grey homespun jerkin was buttonless and worn through at the elbows. His dull eyes were swimming with a greyish fluid, and the tip of his long drooping nose was red. In his hand he was holding a bundle and a knobbly stick, and on his head he had a knitted cap.

'Ugh,' said Marthe, moving her head back again. 'We c'n nivver be left in peace.' She carried on washing, wringing out the finished garments and tossing them into the rinsing water beside her. Then she emptied the dirty soapsuds out into the drainage channel which ran right past her feet, picked up a tub and went into the kitchen.

'In town again, are yer?' She put one foot on the hearth and used a wooden bowl to ladle water into the tub from a boiling pot which was hanging over the fire.*

'Didn' get much for't fish today,' said the peasant in a soft, hoarse voice, shaking his head slowly.

'In God's name, I wish y'd give up this fishin' o'yours,' scolded the woman. 'I can't unnerstan' why they let yer use t'boat.'

'Didn' get much for't, jus' as y'might expec', not much for't,' the old man went on, without looking at Marthe or taking any notice of what she said. 'I's all cursed – so tha's why, i's all cursed.'

'Our li'l Gabriel died, 'ee did,' he lamented, ''ee died an' all.' He went over the the hearth and pulled timidly at Marthe's skirt. 'Six bairns I've buried, five in't churchyard an' one somewhere else.' He had lowered his voice to an almost inaudible whisper. 'I'll tell yer summat' – he stopped suddenly and glanced searchingly around the kitchen with a look of surprise. When he realised that he was alone – Marthe had gone out into the back yard again – his head sank down onto his breast and a snuffling sound came from him. Then he sat down on the hearth, rested his elbows on his knees and his face in his hands without letting go of his bundle or his stick, and sang in a slow, wheezing voice:

What good is there in rising early,
Striving at our earthly chores,
Our efforts neither help nor hinder …*

The street door opened, and Jens came in.

'Well wha's this, is tha' you, our Da, wha' is i' this time?' His tone expressed both sympathy and aversion.

'I'm starvin' till it 'urts, then I'm eatin' till it 'urts, so it's 'urtin' all t'time,' his father whined.

'Out the way, Da, ye're sittin' on me slippers.'

The old man stood up.

'I brought yer a bit o'fish an' a meal o'tatties,' he said, holding out the bundle to his son.

Jens took it, untied it and tipped the contents out onto the kitchen table.

'Didn' ye see anyone, Da? Our Marthe sh'd be a''ome.'

'When Sjur Gabriel comes there's nivver anyone a''ome,' his father complained.

'Wha' you standin' there talkin' nonsense wi'im for?' Marthe exclaimed crossly, as she put her face around the door. 'It'd be be'er 'f you got 'im out of 'ere, 'ee meks t'ole 'ouse stink o' cheap booze.'

'No need ter sit in't 'earth, Da, 'ere's a stool for yer.' Jens pulled a three-legged stool out across the floor. 'Gi' Da a couple'a slices o' bread an' a drop o' coffee,' he said, going outside to Marthe.

'It'd be much be'er not ter feed 'im,' Marthe answered sulkily, as she wiped the soapsuds from her arms and shook the water off her hands. 'We'll nivver get rid of 'im like tha'.'

'Don' be so 'ard on our da', Marthe,' Jens admonished her.

Marthe pursed her lips with an injured expression as she dried her fingers on a dry corner of her sacking apron, and went into the kitchen, where she took a couple of buttered slices of bread out of the hanging corner cupboard. Then she poured a bowl of coffee and passed both to Sjur Gabriel, whose trembling fingers with their black stubby nails had difficulty holding on to it.

'Here's some fish an' tatties for you, Marthe, Granda'

wants ter say,' said Jens cheerfully, pointing at the kitchen table.

Marthe wrinkled her nose. 'I jus' wish 'ee didn' bring any,' she said in a low voice. ''Ee's allus grumblin' as 'ow 'ee's starvin' ter death.'

'Tha's jus' wha' farmers do,' Jens said placatingly. 'Are t'tatties any good this year, Da?'

''F only I c'd keep some,' Sjur Gabriel whimpered. 'Them Kristi an' Anders cheat on't measurin' an' then they steal from us an' all.'

'You 'ear tha', tha's jus' what I was sayin',' scolded Marthe indignantly. 'Why d'you bring some 'ere then, Granda'? Jus' tek 'em 'ome again.' She grabbed the cloth and started gathering the potatoes up in it again with hasty fingers.

'I's cursed, everythin's cursed,' began Sjur Gabriel.

'Stop tha' nonsense.' Jens pulled the cloth away from his wife, so that the potatoes spilled out. ''Ow can you be so 'ard on an old wreck like 'im.'

'Well, you do as you please,' said Marthe huffily, and hurried out again to her washing.

A man in a threadbare dark blue suit with shiny yellow buttons, a round cap and a bag decorated with a gilded posthorn on a strap over his shoulder came into the kitchen.

'Dockworker Jens Gabrielsen,' he read from the top of a bundle of letters which he held close up to his dark red face, which was ravaged by rain and wind and drink. 'That must be 'ere?' he went on, looking at Jens with his rheumy eyes.

'Aye, tha's me, tha' is,' answered Jens quite formally, and stepped closer.

''Ere you are!' said the postman, and gave no sign of leaving.

'Dockworker Jens Gabrielsen in Dræggen, near The

German Church in Bergen, Norway, Europe,' Jens spelt out the address. 'Aye, tha' can't be anyone else bu' me, tha. Wha' d'you think, Marthe?' he called out to the back yard.

'Tha's from our lad,' she said, going pink with emotion. 'So 'ee 'as written to us a'er all.'

'From Sivert, aye!' shouted Jens, delighted that all had become clear. 'Will yer look a' tha', 'ow well 'ee's learnt to write an' all.'

'Has t'postman 'ad 'is shillin'?' asked Marthe.

'Aye, righ'! I quite forgot.' He reached into his waistcoat pocket and took out three half-shillings, which he handed to the postman.

''Ere you are, Jonsen lad, you c'n 'ave an extra half-shillin' fer yer trouble.'

'Put t'letter aside, Jens,' called Marthe when the postman had left. 'I've no' time till I've done washin'.'

'Who's to read it then?' asked Jens.

'Can't you?' said Marthe.

'No, I'll not read as well as you; you 'ad more schoolin' 'an me and you'll be be'er at it 'an me.'

'You know wha', Jens, we'll let Thrine read it out loud this evenin' when she comes back from 'er cleanin'. She'll be best.'

'Aye, tha's wha' we'll do!' Jens clicked his fingers triumphantly.

'But tell Granda' ter be off now.'

'Aye, Granda' – tha's righ'', sighed Jens. 'I'd forgot 'ee was 'ere.'

'You need to see to get 'ome now, Da,' he went over to Sjur Gabriel and put his hand on his shoulder. 'I'll put t'rest o' yer bread in yer bundle so ye c'n 'ave it on't way 'ome.'*

He took the half-eaten slice out of his father's hand,

wrapped it in the cloth which had held the potatoes and fastened the ends together to make a handle.

'See 'ere, Da,' you best toddle off now, or tha'll be dark afore you're there.' He got hold of his arm near the shoulder, hoisted him up from the stool and helped him out.

That evening Marthe was sitting in her usual place by the window, warm and dry after changing her clothes, blowing on her hands, which were chapped and sore after the washing and smeared with candlegrease. Opposite her at the other window sat Jens with his clay pipe, in waistcoat and shirt sleeves, which were unbuttoned so that you could see his knitted woollen undershirt. Over on the wooden bench lay the youngest lad, Simon, asleep with his face in the pillow and a mass of curly brown hair standing out around his head. Nils, the next eldest, was sitting with his arms stretched out over the table and his hands clasped in his hair, so close to the two-shilling candle in the tin candleholder that the flame was singeing his fringe. He was impatiently watching the movements of his sister, who was clearing the table after supper.

'At last!' said Nils, breathing out in relief as Thrine finally carried a chair over to the table and sat down.

Jens stood up, picked up the Bible from a shelf on the wall and opened it.

''Ere it is then,' he said, holding out Sivert's letter to Thrine. 'No, wait a minnit, I'll tek it ou' for you.'

When he had done so, Thrine took the sheets of writing paper, cleared her throat a couple of times and began reading. To start with she faltered and her voice shook a little, but after a while it went better. She read in a flat monotone and pronounced each word as it was written.

When she got to a difficult word she stopped and spelt it out in a whisper.

This was what it said:

> *Kingston the Fiftenth april 1853*
> *On bord in the Bark two friends*
> *aternoon after messtime*

Dear respecful Parents

At last i can Pik up a pen and start a lettr to you Bak home to tell you that, 10 days ago we arived well and helfy and in good order, at our destenashun wich is on the Iland of Jamaica a big fine town cald Kingston as I writ at the Top but they say tun. And here they are all Blak in White cloths exep the wimmin who wear yeller and red and blu and All sorts of colors, you can think of and there hair is Curley like sheeps baks and they have rely thik lips and great big White teeth like on horses.*

''Ave you ever 'eard the like!' exclaimed Jens.

'In't tha' jus' summat 'ee's made up, Ma?' asked Nils.

'Don' be stupid,' Thrine commented. 'Ain't you learnt 'bout blacks in school?'

'Course I 'ave! But Sivert tells such drefful lies.'

''Ush now, so we c'n 'ear wha' the lad writes,' said Marthe.

And ive bin Ashore at the Consuls and many times to the Bucher and the chanler, they live in a street Jus made of sand and its like that in All streets and it Burns rite threw your boots, corse its so hot its jus like bein grild alive. And nites are cooler but Not much –

'Leastways they'll not be freezin'!' Jens interjected

191

excitedly.

And theres trees outside All the houses, but the Leaves begin at the Top, so it looks like an Open umbreller. And theres green wood Shuters over all the windows for the heat and canvas puld down with red edjes, Sølvfest says theyre cald ornings, he knows about it corse hes bin here afor. And we had Terible storms when we were up North so the boson said it was the Worst Wether hed ever bin out in altho hes bin at Sea for 20 Years and they thort we were goin strait to the Botom and they were all so afeard they cud ardly Breth, and they wanted to let down the Lifeboat, corse the forsail was riped from Boltrope wich is the rope round it, but then i came runnin and up the mast jus like that and sekurd the Shreds all alon.

'Dear Lord, 'ave you ever 'eard anythin' like?' said Marthe.
'I reckon 'ee's braggin' a wee bit,' was Jens's comment.

And when i come down agin Captn wept with joy and said thats all thanks to you Sivert, if You hadnt bin here wed have founderd –

'Read tha' bit again,' begged Marthe.
Thrine read the last sentences again, and her mother nodded her head with moist eyes at each word.

And he said at Once that he was puttin me on His own wach. And its niver append that a Cabin boy is put on wach not to mensjun captns own, corse they have to sleep all Nite and work all day. But i dont do that. And we had Storm for 6 days, and We were more under water than over it, corse it piches most in Balast, and Cook refusd to cook corse it was

*Danger to Lif and lim. But who didnt hold bak was Sivert, i
cookd food for the Hole Crew and you can imagin folks was
glad, exep Cook corse he cud have swallerd me hole corse id
done summat Imposibl –*

'Well 'oo's goin' ter believe tha', ha ha,' laughed Jens. 'But
go on readin.''

*So you can see you cud have let me go to Sea afor las
Summer when I wantd and Cook was rely mad anyway corse
captn had tossd all his Shirts in the sea but that was to punish
him for tellin Lyes about me, corse captn wudnt stand for that.
You dont tell Lyes about a lad like Sivert Jensen he said and
out went the shirts as an Awfl Warnin. And now captn has
promisd to Increse my pay and ill not have to pay for things
whats broke, but Normaly a Cabin boy has to pay for anythin
smashd in ruff seas but captn said to me youve bin a Modl for
us all Sivert and youll not have to pay –*

'Ooh, jus' think, a model,' said Marthe, moved.

*But captn is a Roarin Lyon but hes bin good to me and when
he gets Mad he runs after folks with flamin logs –*

''Ee mus' be crazy! Tha's worser 'an t'devil hisself!' exclaimed Jens.

*And boson told me i shud Thrash cook corse hes turribl
jelus of me and cant stand me bein preferd, but i dont want to
corse its not Chrisjun and ive not forgot what i lernt as a child,
but bin tru to Our Lord and said my prayers as i promisd Ma
when i left. And i wasnt a bit seasik jus a litl dizy the first Day*

and boson has bin like a father to me and hes the best Man onbord. And Yesterday i was sent to the conselate wich has a Big Garden round it with enormus birds of all colors and they can talk jus like peple –

'Now I know 'ee's lyin'!' Jens interrupted.
''Ush, be quiet, so's we c'n 'ear.'

And amazin flowers as Big as goosbery bushs and trees the tallest man can Walk under and a water jet comin out of a nakd woman –

'A livin' one?' shouted Nils.
'Aye, 'oo knows?' replied Marthe.

And inside were colord ston tiles to walk on insted of a floor, and a Blak man opend the door and bowd to me as if I was a Prince. Consel isself was same color as bak home and he had shinin White trowsers so smooth you cud see your face in them and pale grey boots with laces and Shirt sleeves, but fine. And i jus had to hand over a leter and tek an anser and he talkd english and i understood but not Evrythin. When they mean gooday here they say howjudu and goodmornin is the same as bak home. Then the consels litl girl came in shes about 6 and she wantd me to stay the Hole Day I understood corse she took my hand and said Come on and mei bois wich means nice lad but her father shook his head and said naa naa Mari wich means dont do that Marie. And then theres a place nereby where folks go and there are Four Halfnakd lasses as sit on there laps –

'Oh, tha's the kind they 'ave there,' sniffed Marthe indignantly.

But the mulatos arent as Blak as the Negro lasses and there hair is Longer and shinyer and theyre pretier too but there cloths i cant tell you what it looks like, and they jus have a skirt you can see thro and not a stich more on them. You cn see everythin theyve got so its rely embarasin.

'Aye, tha's true what you say, Sivert lad,' muttered Marthe. ''Ow c'n such things be allowed? They sh'd be drownded, the 'ole lot o' them.'

But the other day i was in there with Sølvfest who is Best sailer and Drank a glas and then one lass came over and wantd to play games with me, but you cn be sure i sent her packin and then i went as well and ran strait Onbord ship again.

'Tha's good to 'ear!' sighed Marthe.

Corse were moord at the Key, that means the dokside, and i was all upset and her Swet smelt so rank –

'Filthy slut,' said Marthe.

And they all swet here so you can smell it a Long way off and the streets are so narow and teribly long but theres No houses to See corse theyre bilt so far bak jus trees and rely big Gardens on both sides. And in the commen streets you see more of the houses corse theyre Nearer the road, but now i must finish corse its time for Mess and here they say mess and not mealtime, If you want to write and put on the leter Norwegen Bark two friends, swedish Conselat Marseilles corse they write it like that but you can jus hear sei then ill get it when we arive corse were goin to sail there but well be moord here a long time as captn wont take more than 6 men from shore to help. And then it takes longer but he erns more money they say Greetins to my brothers and to Thrine wholl get a box coverd in seashels from

   your lovin faroff son
   Sivert Gabriel Jensen Cabin Boy.

Now ive bin writin since thursday corse most days i only have a short time in the evenin and Today has bin sunday.

'Well, wha' a fine long le'er!' cried Marthe. 'I's amazing 'ow well 'ee's doin'.'

'Aye, 'ee's good at tellin' a story,' said Jens, shaking his head with a smile.

'But you wanted ter stop 'im goin', Jens. Bein' at sea's jus' the thing for 'im, you'll see.'

'Mebbee, 'oo knows?' said Jens.

'You know wha', Jens, I think we sh'd get Thrine to read t'le'er again,' suggested Marthe. 'I can't rightly remember wha' it said.'

'Aye, 'ow about it, Thrine?' asked Jens. 'You no' too sleepy?'

'Not a' all!' answered Thrine readily.

An hour later, after they had put out the candle and gone to bed, Marthe could not get to sleep. She lay there tossing and turning, and feeling more and more awake.

'You awake, Jens?' she asked finally, as she felt him move.

'Aye, I am that, wi' you shiftin' about like that.'

'Aye, tha's a sad thing,' Marthe sighed, 'when I've bin standin' over the washin' since four this mornin'. – But I'm lyin' wonderin' 'bout what Sivert said, 'ow 'e'd saved t'ship. I think t'shipowners sh'd give 'im a reward.'

'Ugh,' said Jens. 'Wha' made you think o' such a thing?'

'Don' you think it'd be only fair for 'im to get summat for it?' Marthe sat up in bed.

'If it really did 'appen the way 'ee said –'

''Ow could t'capt'n be thankin' an' weepin' wi' joy if it weren't the truth?' exclaimed Marthe eagerly.

'I didn' see it,' said Jens, yawning.

'Well you sh'dn't think such things of your own flesh an' blood. 'Ee's not lyin' this time, I know tha.'

'Jus' get some sleep, Marthe.' Jens turned towards the wall.

'Won' you go up t't shipowner's office tomorrow an' tell 'em wha' Sivert did?' asked Marthe.

'No I'll not do tha', corse not. If there's any truth in't t'capt'n'll write to 'em about it. – We don' want ter look fools.'

'T'capt'n, – sh'd think 'ee'd be glad if no-one says owt, then they'll all think 'ee did it.'

'Well, jus' you be quiet now an' let's get some sleep,' Jens pulled the quilt up over his ears. 'Le's see wha' 'appens.'

'I'll go up t't office tomorrow, I will tha,' thought Marthe, as she rested her head on the pillow again. 'I'll tek t'le'er wi' me an' show t'consul.* Then we'll see Jens's face when I'm back. They're bound to gi' me 20 speciedalers a' least.* I'll pu' it in't bank. Then Sivert c'n watch it grow an' 'preciate till 'ee's capt'n hisself one day.'

7

The next afternoon, after she had finished hanging her washing up to dry, Marthe put on her best black dress, which she used only twice a year when she took communion, and a brown apron of fine linen. Then she took her shawl out of the chest of drawers, folded it so that came to a point behind and pinned it in front. She knotted a scarf round her head, pulled on a pair of grey cotton gloves and went up to the attic to fetch her nankeen cotton umbrella. Actually the weather was fine, but she decided she looked more well-to-do with it in her hand. She worked out that she could be back before Nils and Simon came home from school, so she locked the street door, put the key in her pocket and set off.

She decided to take the route along Øvregaden, even though it was longer, because if she went by Bryggen she would risk running into Jens, who worked there.

She walked quickly, but soon felt so warm that she had to stop and wipe the sweat from her nose with a handkerchief she was holding, in which she had wrapped the letter from Sivert. It was the first of June, with clear air and bright sunshine. Marthe's sallow cheeks grew pink, and her narrow eyes sparkled and shone as she rehearsed what she was going to say in the office. She felt so proud and hopeful.

Looking neither right nor left, she hurried down Vitterlevsalmindingen and up across the town square. Then she turned the corner and walked down Strandgaden, where the traffic was so busy that she had to slow down. It was worst by Smørsalmindingen. There the road was being repaired, so there was only a narrow passage for traffic. Marthe had to stand still on the pavement and wait whilst some waggons drove past at a snail's pace. At that moment she caught sight of a stonebreaker who was passing close by her dragging a sledgehammer. Quickly she turned her back. She had recognised her brother-in-law Magne, Jens's youngest brother, and did not care to be hailed by him today. He was even more ragged and filthy than usual, and there she was in her best clothes; and besides, she could not be sure that he was sober, because Magne drank.

As she came closer to her destination, she gradually began to feel more uneasy, and walked more slowly and uncertainly. Her errand was straightforward enough, it seemed to her, but it could be that people like that were not so easy to deal with. She just hoped the consul was not too high and mighty.

'Herman D. Smith and Sons', she read on a front door with a brass plate just by Muralmindingen. Goodness, how fine and elegant it looked, so bright and shiny, as if the whole house had just been lifted out of a chest. Her heart was beating so fast it almost hurt, but then she said to herself: come on, Marthe lass, and she climbed up the two stone steps, opened the front door and walked in. After several queries and hindrances, she succeeded in being shown in to see the consul, in his inner office.

For a moment Marthe thought the office was empty, but straight after she noticed a tall male figure standing over by the window, looking out at the street over the yellow raffia blinds. She remained standing in the doorway unmoving, but when she thought she had been waiting a long time, she coughed gently. The consul didn't seem to notice. 'Mus' be t'row from t'street,' she thought, so she coughed so loudly that it sounded like a horse neighing.

'It's too late for today, my good woman,' said the consul,

turning around quickly and waving his hand. 'The clerks could have told you that.'

"Ow c'n 'ee know what I've come for?' thought Marthe. "Ee can't know 'oo I am?'

She wanted to ask the consul that and a lot more besides, but he had already turned his back on her again.

'Hm,' she said, and coughed again. 'Tha's a pity, that i' is. Wha' time'd best suit t'consul then?'

'You'd better come back between 10 and 11 tomorrow morning, then the cashier will be here.'

'There you see, 'ee knows wha' it's all abou',' Marthe nodded to herself. "Ee's already decided 'ow much to gi' us. Surprisin''ee ain't sent ter tell us ter come. – Thank you very much, Mr Consul Sir,' she said, dropping a little curtsey, and took hold of the doorknob. 'Goodbye Mr Consul, I'll come tomorrow then.'

That evening, after Jens had come home, Marthe surprised him with her odd behaviour. Whatever they were talking about, she finished off by saying: 'Nay, our Marthe, she in't as daft as she looks, jus' you wait an' see,' at which she nodded secretively. Now and then she was so preoccupied that she didn't hear when Jens or the children said something to her; when they tugged at her, and Jens asked if she was dreaming of weddings, she laughed until she had tears in her eyes, and said several times: 'Aye, aye, jus' you wait, I'll say no more.'

The next morning at exactly 10 o'clock Marthe once again made her way to Consul Smith's on Strandgaden.

In the first office there was a man with a grey beard and horn-rimmed glasses right down on the tip of his lumpy nose, standing behind a two-foot-high grille of birchwood, counting out some notes which he had taken out of a cupboard on the wall and handing them to a woman on the other side of the grille, saying: 'Count them so that you can see that it's correct', and straight after in a louder voice: 'Next'.

On the bench over by the window sat several women, each with a folded sheet of paper in her hand, which they seemed to be holding ready. One of them stood up, went over to the grille and handed the paper to the man with the horn-rimmed glasses.

'It's the sailors' wives drawing their pay,' thought Marthe, who had remained standing in the middle of the floor. She felt anxious. No-one had answered her greeting, and no-one took any notice of her. She was worried that the consul had forgotten to let them know, and moved restlessly from foot to foot. Finally she walked resolutely towards the door which led to the consul's private office.

'Where are you going, mistress?' called the cashier, without looking up from the notes he had in his hand, and then went on counting: 'Five, six, seven, eight.'

Marthe stood still with her arm outstretched towards the doorknob.

' You must sit down and wait,' said one of the clerks, who was sitting and writing at a high desk on Marthe's left. 'You have to wait your turn.' He pointed over to the bench.

Marthe obeyed automatically. 'It's obvious they know why I'm here,' she reassured herself.

When the others had been dealt with and the last of the women had left the office, Marthe got up and went over to the cashier without saying anything.

'Authorization,' he said, holding out his hand whilst keeping his eyes fixed on a large account book in which he had just written something.

This was so unexpected that Marthe couldn't say anything, but just stood there gaping.

'Well?' asked the cashier impatiently, looking up at her.

'I ain't got an authorization,' she began, flushing up to the roots of her hair. 'I'm t'mother of Sivert, t'cabin boy onboard *Two Friends*. Didn' t'consul say anythin'?'

'What d'you mean, say anything? If you're not drawing pay, what is it you're after?'

'Aye, cause our Sivert saved t'ship in t'storm when they were sailin' up north, an' I was goin' ter ask if 'ee shouldn' get a reward?'

'Saved the ship, what kind of a cock-and-bull story is that?' said the cashier, exchanging glances with the clerks, who started to titter.

'T'consul knows abou' it,' stammered Marthe. 'I were 'ere yesterday, an' 'ee asked me to come back today.'

The cashier looked at her with a strange smile on his lips. 'I've not heard a word about that,' he said, 'but I can go and ask the consul.' He opened the grille and stepped out. 'Is that a recommendation from the captain?' he asked, holding out his hand for Sivert's letter, which Marthe had unwrapped from the kerchief.

'I's our lad's le'er,' answered Marthe in a trembling voice. 'I brough' it along in case t'consul wants ter see it.'

The cashier looked undecided, and then with an expression that was part embarrassed, part scornful, he said: 'There must be some misunderstanding. But' – he seemed suddenly to come to a decision – 'if you'd like to give me the letter, I'll take it in and show it to the consul.'

Marthe unfolded the letter, and pointed to the middle of the page, saying: 'Tha's where 'ee's written abou' it,' upon which the cashier went off with it. -

'The consul knows nothing about this,' said the cashier as he returned, doing his best to keep a straight face. He folded up the letter and gave it back to Marthe. 'It must be something your son has written for fun, otherwise the captain would definitely have mentioned it in his report.' He went back behind the grille, polishing his glasses with a large red silk handkerchief. 'On the contrary, the captain writes that he had a smooth and easy passage.'

At those words it seemed to Marthe that the whole room began to swing around her, and she could feel the two clerks' sharp eyes jabbing into the back of her neck.

'Well tha's mos' peculiar,' she uttered with some difficulty, whilst her shaking fingers strove to wrap the letter in her kerchief again. 'T'consul said yesterday as I sh'd come back today.'

Even though Marthe felt as shamefaced as she had ever done in her life, she nevertheless thought with irritation of how she had put on her best clothes and walked all that long way two days running, all to no purpose, and what would Jens have to say about it.

'Tha' is mos' peculiar,' she repeated, almost in tears.

'But we don't want you to have come in vain,' said the cashier. 'The consul has instructed me to give you two speciedalers.'

Suddenly Marthe heard a dull rushing noise in her ears. It felt as if she had been lifted up from the floor and dropped down again. 'Gi' me two speciedalers,' her voice shook, and she felt breathless. 'I didn' come 'ere to beg.'

'That was not what the consul meant, my good woman,' – the cashier's tone was polite but reproving. 'But daler notes don't grow on trees these days, and the money will no doubt be welcome.' And before Marthe could react the cashier had put two notes in her hand. With that he turned his back on her with a brief good-bye and bent over his accounts.

Marthe wanted to say something, but could not move her tongue. She wanted to put the money down, but was unable to lift her arm. So she turned around, and shortly afterwards she realised that she could feel the cobblestones under her feet. How she had moved from the office out onto the street she had no idea. On the way home she struggled to remember whether she had said good-bye, whether she had walked across the floor quickly or slowly, whether she had closed the door quietly or with a bang, but to no avail. All she knew was that she had been treated like a beggar who wanted to get money out of the consul. 'The consul has instructed me to give you two speciedalers' – those words echoed continually in her ears, the voice, the tone, everything. The corners of her lips felt tight and her nose prickled. Inside her head it felt like hammer blows. Tears were trying to escape, but she resisted them and swallowed them down.

But when she had arrived home, changed her outfit and put her best clothes away carefully, she sat down and sobbed heartily, asking herself all the time: 'Is i'possible that Sivert was jus' lyin' about i' all?'

In the end she stood up and threw the notes, which she had crushed between her fingers into a clump on the way home, into her chest drawer, went out to the kitchen and folded up the dry washing ready for rolling.*

8

'Oh my lady come down below!'

followed by the sound of hauling and a clunk.

'I have smashed my little toe'

then again hauling and a clunk.

'Oh my lady come down below!
Oh come down in the ice frost and snow!'*

This shanty and the noisy clunks had been ringing out for days from the hold of *Two Friends*, and Sivert could no longer get either the words or the tune out of his head. The worst thing was that he could hear it best of all when it was not actually being sung, such as when they were in the mess or having a nap.

When he was in the hold himself, in a team of three of four led by a naked black man, hauling on the ropes which were made fast to the heavy wooden cleats, he had nothing against it. On the contrary, it seemed to him that the work went more easily because of it, and in all seriousness he bawled out the native song about ice, frost and snow, whilst they toiled in the stifling heat until the sweat poured off them, literally making puddles around them.

The captain had taken on some black workers, who had been recommended to him as 'most brilliant workmen' and 'first rate loaders' to help with the loading,* and the work had in fact progressed so fast that the captain found no reason to rant and swear about it, which really meant that he was rubbing his hands in glee at how things were going. Two thirds of the cargo, comprising various sorts of wood, had been taken on board in eleven days; they were now in the process of getting the remainder of the smooth round blocks of pokkenholt and the trunks of logwood securely stowed.* Tomorrow they would begin loading a consignment of casks of sugar and rum, which were already waiting on the quay, to the captain's satisfaction.

Up from the hold came the workers, semi-clothed or completely naked, dripping with sweat. The crew came first, pulled off their canvas trousers, which were turned up to above their knees, and dived headfirst into the sea. The blacks put their clothes on and hurried ashore. Work was finished for the day. It ended when the sun set at half-past six, when darkness fell suddenly without any dusk.

Sivert, who helped in the hold all the time he could spare from his other duties, had been called up earlier than usual. The captain and the first mate were going ashore, so he had been given orders to serve dinner in good time. That suited him very well, because he himself had asked permission to go ashore this evening, and it had been granted.

He had made an important decision. This evening he would not be as stupid as he normally was over in Princess Street. It was true that the girls were black, and they smelt bad – but the others did not let this put them off, so he would not either. He had been a figure of fun for long enough. If only he could get ashore before the others. He had gathered that both the sailmaker and the cook were intending to go ashore, and he was well aware of where they would be heading. So he made haste to finish his work, and straight afterwards he was standing amidships, stripped to the waist and washing himself in a bucket of fresh water.

Over the fort on Port Royal the moon had risen like a blood-red disc. As it rose higher and became paler in colour, it cast a brilliant stripe across the deck. From one of the narrow streets leading down to the quay came a sound of yodelling and native songs, accompanied by a monotonous tune that sounded like bagpipes. On the quay close to the ship lay some black men, stretched out on bales of cargo and puffing at cigarettes, which glowed red, whilst they flirted with their female compatriots, whose extremely low-cut shifts and colourful calico skirts appeared bluish-white in the moonlight. A little further off in the harbour a black man was paddling a canoe and singing:

I have got no wife
To bother my life
I paddle my own canoe.

From Port Royal came the sound of shots and trumpet blasts, summoning the men to their quarters. On board the ships eight bells was sounded. When one had finished the next one started up; it seemed to Sivert that it went on for ever this evening. Large insects and glittering fireflies buzzed in the air.

'Oh my lady come down below,' Sivert hummed as he bent over the bucket and rinsed the soapy water from his neck.

A tall, slim black girl with a basket on her head, which she held with one hand whilst the other was placed on her hip so that her arm was bent at a sharp angle, came strolling onboard. Around her bare black neck hung many rings of yellow and bright red beads, and Sivert could see her teeth shining as brightly as the whites of her eyes.

'Blimey, wha' a snooty lass,' muttered Sivert as he turned his head to watch her. 'She's carryin' on like a queen, an' she's nowt bu' a washerwoman, an' a black one an' all.' Erect and serious, she walked aft to the second mate, who was sitting on the bench next to the wheelhouse, bare-headed and with his shirt unbuttoned, smoking his evening pipe and cooling off after the day's work.

'Good evening, captain onboard?' Sivert heard her say in her broad, lazy English; to that the second mate answered that he could take the washing, and asked her to bring it downstairs.

'Scorpion!' yelled Sivert at the same moment. 'A big fat scorpion! I saw 'im clear as day, 'ee were abou' to sting me foot.'

'Is that all? Now if it'd bin a snake, that'd be summat else,' said the second mate scornfully.

'Bu' they're poisonous,' Sivert muttered, taken aback.

'Well, why're you walkin' round barefoot? Didn' I say we get loads of snakes an' scorpions onboard wi't logwood? Anyway, it was probably nothin' more'n an innocent li'l cockroach.'

Sivert protested, then slunk off to the cabin, where a lamp had been lit. He sat down in front of the second mate's cracked six-inch mirror, which had black spots where the quicksilver had worn away,* and wrestled with his thick brown hair. The parting was meant to run from his temple and round past his ear in a curve. He dipped the toothless horn comb in a bowl of water, pulled it through his hair, and smoothed it down with his fingers on both sides, holding the lamp close to his reddish-brown face which was still shiny from washing; but his tightly-curled, rebellious locks refused to lie down. Eventually he decided it would do. Then he knotted his confirmation necktie round his neck, turned his shirt collar down over it, and pulled on his black jacket, after giving the patches of greenish mildew a rub. It was astonishing how much he had grown on this journey. He tugged at the sleeves to make them longer, but the moment he moved they crept up again past his bony red wrists. Then he took down from a hook a beige hat with a pointed crown and a wide brim, which the blacks constructed from thin bark and sold for sixpence apiece, put it on at an angle, looked in the mirror again, pulled up his shirt to make it balloon out over his trouser waistband, nodded to himself in satisfaction, and set out.

He walked quickly across the quayside, turned the corner up into Victoria Street with its multitude of offices and shops, and then turned right into a side street which had a more rural character. Most of the houses had an area of fenced-in land in front with ancient, twisted palm trees and bamboo sheds, and they looked ramshackle and run down. They seemed to be scattered here and there with no planning. One house stuck out into the street, the next lay further back; some resembled Indian tepees or fishing cabins, whilst others had two floors with shaded balconies, enclosed on both levels by closely woven lattices of green rushes. The light from the houses was as bright as the light of the moon, and Sivert could see the inhabitants in their airy garments going about their lives both indoors and out.

In front of one of the smallest huts there hung a number of ropes fastened to posts and palm trees. An old black woman was hanging washing up to dry. In the doorway of the hut sat a younger woman, bathed in moonlight, wringing out washing from a butt. In front of her stood a stark naked black boy with a large, protruding stomach, drinking from her breast. Each time the boy lost his grip because of her movements he hit out, screaming with rage. Then the woman splashed water at him, and that made him so furious that he pulled her hair with both hands and kicked out backwards like a cockerel, while the woman roared with laughter.

Sivert joined in the laughter, and then directed his steps towards a building which was set back a little from the street and surrounded by a narrow enclosed verandah. The many irregularly pointed gables looked as if they had been dropped at random over the flat roof of the lower floor. Immediately over the entrance door in the middle hung a light with red and green glass, on one side of which was written:

Appartements to be had*

and on the other:

Well aired beds

Sivert had spelt out the words to himself the first time he was here, and translated them after a fashion.

He put his hand on the latch of the gate to the front enclosure, where a tethered goat lay sleeping beneath the tall trunk of a coconut tree with a kid beside her.

The light from the windows and the open door beckoned him in; through it he could see the large, bright green parrot called Old Bob swinging on his ring which hung down from the roof. But despite that he stood still. His heart was beating wildly and his head was burning. Now he intended to be resolute and go in, but he suddenly felt the urge to scratch the mosquito bites down on his ankles.

'Good evening gentlemen, good beds, nice girls!'

Sivert gave a start, although he knew that it was the parrot speaking; it always said the same thing, over and over again.

Suddenly a substantial black girl appeared in the doorway. She was the one they called Miss Louise. She was dressed like a tightrope walker, with shiny shoes and crossed ribbons all the way up her sturdy calves. In her hand she was holding a harmonica, on which she at once began to play 'God Save the Queen', whilst casting searching glances down towards the main street. Two other girls in similar costumes appeared. They put their hands on their hips, moved their legs and swayed their hips in time to the music, singing along to it. The one in blue with a nodding feather in her hair was Nancy, and the one in red with flowers and a fluttering ribbon round her neck was Annie, but where could Emmeline be, wondered Sivert. She was the prettiest, or anyway the least ugly. If only they would move away from the door so that Sivert could go in, because he was too embarrassed to go up there whilst all three were in the way. Then all at once they set off across the verandah and down towards the gate, still playing and singing.

Sivert ducked down in order not to be seen, and quickly walked away. When he had gone a short distance he straightened up again and walked back with a confident air, as the blood ran hot in his veins.

As soon as the girls caught sight of him they opened the gate and surrounded him with cheerful cries and affectionate greetings, before leading him between them up to the house and into the large central room, with doors leading off in all directions. Here they made him sit down on a monstrosity of a rattan sofa, which stood in the corner by the window with a rough-hewn table in front of it. In the opposite corner stood a similar sofa and an identical table. On both sides of the entrance, two hammocks were slung across the room on long ropes which were fastened to the wall and trailed along the rush matting on the floor, which was full of holes. Along one of the walls stood a kind of sideboard, its doors hanging open to show some glasses and some chipped crockery, with drawers above and below, out of which pieces of material and ribbon were spilling. Above the cupboard hung coloured lithographs of Queen Victoria and Prince Albert in coronation robes, together with a flyspecked mirror. On the table stood glasses and empty bottles, a half-eaten coconut lay on a stool, and there were some gnawed chicken bones and a piece of bread on top of the sideboard. In front of the windows hung muslin curtains with long rips in them and frayed edges. The room was lit by two lamps with smeared glass and cracked globes.

'Something to drink?'* asked Louise, picking up a glass and holding it to her mouth to demonstrate what she meant.

'Ah yes,' answered Sivert. 'A drink, you mean.' He picked up a glass and made the same movement as Louise.

The girls cackled with laughter and clapped their black hands. All at once Sivert forgot his awkwardness.

'Ah yes,' he repeated, joining in the laughter. 'You and me drink, together.' He pulled a coin out of his pocket and tossed it on the table.

The girls laughed more and more. Then they put their arms round his neck and tried to kiss him. But Sivert shook them off and looked round for Emmeline.

Fat Louise opened a door and called: 'Jack, old boy, come here.'

An old, stooping black man with a heavily wrinkled face, bare feet and red canvas trousers appeared from an alcove at the back of the room.

'Yes sir, ma'am,' he said in an indifferent, cracked voice, and stood there with his arms hanging down.

Miss Louise pointed at a bottle and ordered him to fetch some rum.

'Let us have a dance!' called Nancy, pulling Sivert up off the sofa.

'No, no, cannot!' Sivert protested, pulling away.

'Nonsense!' laughed Nancy. 'Me teach you.' She put her arm round his waist and danced round with him.

'Too warm, too warm!' cried Sivert. 'Too much svet, you know!'

The girls roared with laughter, and Nancy buckled at the knees.

Louise threw down her harmonica, ran across to Sivert and unbuttoned his jacket. 'Take this off, you don't want it.' She pulled off his jacket, untied his necktie, undid his collar and asked him if that was not cooler. Then she began to tickle him. Nancy and Annie joined in. Sivert laughed and yelled and defended himself, but finally he pulled himself free and ran around the room pursued by the shrieking girls.

They carried on like this until the black man returned.

Then they sat down to drink rum, which they mixed with water, and sent the old man out for cigarettes.

When Sivert had swallowed a few mouthfuls from the glass he plucked up the courage to ask about Emmeline.

'Got business,' was Louise's brief answer.

Straight after that a door was opened in the opposite wall and out came a middle-aged, well-dressed black man in a nankeen suit, with an enormous stomach, short bandy legs, rings on all his fingers and a thick gold watch chain festooned with baubles. He walked straight across the floor and with an indifferent 'Good evening ladies' left the house.

A moment later Emmeline emerged from the same door. She was wearing a short-sleeved shift and a short white muslin skirt with a sprigged pattern; her neck and arms were decorated with rows of beads and her long loose hair was tied at the forehead and at the back of the neck with lurid yellow silk ribbons. Her skin was a bit lighter than the others', and her mouth less protruding. Sivert thought she looked almost pretty this evening.

'Are you there my sweet boy,' she cooed to Sivert, sitting down next to him and stroking his chin. 'Your beard don't scrape.' She put her face against his cheek and rubbed it.

Sivert, who had gained courage from the rum, put his arms around her and kissed her neck.

The others were not pleased at this. They shouted that she had taken their place, and pulled and tugged at Emmeline, who held on to Sivert and tried to push them away. But when Louise bit her arm and trod on her toes at the same time, Emmeline let go of Sivert and gave Louise a resounding slap. A moment later all four were writhing on the floor in a furious battle.

'Halloa, halloa! Take it coolly, folks!' someone suddenly shouted.

Sivert thought he recognised the voice, and as he let go of Louise's hair, which he had been pulling to try and get her away from Emmeline, he looked up and saw the sailmaker and Sølvfest standing in the middle of the room.

'I think there's too many hens around one cock here,' grinned Sølvfest, grabbing Nancy around the waist and leading her over to the sofa. 'We got here just at the right time, don't you think, sailmaker?'

'Good evening my dearest darling favourite gentleman!' cried Emmeline, as she caught sight of the sailmaker, and she ran over to him. She threw her arms round his neck and kissed him over and over again with a loud smacking sound. Louise and Annie had also run over to the sailmaker; now they were pulling on his arms and caressing his hands.

Sivert, suddenly left alone and ignored, was on the verge of tears. He felt like seizing the sailmaker by the throat and murdering him on the spot. He looked over at him, trembling with rage – and it suddenly struck him how handsome the sailmaker was, tall and broad-shouldered, with fair curly hair, a curved nose and bright blue eyes, his beardless cheeks tanned by the sun and with a pure white forehead above the line where his cap had reached, with a mouth as small and red as a rowan berry and white teeth. And how well his clothes sat, with his v-necked shirt leaving his throat bare and a big blue collar hanging down at the back, like a proper sailor.

Sivert went over to the table, drained his glass and lit a cigarette.

'Aye, you'll 'ave to console yourself with the bottle now, sailmaker's pushed you out,' laughed Sølvfest. 'The lasses all go ravin' mad for 'im, whether they're white or black, red or blue.'

'Here is the beauty of them all,' said Emmeline, coming over to the table and pulling the sailmaker along with her. She poured some drink into two glasses, gave one to the sailmaker and clinked glasses with him. Then she ran over and jumped up into a hammock, holding out her arms to the sailmaker to show him that there was room for him too. He accepted the invitation, climbed in beside her and started the hammock rocking with the help of a hanging rope.

'You'll 'ave to make do with that skinny one there,' Sølvfest consoled Sivert, pointing to Annie, who was standing beside him running her fingers through his hair. 'She's not got much flesh on her bones, but by God she's better than that fat sausage there.'

'What did you say?' asked Louise with her apoplectic smile.

'Your skin is as white as milk,' exclaimed Emmeline from the hammock. In her admiration for the sailmaker's white skin she had pushed up his shirt sleeve, and was now caressing his arm.

'Shall I sing for you?' asked Annie, and pushed her round face under Sivert's nose; he was sitting with his elbows on the table and his cheeks in his hands. When he made no answer, she launched into 'The Captain and his Loving Girl'.

Louise picked up her harmonica, sat on the edge of the table and played the accompaniment to the song, as she beat time with her dangling legs, all the time showing her large teeth and her glistening red gums. At the chorus of each verse, which went like this:

And the captain with the whiskers
Took a slight glance at me!

all the girls joined in, and even Emmeline from over in the hammock made sure to take part.

Before the song was quite finished, Emmeline and the sailmaker jumped out of the hammock and ran arm in arm into one of the adjoining rooms. –

I am going to get me a sweetheart tonight.

Sivert turned his head and saw an English sailor from a ship which was moored alongside *Two Friends* for loading, standing on the threshold and looking around with a calculating glance. Then he went over to the table, put down a coin and asked for a drink.

'See here,' said Sølvfest, pushing the bottle of rum over to him. 'When that is empty, you give another.'

The sailor poured a drink, held the glass up to the light and examined the contents, whilst he sang:

I am going to get me a sweetheart tonight,
May be black, may be white, may be yellow.

On that he drank it down, caught Louise around the waist and continued, as he danced across the floor:

And I will love her because her complexion will keep.
She is black, but that is no matter.

Then they disappeared through the door beside the one that Emmeline and the sailmaker had gone through.

Straight after that Sølvfest went through a third door with Nancy.

Sivert found it difficult to breathe, and the room danced in front of his eyes whilst Annie sat nudging him and whispering in his ear.

'Oh yes come on,' he said in a thick voice, standing up suddenly and walking resolutely across the room, holding Annie's hand. But suddenly Annie was grabbed from him and he was pushed aside; before he could grasp what had happened, he glimpsed the back of the cook who was walking off with Annie, and heard her say: 'Not there, this way'. The next moment one of the doors had closed behind them.

Sivert stood staring open-mouthed and wide-eyed; he felt frozen to the spot. But when he realised it was the cook who had taken her from him, he flew into such a rage that all his limbs shook. He clenched his fist, raised his arm and leapt towards the door, pushed it open with a bang and stormed in. But the next second he was ejected by the cook with such force that he flew across the floor like a ball and crashed into the far wall of the room. At the same time he heard a bolt being pushed across the door behind him.

'Good beds, nice girls,' chattered the parrot from up on its ring.

Sivert shook his fist at it and shouted at it to shut up.

He felt a violent desire for revenge. He would set fire to the house and burn everyone in it. He stuck his hand in his pocket for matches, but found none. But he would and must do something; his eyes scanned the room. The bottles and the glasses, he would smash them against the closed doors. He ran over to the table and seized one of the bottles. As he turned to hurl it, the old black man came gliding towards him. So he put the bottle down again and stood there irresolutely.

'All gone?' lisped the man, looking at him pityingly. 'Your turn by and by,' he added, nodding with a repulsive smile.

Sivert was filled with shame and disgust. He looked

round for his jacket and hat and found both on the floor by the sofa. He went over and picked them up, put his hat on, threw his jacket over his arm and hurried out.

But he would have his revenge on the cook. Now he would get his own back for everything at once. Tonight the battle would take place. He would wait for him outside the house, even if he had to wait until tomorrow morning. He lent on the little gate through which the girls had led him in triumph only an hour ago, and looked up at the lighted windows. Gradually he was filled with a consuming feeling of abandonment and humiliation. Here he stood like a reject, while all the others, – even though he had been there first!

But it had always been like that. He had always been pushed aside. All the time he was at Bethelem School,* when they were playing games in the playground, and especially if the little girls were there too, he was always left out in one way or another. Like that time up on Skansen, when they were going to play mummies and daddies.* The biggest and prettiest of the little girls had said to him: we two are husband and wife. And then the whole group had joined in and lain down in a long row, couple by couple – they were pretending that it was night-time and they had gone to bed. And the pretty girl had laid her head on his arm and said that she wanted to lie like that, because all parents did that. Then along came a boy who hadn't got a wife and pulled him up by the arm, shouting: "'urry up, 'urry up, yer grandma's down there, she's so drunk she can't stand up, you 'ave to 'elp 'er 'ome!' And he had jumped up and pretended that he thought it was kind of the boy to warn him, even though he could have killed him on the spot, because he knew it was a lie and made up just so that the boy could take his place. He had run straight home and shut himself in the woodshed in order to hide how miserable he was. He couldn't have been more than seven at the time, but he had felt the shame and the humiliation just like an adult. It had scorched and festered in him, and at moments it felt as if something was bubbling up inside him, as if he was going to drown in it. And still today, whenever he thought of it - -

A shudder ran through his body, and he felt a sinking feeling in his breast which reached right down to his stomach; his shoulders began to move slowly up and down, and he broke into a stifled sobbing. But it soon passed, and he dried his eyes with his blue-checked handkerchief, which he had folded into a small square, thrust his hands into his pockets and took up his previous watchful position.

Ugh, his grandparents! For as far back as he could remember, every time he got involved in a quarrel, or someone wanted to get at him, they had been thrust in his face. They had weighed him down constantly, like a terrible shame. He would never be able to become a decent person. Just look at how he had been bullied this evening, even though he was thousands of miles away from them! First of all he let the sailmaker take Emmeline from him – although that was understandable, the sailmaker was such a fine handsome fellow – but that red-haired, squinting, bandy-legged cook!

He swore out loud that he would beat him black and blue.

Just then he felt something stinging his neck. He reached up and felt a number of itchy, burning bites. 'Tssss,' sang the mosquitos around him; he waved his arms about, but the sound went on: 'Tssss'. They were settling on his nose, his forehead, his hands; it made no difference if he brushed them away. When he thought about it, he had heard their buzzing the whole time, but he had been so lost in thought that he hadn't paid it any attention. But he couldn't stand still here any longer; he would be eaten alive under the trees. It would be better to walk up and down out on the road.

He opened the gate and went out. Now it was completely quiet everywhere. The houses were shuttered and dark, but the moon had risen further in the sky, and its bright gleam made everything as light as day. Sivert walked along the fence outside, past the house, turning round constantly to see whether anyone was coming out of the place he was watching. And it was not long before he saw a long, slim shadow falling across the gate and out onto the street. Sivert stole round the corner of one of the small houses which jutted out into the road and peeped out. It was the English sailor. He walked off rapidly in the direction of the harbour, cheerily humming the ballad of 'The Black Sweetheart' and rolling his hips.

Shortly after another man emerged. It was Sølvfest. He staggered from side to side, his erratic hops and skips making the sand fly up around him, whilst he held on to random trees and fences. Once he tripped and fell forwards, caught himself with his hands on the sandy road, and after crawling on all fours for a while managed to pick himself up again.

Before he was even out of sight Sivert saw another shadow falling across the gate. This time it must be the cook. He crouched down, put his fists up in front of him and was poised to leap out. But then he realised it was the sailmaker. His hands fell down limply, and he was about to move further back, when at that moment he heard the voice of a woman crying and pleading. Sivert moved forward far enough to see around the corner of the house wall he was hiding behind. In the gateway stood the sailmaker, struggling to break free from Emmeline, who was clinging to him with both hands round his neck. Her head was tilted back and she was looking up into his face as she spoke urgently, almost shouting. The sailmaker replied with one or two words, pulling at her arms to loosen her grip around his neck.

'Take me with you when you leave this country!' Sivert heard her say, as she sobbed: 'Oh, oh, oh! Me so unhappy, so miserable, my darling boy, oh, oh, oh! Fancy such conditions! Me shall die, when you part with me. You needn't be ashamed of me – me not negro, look at me, just a little brown, and my hair is soft and smooth.'

'Get away with you, I can't stay here any longer!' the sailmaker burst out more roughly than before. 'Do you hear, I must onboard,' and with a sudden jerk he freed himself and started to run.

'You come back, you come back! Will you not!' Emmeline called after him with such despair in her voice that it pierced Sivert's heart.

The sailmaker, who was already some distance away, turned round and shouted: 'Yes, I come back by and by!'

'Just think, she's not ashamed to show how fond she is of him,' thought Sivert. He had such a strange feeling, both moved and embarrassed at the same time. It was odd that one person could be reduced to begging another like that, even if they were black or mulatto. But perhaps that was what they called love. He was startled by the word, and pondered it for a long time. Love – but she was one of that kind; was it possible that they were the same on the inside as others? 'Aye, only our Lord knows how things stand,' he muttered finally, and peered out once more.

Emmeline was still standing by the gate with her back towards Sivert, looking in the direction the sailmaker had run off in. She was weeping so violently that she was shaking, and wiped her face with her hand repeatedly. Eventually she turned round with a shuddering sigh, and went slowly back into the house.

Sivert began patrolling along the fence, making frequent turns. That damned cook wouldn't show himself. You would think that he knew what was waiting for him.

Suddenly he noticed a tall, broad-shouldered black man in a white uniform with a helmet walking towards him and stopping a little way off. Sivert recognised the police uniform, and was startled.

'No doubt he'll go away again,' he thought then, and calmly carried on patrolling. Each time he had his back to the man he hoped that he would have gone when he turned round, or at least have moved off in another direction, but the constable remained in place, as stiff as a statue, and Sivert noticed that he was watching him constantly. In the end it became unbearable to feel those eyes on his back, and to see that threatening ghost standing there spying on him every time he turned round, and he decided to retreat. He would go aboard and wait there. He could just as well thrash the cook there as on land; at any rate there would be no policemen there to interfere, and the crew would be asleep in their quarters. No-one would notice there.

Once he had made his mind up, he set off at a run. Just as he was about to turn the corner into Victoria Street, he looked back involuntarily. There was the constable, striding quickly after him. 'That's because I'm running,' thought Sivert, and slowed down. At the end of Victoria Street, where the quayside began, he looked round again. The policeman was right on his heels, and it was clear that he intended to see where Sivert was going.

'Well, if you've not been on a fool's errand afore, you 'ave tonight,' mumbled Sivert, as he stepped onto the gangplank and jumped aboard.

The constable had followed him right to the ship. Now he was standing still on the quay, looking up at Sivert.

'Wha're you gawpin' at, you lanky p'lice devil?' Sivert called down to him. 'Are you after summat?'

'He?' said the constable, putting his hand to his ear and coming a step closer.

''Old yer tongue!' answered Sivert, who now felt safe and cocky. With that he turned on his heel and walked aft at a measured pace, whistling, into his cabin, from where he could keep watch.

9

Quietly and carefully, so as not to wake the second mate who was sleeping in the lower bunk, he changed out of his shore clothes, which seemed to him too good to fight in, and then he sat down on the chest by the little open window at the front of the wheelhouse. From there he could see over just about the whole deck, as well as the gangplank and part of the quay.

'Why, God 'elp me if tha' p'liceman in't standin' there still,' he exclaimed in a whisper, and let his hand fall on the little shelf under the window, which was screwed to the wall and served as a table. 'I reckon 'ee's rooted to't spot – . Does 'ee expec – oh no, ee's shufflin' off – bou' time an' all.'

After Sivert had been sitting there for a while, he began to feel sleepy. His head felt heavy after the rum he had drunk. "F only I 'ad some baccy ter chew," he muttered; he put his hand in the pocket of the mate's waistcoat which was hanging on the wall, found what he was looking for, bit off a piece and put the rest back. That helped; at once he felt as alert and ready for a fistfight as ever.

A figure appeared on the quay, making straight for the ship. Could it be the cook? No, he was too tall. Now he put a foot on the end of the gangplank and came on board. It was the first mate. He looked to be in a bad mood. Without looking to right or left he walked aft, talking to himself in an indignant voice: 'I wish to God that Satan would take the 'ole cartload of 'em. Bloody lasses … i's robbery, tha's wha' it is, dayligh' robbery.' Sivert heard him go aft into the cabin and slam the door after him.

"Ee who pays t'piper calls t'tune," sighed Sivert, smiling maliciously. 'Tha's 'ow i' is – ee's mad cause ee's spent 'is money an' I'm mad cause I still got mine.'

'But in't tha' t'capt'n comin' along there? I do b'lieve i' is.' Sivert put his face right against the window and opened his eyes wide. 'No, 'ee looks too li'l fer tha'. - - - 'Ang on, 'onest to God, tha' is t'capt'n, bu' wha's wrong wi' im? 'Ee's drunk, ab'slutely sozzled. I bet 'ee can' even find t'ship. Well, if 'ee in't comin' up t'gangplank after all – . Ups, now ee's fallin' over.' Sivert covered his mouth with his hand and chuckled merrily to himself as he watched the captain, who time after time kept putting one foot on the gangplank without being able to bring the other one along as well, which meant he kept hopping up and down and waving his arms about, until he finally knocked off his own hat. After a number of fruitless efforts, many bowings and misjudged grabs in order to pick up his hat again, he seemed suddenly to forget what he was trying to do. He stood still for a minute, looking at his feet as if in utter amazement at something or other. Then he recommenced his attempts to climb onto the gangplank. Sivert laughed until he ached.

'I think I'd best go down an' 'elp 'im,' he said to himself after a while. 'It'd be best ter shift 'im afore t'cook arrives.'

'Good evenin', capt'n, 'ere you are, 'ere's yer 'at.' Sivert had gone down onto the quayside past the captain, who hadn't seemed to notice him.

The captain uttered a hoarse growl, waving his arms about as if he was swatting flies, and then snatched his hat from Sivert as if at random. But instead of putting it on his head, which seemed to have been his first intention, he suddenly thrust it under his arm and squashed it flat with a bang, after which he held all ten fingers up in front of his nose and stuck out his tongue.

'It'd be best 'f you gi' me yer 'and, capt'n,' said Sivert in a voice which was weak after the hearty laughter which he was doing his best to stifle. "S no' easy walkin' on't gangplank this late a' nigh." The captain seemed neither to hear nor to understand, so Sivert simply took him by the arm and with some difficulty managed to get him onboard in one piece.

'Sh'd I see yer downstairs, capt'n?' asked Sivert, after having let go of him.

The captain folded his arms across his chest, leaned backwards, sticking his chest out, and took a couple of paces aft with a stiff bearing and pointing his feet as if he was going to dance the Lancers.

'Fine ship, *Two Friends*, grea' ship,' he pronounced with a thick voice, standing still. 'Tight as a drum – an' look at these seals.' He bent over to examine the deck, but lost his balance as he did so and would have fallen if Sivert had not grabbed him.

'Captain of *Two Friends* 's a goo' man,' he snuffled. 'Gen'leman, first rate fellow. Don' bother abou' 'im drinkin' a li'l bi' this evenin'.' His voice became humble, almost entreating, as he stood there leaning over and rocking slowly to and fro.

'You sh'd go to bed, capt'n, see 'ere's t'door.' Sivert walked over and opened the companion door. 'Come on down, capt'n, i's very late.' Sivert went over to him again, took his arm and pulled him along.

'Jus' one thing I'll say afore I die,' announced the captain, suddenly solemn, as he stumbled down the steps with Sivert practically carrying him. 'Never visi' loose women in foreign ports, never, I say. – They tek blood money an' tempt yer to drink, to dri – ' here he was interrupted by a violent hiccup, after which he carried on saying 'to drink' long after Sivert had tipped him over onto the sofa in his cabin.

As soon as Sivert stuck his head out of the companion door he caught sight of the cook coming onboard up the gangplank. From his unsteady gait and eagerly nodding head he could see that he too had drunk more than was good for him.

After the episode with the captain, however, Sivert was in such a merry mood that he was no longer so determined to thrash the cook. It would be best to wait until another time, he thought, or would it be better to deal with it straight away? Undecided, he walked a little way along the deck, keeping his eyes on the cook, who had now come aboard and was slowly walking forrards. "Ee can' see nor feel 'owt tonigh", Sivert muttered, and was going to go, but at that moment the cook turned round and shouted with a drunken slur: 'Annie said t'say 'ello to our li'l toddler!'

He had hardly turned his back in order to keep walking forrards before he had Sivert's hands round his throat, and the next moment he was lying sprawled on the deck with Sivert on top of him.

There was a violent tussle. The cook hit out with his fists; the sudden fright had made him almost sober. But Sivert, who was kneeling on his chest, had the upper hand. With one hand he lifted the cook's head up by the forelock and banged it down on the deck repeatedly with all his strength, whilst with the other he hit him in the face without stopping, and he did what he could with his feet as well. The cook tried to throw him off, but Sivert was not to be budged, despite the fierce blows from the cook. Finally the cook managed to shift him so far forward that he could get in a kick from behind, and he propelled Sivert straight over his head, headfirst into the deck a couple of feet away. Quick as a flash the cook was on his feet and on top of

Sivert. And now the roles were reversed. The cook grabbed Sivert by the forelock and banged his head on the deck, but the third time he lifted it up, Sivert seized the chance to bite his nose so viciously that the cook, with a bellow – the only sound either of them had made during the battle – let go of his hair and rolled onto the deck beside Sivert, where he lay still and apparently lifeless.

'There 'ee got what was comin' to 'im,' muttered Sivert, getting up and examining his victim. The cook lay on his side with his head bowed down towards his chest and his face turned to the deck so that you could hardly see it.

Suddenly Sivert was seized by fear. With a shudder running through all his limbs he jumped into his cabin to get undressed and go to bed. But as he opened his hands, which had remained clenched as though for a fight, he found that the right one was full of red human hair. With a fresh shudder he opened the door and shook his hand out through it. Then he caught sight of a sallow face in the mirror, smeared with blood. With staring eyes and hair standing on end he was about to turn his head to see whether anyone was there, but before he could do it he realised that the face was his. He got hold of a corner of the towel hanging on the wall and started wiping the blood off, holding the mirror in his other hand. He couldn't discover any wounds, and he hadn't had a nosebleed either. So it must have come from the cook, as he bit him. His hands shook, and his teeth began to chatter in his mouth. What if the bite had killed the cook? It felt as if everything stopped inside him. Just sixteen years old and perhaps already a murderer. He looked out through the window. There lay the cook on the same spot and in the same position. Cautiously he crept out, tiptoed across the deck, bent over the cook and listened. He could detect no sign of breathing. He walked around him several times, leaning over, listening and staring.

Senseless with terror, he finally picked up the bucket by the cabin door and poured some water over the cook's head. After he had repeated this several times, the cook started to move. 'Thank God, 'ee's not dead,' said Sivert to himself, letting out his breath in unspeakable relief, after which he carried on pouring water over him until he came round properly. With a moaning sound the cook slowly moved into a sitting position, pulled up his knees and rested his elbows on them, putting both hands to his head. Sivert had seen a glimpse of his face. It was in a dreadful state, the nose swollen and caked in blood.

But Sivert was so overjoyed that the cook was still alive that he could almost have started singing. Quickly and quietly he put down the bucket and ran lightly back to the cabin. Before he got into his bunk he peeped out onto the deck. The cook had finally got to his feet. Leaning on the galley wall, he dragged himself forwards and disappeared round the corner of the forecastle.

'Tomorrow mornin' 'ee'll be righ' as rain,' Sivert comforted himself, as he laid his head on the pillow and turned to the wall. Straight after that he was asleep.

10

The next day the captain woke up with a headache and a nasty taste in his mouth.

'How in the devil's name did this happen?' He sat up on the edge of the sofa with his arms hanging down and pondered how it could have come about that he was fully dressed and not in his bunk. He pulled his watch out of his waistcoat pocket and saw that it had stopped. Then he raised his head slightly and looked out of the skylight at the ship's clock. It was eleven o'clock.

'Blow me, what does that look like!' He had caught sight of his hat, which lay on the floor as flat as a pancake; then suddenly he had a vague memory of walking somewhere hanging on to Sivert's arm. Whether it was on land or on board he couldn't work out.

'You must've had a real skinful, Hans Jørgen Hansen,' he said to himself, as he passed his hands over his aching head and bent down to pick up his hat.

'If only I had some sour milk!'* He stood up, went into the inner cabin, dropped his hat into a chest drawer, locked it and put the key in his pocket.

He wished he could work out how it was that he had a feeling he had been hanging on Sivert's arm. It must have been something he had dreamt, although it was a devil of a mystery.

'Ah, I'm parched!' But whatever he felt, he had to get changed into his everyday clothes before anyone saw him, and carry on as if nothing had happened.

Finally he managed to get changed, and called Sivert to demand coffee.

'Aye aye, capt'n, t'coffee's 'ere,' announced Sivert.

The captain pulled himself together, walked smartly out into the forecabin, sat down at the table and poured himself some.

'Well, you were late gettin' back on board last night, eh?' he said to Sivert without looking at him.

'No – o,' answered Sivert as if thinking about it. 'It weren't tha' late.'

'Weren't tha' late,' mocked the captain. 'What d'you call late, if I might ask?'

'It weren't even midnigh.'

Then I must have dreamt it, thought the captain in relief. It was almost two before I came out of that Sodom up there. I reckon he'd have had more of a glint in his eye if he'd had me hanging on his arm.

'You better come and see to the peas, Sivert!' a voice called down. 'They'll be burnin.' The second mate's head came into view by the companion.

'What's all that about? Isn't the cook in charge of the peas?' asked the captain.

Sivert stopped on the stairs and looked embarrassed.

'What's wrong with the cook?' the captain went on.

'He's sick, capt'n,' said Sivert, turning his head away and running up the stairs.

'I guess he was drunk, the pig,' muttered the captain. Shortly afterwards he went up on deck with a pot of English salt in his pocket.

Work was in full swing on the deck. Two of the crew were standing on the quayside, where they were looping hawsers around the barrels of rum and making sure they didn't bang against the side of the ship. By the main hatch seven men were busy hoisting provisions on board with the help of a block and tackle. In the hold beneath the hatch some black workers were stowing them.

The captain stopped for a while and watched the work. Nothing was right for him, and he grumbled at both the mates and the crew. The tackle squeaked because it wasn't oiled, and a new hawser was being used without permission.

When the captain came down into the forecastle, where the cook was lying in a lower bunk next to the door, he took a step back in shock. The cook's face was all bloody, and the tip of his nose was a gaping wound. In a whining, indignant voice the cook told him about Sivert's attack the night before.

'You've been baiting him all this time,' said the captain. 'I'm not surprised the lad gave you a thrashing, but biting someone's nose off is taking it too far.'

'I've 'eard that bites can be fatal,' said the cook. 'I jus' 'ope you'll get 'im put away for murder if I sh'd die of it.'

'Die of it – that's a likely story! But now we'll get a dose of English salt into you.'

'Tha's not wha' I need, not a' all,' said the cook, recoiling.

'English salt is good for everything.' The captain took the pot out of his pocket, shook a portion of the contents out into a pewter mug, poured water from a flask onto it, stirred it with his finger and forced the cook, who was protesting vehemently, to drink it. After that he departed with an order to the cook to get dressed quickly. He would take him off to a doctor.

Then Sivert was summoned to the cabin and had to explain what had happened. The captain reprimanded him and asked him whether he thought it was acceptable to use such a dirty trick in an honest fight. Sivert defended himself, saying that the cook had almost killed him.

'Well now it's a good thing I let you off payin' for the crockery you smashed,' the captain concluded. 'Now you'll have to pay for a new nose for the cook.'

There was something in the captain's voice which gave Sivert fresh courage. 'I sh'd think they'll be able to mend it,' he said, and risked a small smile. But the captain bristled and promised to put him on bread and water when they got home.

A little while later it was dinnertime. The crew went to and fro from the galley, holding out their bowls to Sivert, who put a chunk of meat in the bottom and ladled out peas on top. On the spar by the gangway sat the cook, waiting for the captain, in his best clothes and with a scarf wound round his nose and forehead so that only one eye was visible. He was leaning over with his head in his hands, staring darkly and inertly out of his one eye.

When the crew had all been served, the black workers came along to collect their meal. They brought their own food, but had it cooked on board. With their bunches of fried bananas and a thin slice of roasted meat, which one of them carried on a loaf of white bread, they climbed down into the hold to eat, after which they stretched out on the cargo for a nap, completely naked.

Sivert came out from the galley, drying his hands on a damp teacloth. The sun was intense, burning and baking; nowhere was there the slightest shade or any breath of wind. 'It's burning inside and burning outside; it can't be any hotter in Hell,' thought Sivert, as great drops of sooty sweat trickled from his face down over his neck and his bare chest. Then he picked up the full tureen which was intended for the deckhouse and carried it aft. As he passed by, the cook kicked his ankle, which was bare above the flat-trodden sandal.

'You tryin' to trip me up, can't you see wha' I'm carryin'?' shouted Sivert crossly, and walked on. The cook looked after him with fury in his eyes, and shook his fist at him, muttering a curse behind his scarf.

When the cook returned from his visit to the doctor later that afternoon, he had a large bandage over his nose. It was just around the time of the afternoon break, and the crew were sitting forrard on upturned buckets and coils of rope, up against the side of the wheelhouse, which provided a little bit of shade, chewing and drinking, with the coffee pot perched on the chopping block between them.

When the cook appeared, a storm of laughter and jokes broke out.

'Looks like you'll be a clown in't circus now?' called out the bosun.

'Or a tightrope walker!' remarked Sølvfest, laughing until he had tears in his eyes. 'I've never seen a snout like that!'

'Won't you take me wi'yer?' said another. 'I can stand on me 'ead and walk on me 'ands, and I'll do it for free.'

The cook walked past them with a sullen expression, and went into the forecastle, where he filled his pipe and lay down on the bunk.

'Letters from home!' shouted the captain as he jumped down from the gangplank and stopped amidships.

'Did 'ee say letters?' shouted the sailmaker, as he leapt up and began mimicking a native dance.

'Let's go over and hear whether there're any for us,' said Sølvfest. 'Looks as if the captain's waiting.'

So they drifted slowly along the side of the wheelhouse, one by one, awkward and uncertain, as if they weren't sure whether to go forwards or back, and came to a halt a few steps from the captain.

'What're you after?' asked the captain, looking slyly at them.

The crew looked at one another and smiled self-consciously.

'We jus' wanted to ask if there was anythin' for us,' the bosun finally managed to say.

The captain put his hand in his breast pocket, took out a packet of letters and looked at the envelopes.

'Able Seaman Sølvfest, Zacharias Nilssen,' he read out, 'Sailmaker Anton Marius Selsing, Bosun Torsten, Rasmus Christensen, Ship's Cook Pitter, Christian Hybenetten – no, the rest are for the officers,' he finished.

Those whose names had been mentioned had taken a step closer.

'You'll not get 'em till after work's done,' said the captain. 'Just so's you don't sit and mumble over 'em all afternoon!'

'We'll not read 'em till this evenin', capt'n,' the sailmaker put in. He was looking down at the deck, running the tip of his shoe to and fro along the join between the planks.

'I s'pose you're waiting for a letter from your sweetheart,' said the captain teasingly, 'since you're so fidgety.'

'Aye, 'ee's got a girlfriend in every port,' remarked Sølvfest, looking sideways at the captain to see whether he took the joke in good part.

'Aye well, enough o' that, you'll not get 'em till this evening,' said the captain. 'It's good to have something to look forward to.' He walked a few steps aft, then stopped and called back: 'Here, give the cook his, he's having a day off anyway, since his nose is bent out of shape!' With that he gave the letter to the bosun, who took it forrard. –

Sivert was crouching in the galley, sweeping up the

crumbs from the floor. He kept sighing and shaking his head. Even though he had not expected a letter to this place, and up until now had not even thought about it, he felt strangely bereft at having missed out. When I get to Marseilles, there'll be a letter for me, he comforted himself. I wonder who will have written it? I suppose it'll be Thrine they'll get to do it, and what will it say? 'Dear Brother Sivert, we are all well and getting on fine, I am sending greetings to you from me and our parents.' All at once he was seized with longing for those back home, and at that instant they appeared to him so vividly that it seemed to him that they were standing beside him, and all he needed to do was reach out his hand in order to touch them, and he could hear their voices so clearly. Just think, he had a father and a mother and a sister and a brother! It felt as if he had not really known that until this moment. He had never thought it meant anything, but now it came over him with a feeling of fortune and happiness. When he got a letter from them in Marseilles just like all the others, a letter with his full name and postmark on, that would be a proud moment.

He was lost in thought. His hand with the brush lay at his side, and the dustpan slid down onto the floor. Then all of a sudden Emmeline's weeping and wailing from last night, when she had taken leave of the sailmaker, rang in his ears. Just think of being so much in love with another person. Would anyone ever feel like that about him? That would be wonderful.

'Is it ol' Madam Tosspot, yer gran, wha' walks t'streets wi' Tippler Tom, wha's taught yer to bite so well?' came a voice suddenly from just over his head, and at the same moment he felt a shove from a sharp knee in his back, so that he had to put his hands out to prevent himself pitching forwards.

'These drunken old Stril women are terrible bad at bitin', so I've 'eard,' went on the cook's voice, 'an' t'apple don't fall far from't tree. Course yer Da' drinks an' all, don''ee, 'ee'll 'ave bin reared wi' a dummy full o' brandy, no' a't' breast.'

Sivert felt as if he had had a knife plunged into his heart. The sensation surged up inside him so powerfully that he stopped breathing, and then it blocked his throat like a cork. In a single flash he saw all the insults and taunts he would have to face from now on. And he had been so furious about what happened with those girls last night. Now the boot was on the other foot. If he had been able to crawl down into the floor and hide beneath it, he would have done so. But the floor would not open. There was nothing to do but remain where he was. Fumbling, he picked up the brush and pan, swept up the rubbish carefully, went out and emptied it overboard.

As if in a mist he saw the cook standing by the galley door staring at him, and the sound of his voice struck him like agonising strokes of the whip from far away, as he shouted after him: 'You sh'd 'a said a' once wha' kinda family you're from, so we'd 'a known wha' stuff ye're made of! Well now 'ere's a thing! – So ye're Madam Tosspot's gran'son, are ye? 'Ave you seen wha' she looks like when she strips off in't marketplace ter buy some brandy? P'raps you 'elped 'er sell 'er rags, did yer? An' wha's 'is name, yer grandda'? 'Ee drinks like a pig, 'im an' all! When ye're thrown in jail for attempted murder, I sh'd think yer'll meet yer family there. – Tell 'em I said so!'

Sivert heard no more. He had gone into his cabin, where he sat down on the chest with his shoulders drawn up and his head right down on his breast. Now it had reached him right out here in the wide world, what he had run away from. How could he ever have felt himself to be safe? How could he not have known that it had to come some time, that it had to strike him like lightning from a clear sky. Now it had happened. In the first letter the cook had from home it had been mentioned. And he had wanted to be a big man, wanted to behave as if he was just as good as the others. He was marked from the moment he was born. What was it that it said in the Bible: some vessels are created to dishonour, others to honour.* He was one of those to dishonour, but why him?

Well, there was no point wondering about it. It must have been decided by God's wise judgement from time immemorial. But was there no way he could ever be rid of it? If both of them actually died, then no doubt people would have to forget it eventually. They were old now, after all, although no older than that they could easily live for another twenty years; then they would be eighty, if an accident didn't finish them off before then.

Suddenly he slid down from the chest onto his knees with his folded hands raised high and his head bent back, and while the tears streamed down over his face he prayed quietly but earnestly to God that He should let his grandparents perish in an accident as soon as possible. Or at least that she should. He begged and pleaded in passionate words, and kept repeating: 'In the name of Jesus and for His sake, for you have promised us, Lord God, that we will be given everything we ask for in the name of Jesus.' Suddenly it occurred to him that it was also written that they should add: 'Thy will be done, and not mine.' But he pushed that thought aside at once and pretended he had forgotten it.

11

They had filled up the freshwater tanks and loaded the provisions. Now they were just waiting for the captain, who had gone up to clear customs, before they were towed away from the quay and tied up by a buoy a little way out, where they would wait for the tide to turn in a couple of hours.

When the captain arrived they were given orders to delay casting off. At the last moment the consul had persuaded him – in return for a substantial payment – to make room for two Frenchmen, a botanist and a zoologist, who were travelling for Jardin des Plantes, and were now returning home with the specimens they had collected. The second mate was ordered to move into the first mate's cabin on the port side, where there was an empty top bunk, and Sivert was to move forrard and share a bunk with one of the crew. The Frenchmen were to have the starboard cabin.

Shortly afterwards the passengers arrived with two large waggonloads of baggage, in addition to the various packages they were carrying in their hands. At that point the captain had gone down into his quarters in order to write and inform the shipping company of their departure, so the first mate told some of the crew to help bring things on board. There were live birds in cages, lidless rectangular crates in which turtles lay in green, slimy water, six in each, side by side, and tall square crates with steel wire over the top; some contained snakes, both large and small, and others crocodiles. Sivert, who was helping to carry the items onboard, stared wide-eyed at it all. Two cages with iron bars around the sides were placed on the main hatch.

Sivert bent down to look into them, but hurriedly pulled back when some ocelots hissed at him, baring their teeth. One contraption, which resembled a dog's kennel, housed a couple of black porcupines. Then there were a large number of rectangular zinc cases with glass lids, full of the strangest fish and all kinds of ugly creepy-crawlies. In addition there was a huge stack of cigar boxes with eggs and larvae in cotton wool, and bundles as tall as a man wrapped in matting, with bits of rushes and shrivelled leaves sticking out. On everything there was written in large letters: *Mss. J. Beauvais & Pierre Bouvier, Voyageurs pour Jardin des Plantes, Paris.*

When the captain came on deck and saw how much baggage the Frenchmen had with them, he felt a strong urge to put his foot down and refuse to take them; but in view of the fact that there wasn't time to inform the consul, whom he had promised to take them on board, he resorted to effing and blinding in English and Norwegian, cursing the Frenchmen to their faces and threatening to chuck them and their junk into the sea as soon as they had left harbour. The Frenchmen, who were preoccupied with getting their property securely stowed, had no time to consider what the captain's strange behaviour was all about. Now and then they uttered a short 'Hé?' and sent the captain a brief puzzled glance, whilst they lent a hand with the crates and measured out the space on deck.

'All right, plenty de space, capitaine,' one of them said, once they had finally got everything onboard, as he took off his straw hat and wiped his bald head with his handkerchief.

'Aye, that's what you think, you French cockroach!' the captain answered, exasperated. 'Come over here and get a hold of this, Sølvfest!' he then shouted, getting hold of one of the crates. 'If they'd been able to spread them out some more, I reckon they'd have done it. Up with it!' And with Sølvfest's help he lifted up the crate in order to place it on top of one of the tall cages with steel netting, containing two crocodiles. But at that one of the Frenchmen rushed over and seized the captain by the arm, and with a face alight with alarm and indignation he protested with sweeping gestures and a ceaseless torrent of words against the captain's intentions.

The captain was so astonished at this energetic performance that with a vexed 'Bloody pest!' he let the crate fall back on the deck.

'Il leur faut du soleil!' the Frenchman expostulated. 'Considerez donc, Capitaine!'

'Oh, go to Hell!' the captain burst out. 'What riffraff, they can't even talk so's Christians can understand.'

'Ils want du sun, sunshine, you know,' began the Frenchman again more calmly, as he scoured his memory in order to remember the little bit of English he knew. 'Sans, without I mean, sun, you know, ils,' he pointed at the crocodiles, 'shall die you know.' The word 'die' he pronounced with long drawn-out deep emphasis, as he tipped his head back and closed his eyes.

'Yes, I understand, they must have sun for not to die,' replied the captain more amenably. He had been surprised to realize how easily he could understand French.

'Précisément!' exclaimed the Frenchman with a brilliant smile. 'Just so! Magnifique Capitaine.' He laughed merrily and looked delightedly at the captain.

'Oh yes, all right!' returned the captain, as he sprang aft and up onto the wheelhouse roof to oversee the embarkation, which was now well underway.

One of the two Frenchmen had a full black beard, a flabby stomach and a slight stoop, and looked to be middle-aged, whereas the other was young and slim, with a fine blond moustache and smooth fair hair; they busied themselves with their crates and packages, which they sorted out and moved around, consulting each other all the while, chattering away non-stop.

When they could find no more to adjust, they began watching the manoeuvres, which clearly interested them deeply. In the wheelhouse the pilot was standing beside the captain, yelling out his orders in Jamaican patois to the crew, who ran from bow to stern, grumbling and cursing the cluttered deck, and continually bumping into the Frenchmen, who wandered about looking up into the rigging, where the sails were being hoisted one after the other. They kept moving about, but everywhere they were in the way. In the end they sat down on the edge of the main hatch with their feet tucked in under them, smoking cigarettes. After about half an hour they grew tired of their cramped positions and started looking around for their quarters; the companionway was hidden by their birdcages.

'La chambre en bas, hé?' one of them enquired of the cook, who was now free of his nose bandage, and was standing close by pounding stockfish.

'Aye, come to me an' I'll teach you a thing or two,' he said under his breath, without pausing in his work or giving any sign that he had heard.

The fair-haired man got up and came right over to him.

'La chambre, you understand, la cabane, you know?' The Frenchman mimicked the action of going through a door, whilst tapping the cook's shoulder with his knuckles.

The cook straightened up, and brought his face close to

the speaker's ear, whilst he yelled as if to a deaf person: 'We don't speak gibberish onboard!'

'Lourdaud,'* growled the Frenchman, shrugging his shoulders, and he rejoined his companion.

'Look here, cabane en bas?' the bearded one called straight after to a sailor who was running past.

No answer.

This scene repeated itself four or five times. They looked at each other, discouraged, and then one of them said something which made them both burst into laughter.

Shortly after Sivert came past.

'Pst, pst, look here, good boy!'

Sivert stopped and touched his cap.

'You tell me, où est la cabane?' asked the older man, as he got up and put his hand on Sivert's shoulder.

'Kaban, not understand that,' answered Sivert.

'Chambre, salon,' the Frenchman insisted, putting his face close to Sivert's.

'Saloon, oh – you mean the cabin!' Sivert realized with a smile.

'Si, si! La cabine, la cabine, clever boy, thank you!' shouted the Frenchman, opening his arms as if he intended to embrace Sivert.

'Very well, come with me,' said Sivert; he went aft and down into the cabin, followed by the grateful Frenchmen, who when they had got downstairs, made him understand that they would like something to eat.

Later on, when they came back up on deck, the pilot had gone ashore and the ship was underway with all sails set and a fresh breeze, moving away from the island whose high mountains with their sharp contours stood out blackly against the cloudless sky, in which the stars had begun to appear.

After a short time they got hold of Sivert again and explained with signs and a mixture of monosyllabic English and French that they would like to go to bed.

Sivert went over to his former berth. 'Here, please,' he said, inviting them with a wave of his hand to step inside. Then he lit the lamp and began to make up the bunks. The Frenchmen got out two bundles tied up with straps, out of which they pulled plaids and inflatable pillows and various small articles.

'Votre name, good boy, comment vous appelez-vous?' asked the eldest, as he pulled on a nightcap over his bald head.

'Not understand,' said Sivert, who was standing in the doorway. The cabin was so small that there was not room for more than two at a time.

'Look here,' the Frenchman went on. 'Name of this ship, Toe Friends, hé?'

'Yes,' nodded Sivert.

'And your name, hé?' He tapped him on the chest.

'Sivert,' he exclaimed with a broad smile.

'Sivvert,' repeated the Frenchman, pleased. 'My name,' – the Frenchman touched his forehead – 'Jean Beauvais, you call me Monsieur Jean. Understand?'

'Yes, I call you Misser Jang,' said Sivert.

'And that gentleman there,' he pointed to the fair-haired man who was sitting on the edge of his bunk putting on his slippers, 'his name Bouvier.'

'Monsieur Pierre,' the other man interposed, looking at Sivert with a friendly expression.

'You call him Monsieur Pierre, understand?' asked the other.

'All right, thank you, good nigh,' answered Sivert, and left them to it.

'Strange fellows,' said Sivert to himself, as he went forrard, 'but they're kind an' friendly.' He laughed at the thought of their speech and gestures. 'I's a good thing we got 'em onboard,' he thought further. 'Now I c'n potter around wi' them on't voyage, an' they'll not be slingin' dirt 'bout me family. They know nowt, an' understand nowt even if someone said summat – so tha's good.' - -

'Yep, tha's righ,' she asked me to tell you she's weepin' for love o' you,' – Sivert heard Sølvfest's voice as he turned the corner of the forecastle and looked in on the crew. They were sitting on their chests smoking their evening pipes in the flickering half-light spread by the smoking oil lamp which hung from the ceiling under a sooty metal shade with no glass.

'"Tell him that his own Emmeline is going to die," she said to me,' continued Sølvfest, looking at the sailmaker.

'Oh, her,' said the sailmaker with a condescending smile, 'she was pretty crazy. She swore to me she was goin' to kill 'erself.'

'Aye, would you b'lieve that,' said the bosun, spitting.

'Lord knows,' declared Sølvfest. 'I once knew a lass who drowned 'erself 'cause 'er sweetheart broke it off.'

'Aye, there's no knowing wi' women,' agreed the sailmaker. 'Some thinks one thing and some another, but most o'them are just as fickle as we men, that's what I think.'

'If only they dared let themselves go,' said Sølvfest with a knowing expression.

'Let themselves go! They do that all right!' the sailmaker laughed, letting his clenched fist fall onto his chest.

'Oh aye, them as is in't profession, who's talkin' about

them!'

'The others an' all,' said the sailmaker, nodding, 'it's often them you'd least believe it of. Them from good families, I can tell you the finest are the worst.'

'Aye, I s'pose you'd know 'bout that,' said the bosun scornfully.

'More 'an anyone'd b'lieve,' answered the sailmaker, nodding secretively.

'Are you tellin' us you've played sweet'earts wi' a fine lady?' asked the bosun, looking at him through narrowed eyes.

'Aye, I've done that good and proper,' said the sailmaker, clapping his hands together.

'Tell us!' exclaimed Sivert, who had lit his pipe and was now sitting on the high doorstep.

'Now the nose-eater's woken up!' laughed Sølvfest. 'See 'ow greedy 'ee looks, jus' like 'ee's goin' to take a bite out o'it! Ye're daft,' he turned to Sivert, 'don'cha see 'ee's jus' lyin'!'

'Lyin'! Strike me dead if I am, I'll swear to it!' said the sailmaker, 'an' now I'll tell you 'bout it to prove it.'

'It were three years ago,' he began, 'the winter I signed off the *Hope*, you know, that brig o' Tønnesen's. When I'd finished trainin' wi' sail-mendin' I sometimes ran errands for Consul Hoff and his house, 'cause my Ma was a cleaner there, and that's 'ow it 'appened. Their daughter, she's called Thora and is married now to some military feller from Kristiania, she was allus up to some tricks wi' me. If I weren't goin' up to 'er room to move the chest of drawers, I were to take a nail out of 'er boot 'cause it were stickin' into 'er 'eel. An' she kept wantin' me to stay, an' brushed against my 'ands an' stood right up against me, an' many's the time she'd bend down so close to me she'd tickle my nose wi' 'er 'air, an' I c'd smell the fine smell of 'er. But who'd a thought anythin' like that? 'ow c'd I 'ave such sinful thoughts, as it says in the good book.' The sailmaker chuckled, and then lit his pipe before he went on: 'I'd never 'ave 'ad any such ideas, 'cause she were dressed in silk an' fine clothes an' were one of't poshest misses in't town. Then it 'appened one afternoon she asks me to come an' pick 'er up that evenin' from Røjs on Kalfaret.* What time sh'd I be there, I ask 'er. Around 11 o'clock, she says, an' I says: Right Miss, I'll be on the dot. No sooner said than done. Off we set, 'er in front, an' me after. But when we get through t'town gate, down by t'cemetery, she wants to walk beside me. Di'n you see something down there between the graves, Anton, she says in a whisper, an' wi' that she gets hold o' my arm and clutches it so 'ard I nearly yell ou'. Where's that? I says, an' I want to stand still, but she pulls me along wi' 'er, 'er 'ole body shakin'. I were quite scared, 'cause I thought I c'd see summat white amongst t'trees in't moonlight. So all at once we sets off runnin' all t'way to t' Seamen's Poor'ouse. Then she's so breathless she 'as to stop, an' she leans over so 'er 'ead's righ' on my shoulder. Then jus' like tha' she starts laughin'. Lor', 'ow she laughs; I can' do nuffin 'cept join in, an' I laughs good an' proper. 'Ow stupid we are, Anton, she says, come on let's walk prop'ly. Righ' then we see a watchman in a sentrybox keepin' an eye on us, an' she's so shamefaced she sets off runnin' again, 'oldin' me 'and. Tha's 'ow it is the 'ole way, right till we get to t'corner o't square where she lives. That was the strangest walk I ever 'ad, but t'best is still to come, 'cause when I'd get t'key out o' me pocket an' open t'door for 'er, an' teks off me cap to say goo'night p'litely, as y'd expect, she grabs 'old o' me arm again an' says jus' as quietly as up at t'cemetery: Anton, I'm so scared to go in

alone, you mus' come up wi' me. O'course, so I go up wi' 'er
to 'er room. Ooh, it's so dark 'ere, she says, you mustn't go till
I've lit t'lamp, come in, so she pulls me in an' shuts t'door.
Then she stands there a bit an' fiddles wi't matches an' drops
'em on't floor, an' then, afore I knows wha's 'appening, she
throws 'er arms around me neck an' starts cryin' an' sayin'
summat like I mustn' think she's like tha' or think bad things
about 'er, an' Lord only knows wha' she said, 'cause I start
puffin' an' sweatin', an' I'm not sure but I might'a cried an' all.
An' then wi' that she kisses me right on t'mouth and says
goodni' an' I 'ave to go now, but she's driven me mad, so I
get 'old of 'er an' 'ug an' kiss 'er, till she cries she can' breathe.
I don' think about anythin' any more, an' ye' c'n be sure we
'ad a right ol' time.' The sailmaker smiled and scratched his
head, seemingly quite lost in his memories.

'Well I nivver 'eard the like in all me born days!' – 'Tha'll
'ave suited you all righ', yer young striplin'!' said Sølvfest and
the bosun at the same moment.

'Wha' next, wha' next!' shouted Sivert, wide-eyed and
with a voice that sounded as if he'd just heard a ghost story.

'Next!' echoed the sailmaker mockingly. 'Don'cha think
tha' were enough to be goin' on wi'?'

'But wha'd she say after?' Sivert wanted to know.

'Not a peep,' answered the sailmaker. 'Whilst I'm gettin'
ready to go, she's lyin' there in t'bed, all shiny white in
t'moonlight, 'er 'ead buried in t'pillow still as a corpse, an'
when I take 'er 'and to say goo'bye she was cold and numb-
like. I crept away as quick as I could. To tell the truth, I wasn't
sure whether to be glad or not.'

'But 'ow was she later on?' asked Sølvfest.

'I didn't talk to 'er any more but the once. There was no
more summonses an' playin' games after that day, an' tha'

was fine wi' me when I remembered 'oos daughter she was.'

'Jus' the once, you said, what 'appened then?'

'Aye, it was two weeks later, one evenin' I was comin' 'ome she was waitin' for me in t'passage. There was light from a lamp in t'ceilin', so I could see 'er face easy, even though she was pushed righ' up against t'wall in shadow; she was white as a sheet, an' 'er 'air was 'angin' down in 'er eyes wi' no life in it. When I passed she reached out 'er 'and, but pulled it back again as if she'd been stung. I stopped an' said: "Good evenin' miss." "I want to ask you," she said to me, "if you," then she went quiet an' covered 'er eyes wi' 'er 'and. "Wha' is it, miss?" I said, all nice an' p'lite, she couldn' complain abou' that. Then 'er knees started to tremble an' she sank down, jus' as if she was goin' to fall, so I went over to 'elp 'er up, but then she straightened up an' was twice as tall as before. "I just wanted to ask you to keep quiet about – about the other thing," she said, an' tossed 'er 'ead. "When it comes to tha', there's no need to worry, miss," I replied. Suddenly she rushed at me, grabbed my shoulder an' shook it so the bones creaked. "Are you sure, do you promise me?" she said, grindin' 'er teeth. "Shall I swear to it, miss?" I asked. "I'll kill myself if you say anything," she said, rollin' 'er eyes so I could only see t'whites. "I'll be silent as a mouse," I answered. "Good," she said and pushed a five-daler note into me 'and, "I'll trust you." Then off she went, and I never set eyes on 'er again.'

'Well she could've saved 'erself tha' money,' remarked the bosun drily.

'I've kept me promise right up till this evenin',' said the sailmaker, 'an' I'll ask yer to say nothin' to no-one.'

Before the sailmaker had even finished speaking, Sivert felt a kick in his back, and the cook stepped in over the threshold beside him, yelling: 'Out the way, li'l tosspot!'

Sivert grabbed hold of the doorpost and stayed sitting where he was. He was so absorbed in the sailmaker's story that he hardly noticed the cook's hostility. His thick, rough hair was standing on end like an electric brush, and although it was 31 degrees, he felt a chill in his bones, and his skin felt like gooseflesh.

'You sh'd be displayed in a musuem, sailmaker', observed Sølvfest, filling his pipe for the second time. 'There'll not be many who c'n boast of a thing like that.'

''Ow old were you when it 'appened, sailmaker?' asked Sivert.

''Ee's reckonin' whether 'ee's old enough!' laughed the bosun.

'Old enough fer wha'?' the cook put in, sending Sivert a malicious glance. 'Is 'ee goin' ter sail to New Zealand an' become a cannibal? You be'er take yer gran wi' yer – get t'natives to chop up Madam Tosspot, an' I reckon they'll get fallin' over drunk, them as feasts off 'er.' The cook cackled noisily and looked around for applause, as he touched the scar on his nose with his fingertips.

'I reckon you're after fightin' wi' me for a third time,' shouted Sivert, jumping up. 'I thought you'd 'ad enough that time when you lost yer snout!'

'Not righ' now,' said the cook, who was sitting on his chest pulling off his trousers, 'I'm off ter bed now. 'Oo's li'l tosspot sharin' with?'

'Wi' me,' said the sailmaker.

'You'd best rub some pitch on yer nose! Then it won' be so tasty,' snarled the cook as he toppled into his bunk.

Sivert made for the cook's bunk with his fists raised, but was stopped in his tracks by the bosun, who said: 'You two're makin' one 'ell of a fuss.'

'Why can''ee shut up then,' yelled Sivert in a rage. 'Is it my fault if my gran drinks?'

'Jus' say t'same thing back to 'im,' said the bosun. ''Oo knows whether 'is gran weren't a drinker an' all?'

'A likely tale! Ha, ha, ha!' laughed the cook from his bunk.

'She c'd 'ave been a ragin' tramp for all we know,' went on the bosun. 'If 'ee slanders your gran, you slander 'is, an' tha's an end of it. Now that's strikin' eight bells, an' I've other things to think about, I'm on starboard watch.'

I wonder if bosun 'as really 'eard summat, thought the cook before he fell asleep. 'S no' possible – it's 16 year since she left prison, an' then she died right after.

It was a long time before Sivert fell asleep that evening. He couldn't get comfortable, and he was almost stifled with the heat in the lower bunk where he lay behind the back of the snoring sailmaker, despite the fact that he had no coverings and the fresh breeze from astern wafted continually around the corner of the forecastle and in through the open door.

Just think that such things could happen, that fine ladies could be like that. Imagine if he'd been in the sailmaker's place, if he'd happened to be running errands for a fine house where they had a daughter. He was handsome enough for that, he'd picked that up from the girls on land, and from others as well. 'Fine cabin boy you have there, Captain,' one of the chandlers had said once when he went up with the captain to collect some provisions. 'Here is the pretty boy I spoke of,' the consul had said on the verandah, the last time he went up with a note from the captain, and then a fine lady had come in and spoken to him.

He only had to walk up the street, and he noticed how

both the black girls and the white ladies on the verandahs turned as he passed. He had never had any idea what he looked like, but now he had realised that he was what people called handsome, just like the sailmaker, even though they were as different as night and day.

Just think, if he had been born amongst grand folk, the son of a rich merchant for example. He might just as easily have been that as what he was, for no-one could have any say about things like that. But who knew what good fortune he might find in the world. He had once heard the story of someone called the Ash Lad, a simple lad, even the son of a peasant, who had finished up with the princess and half the kingdom.* – Even if it wasn't a princess, because there weren't so many of those about these days, it could still be a fine rich lady, even though he was just called Sivert Gabriel Jensen; he could get rid of the Jensen and call himself Hellemyren, or Myren – no, just Myre, that sounded more refined: Sivert Gabriel Myre. It was probably stupid of him to go to sea anyway, because the most he could expect to be was a captain. If he had stayed ashore and perhaps gone into trade, he could have got higher up. Yes, he regretted it, especially now that it was clear that the story of his gran had followed him. And it always would! Not even if he travelled to the ends of the earth would he escape it; he was beginning to understand that now.

But it was a good thing that he had beaten the cook in their second fight anyway. Now the cook could no longer say that he had been bested because he was drunk, because the last time it had been according to the cook's own rules and regulations, and the crew had witnessed it and agreed unanimously that Sivert was the strongest. 'Here's a lad wi' meat on 'is bones,' he said in a low voice, holding up his clenched fists, 'if it weren't for tha', t'cook would've beat me so's I'd 'ave been done for. Now 'ee'll 'ave to 'old back a bit, thank the Lord.'

12

Sivert pushed open the door to the passengers' cabin quietly and carefully, as he usually did in the morning, in order not to wake them when he put their shiny polished shoes inside.

'Pst, pst, talk to you.' Sivert had pulled back his hand and was about to close the door when these words, spoken in a sleepy voice and accompanied by a long yawn, made him stop.

'I besoin of a bouton,' said Monsieur Jean, who was lying in the upper bunk pointing to his buttonless shirt cuff as Sivert put his head round the door.

'Button, you mean, all right,' answered Sivert.

'Button, hé? That right?'

'Yessir,' said Sivert, and disappeared.

Straight after he came back with a button which he had cut off his best shirt.

'Here, look,' he said, holding the button up between his thumb and forefinger.

Monsieur Jean was lying in his bunk threading a sewing needle.

'Ah yes, yes,' he said, keeping his narrowed eyes focused on the eye of the needle and the thread, the end of which he had rolled into a point. 'Ah, c'est bien, many tanks.' He knotted the end and passed the thread to Sivert, who pushed his fingers between the shirt cuff and Monsieur Jean's hairy wrist, sewed on the button with slow, careful stitches and bit off the end of the double thread with his teeth.

'Merci, many tanks, clever boy, but not use de teet,' and

the Frenchman tugged his earlobe. 'Voilà des ciseaux, you know!' He pointed up at an oilcloth sewing box which was hanging on the cabin wall.

'Scissors,' nodded Sivert.

'Sissers,' repeated Monsieur Jean, 'yes, I know, hé?'

Later that day, when Sivert carried their dinner down, the Frenchman were sitting on ships' stools with their backs against the front of the forecastle, reading.

'Here you are, please come and dine,' said Sivert, approaching them cap in hand.

They got up at once, closed their books and put them in their pockets.

'Tursday today – today stockfish, yes?' asked Monsieur Pierre on their way to the cabin.

'Oui, yes,' answered Sivert.

'And plum soup, oui, yes?' added Monsieur Jean, 'we clever boy, hé?'

'Boys,' Sivert corrected him.

'Yes, boys, for we are toe!' exclaimed Monsieur Jean, beaming with pleasure. 'Moi, I know!'

Sivert laughed so much that he nearly tumbled down the stairs.

After dinner he brought them coffee on deck.

'Today the turtles must have water, you know,' said Sivert, putting down the tray on a water butt.

'Si, si, si!' nodded Monsieur Jean.

'Three days no water, fourth day water, right?' continued Sivert.

'Précisément! I like you très much, Sivert.'

'Very much,' Sivert corrected him, and when they both repeated that, his face opened in another laugh from ear to ear, as he clapped his hands in merriment.

That's how things had been for the whole trip. 'They toddle after Sivert like a mother hen after her chicks,' said the captain now and then to the bosun, 'but that's fine, then they'll not bother the rest of us.'

With those words relations between Sivert and the rest of the crew and the Frenchmen were settled. Sivert was the only one who from the very first day had bothered to look after them. The Frenchmen had felt this at once, so they stuck to him as their provider and providence. Sooner than turn to anyone else with a wish or a question, they would wait for Sivert, however long it took, as they wandered around unobtrusively searching for him. When he appeared unexpectedly from the hold carrying a piece of meat which was dripping with brine, or from the companionway with the crew's bread and butter rations in two buckets hanging from a yoke over his shoulders, then the Frenchmen's faces would brighten as if they had suddenly caught sight of their sweethearts, as they hurried towards him. When Sivert was washing up after meals, they would sit on the main hatch beside him to 'learn Norwegian', painstakingly repeating the phrases he gave them to practise and joining uproariously in his laughter at their pronunciation. When the animals were to be fed or the porcupines to be cleaned out, Sivert always had to be present. On the stroke of half-past seven every evening he brought them hot water and sugar for the grog they made from their own store of liquor, and never drank without inviting him to join them. Each day they came along to guess what they were going to have for dinner, and when he was making up their bunks they stood around chatting to him.

'These are the best days of your life, Sivert, now you've got these French leeches to play with,' the captain said to him frequently, smiling good-naturedly; and Sivert smiled and thought that was true enough, even though he had more to do than ever before, now that he had these Frenchmen to look after as well. But he found it was all as easy as pie. A constant stream of fun and laughter seemed to flow between him and the strangers. Especially Monsieur Jean was charmed by Sivert, and often asked him whether he would accompany him to Paris and work for him, to which Sivert replied every time: 'Oui, aye Misser Jang.'

This intimate companionship with the fine French gentlemen enhanced Sivert's reputation on board. The crew watched with a certain amount of amazement and envy this ability to get on with such difficult people, who didn't even understand English, and the captain had to admit to himself that it was thanks to Sivert that things were going so well with the passengers. No doubt they would write to the consul, and it would be good to have a positive report for the next time; the money for such passengers was easy to earn and a welcome addition.

Sivert for his part was enjoying himself so much that not even the cook's gibes could seriously knock him out of kilter any longer. The fact that his grandmother drank and his father was only a dock worker did him no harm after all. He had just as good a grasp of how to behave with posh folks for all that. It was only now that he realised what he was capable of. He was fit for more than polishing brass and scrubbing decks. But they really were odd people, these two Frenchmen. If only he could just show them properly how much love, yes it really was love, he felt for them. But no doubt there would be no chance of that. The only thing might be if the snake got loose, the grey-spotted one which they said was the most venomous, so that he could dash over and throw himself between them and get bitten instead of them. He almost had tears in his eyes, so moved was he by his own readiness to sacrifice himself and by sadness at the fact that they would never know of it.

In general things were going well on board ship on this voyage. There was an atmosphere of comradeship and contentment in the air, which stretched from bow to stern. They had had a following wind for eleven days in a row. When the captain reckoned their position according to the meridian every twenty-four hours, he could put the point of his dividers on the map a few degrees further away from the West Indies than the day before. In the blue sky fluffy light clouds scudded from southwest towards northeast with promises of continuing favourable wind. The temperature was mild and pleasant, the nights light and fresh. Every Saturday evening the captain treated them to rum toddy both in the forecastle and in the deckhouse. And then they were heading for home, not directly to Norway, it was true, but still a good bit of the way.

13

Sivert came along with a lantern and placed it on one of the turtle crates, over the end of which some planks had been laid to form a table. Then he went and summoned the Frenchmen.

Soon after they all three came back with lit cigarettes, a folded stool under one arm and a glass of grog in the other hand, and made themselves comfortable around the improvised table. Monsieur Jean took a pack of cards out of his pocket and shuffled them, then he placed some copper coins in a pewter mug; the others did the same, Sivert cut the cards, and the game was under way. They had fallen into this habit within a couple of days of leaving port, and since then it had been their regular evening entertainment between eight and ten. At first Sivert had just been an observer, but then they had taught him the game and persuaded him to join in.

As soon as they were at sea the captain had said that Sivert was released from watch duty now that there were passengers onboard; and Sivert, who at first had felt slighted by that, had become more and more content with it as he got a taste for the card game. He had sometimes won and sometimes lost, but eventually the evening came when he had paid out his last coins. He felt quite dejected at the thought that he now had nothing more to invest in the game, so he could not join in any longer; he would have to find an excuse to leave, because it was too embarrassing to admit the truth. Monsieur Jean, who had noticed the way Sivert's eyes followed his hand as he picked up the small coins that evening, had suspected the reason and tried to share his winnings with him, but Sivert had protested volubly and assured him that he had 'plenty of pennies' in his chest.

But where was he now to get some cash for the following evening? Suddenly the thought struck him that he could retrieve the money he had lost whilst the Frenchmen slept. Just so that he had enough to play. The more he thought about it, the more reasonable it seemed. What did they care about a few coppers? Monsieur Jean had even wanted to give them to him, so there was no way it could be called stealing. He was only taking what could have been his, if he hadn't been stupid and refused.

That same night he carried out his plan. It was so easy and quick. During the middle watch he crept out of his bunk, tiptoed aft without being noticed, opened the door and felt along the wall, stuck his hand into a trouser pocket and got hold of a wallet, out of which he took what he needed. This was repeated several times, because he had kept losing on recent evenings. But eventually Monsieur Pierre became aware that his small change was disappearing. It was his purse which kept on being raided, because his trousers were the closest to the door. Then one night, when he woke up for a moment, he caught a glimpse of Sivert in the doorway. He was too sleepy to think any more about it then, but in the morning, when he realised a gold coin had also gone missing, he became suspicious and had the idea of secretly making a small cross with his penknife on his copper coins, in order to see whether Sivert paid with the marked money.

That evening they played as usual. Sivert's eyes were shining and his cheeks were rosy, and he was livelier and more cheerful than ever. For the first half-hour he was winning, but his luck didn't hold, so he lost what he had wagered and then even more.

When Monsieur Pierre went to his cabin that night, he held the coins which Sivert had lost beneath the lamp, and sure enough, they were marked with the little cross. Then he recounted the whole thing to Monsieur Jean, but the latter maintained that he must have made a mistake, and turned towards the wall to sleep. However, Monsieur Pierre decided to stay awake that night and keep watch.

Sivert was also lying awake. He was possessed by a vague sense of dread. Monsieur Pierre had looked so strange as he picked up the money, and then he had dropped it into his waistcoat pocket instead of into his purse. Why had he done that? One moment Sivert was worrying about it, the next he decided it must have been a pure coincidence. But it was also weighing on his mind that the previous night he had taken a gold coin by mistake. He had thought it was a halfpenny, and it was not until morning that he had discovered his error. There was no way he was going to hold onto it. Whatever happened he had to replace it, and after that he would not touch a single penny more of what belonged to them.

Later that night he got out of bed and threw on a few clothes. Then he stole out of the forecastle and slowly crept aft, with the gold coin held tight between his thumb and index finger down in his trouser pocket. The sailor on watch on deck had his back turned. On the boom to windward the watch was sitting half asleep. The first mate was strolling to and fro in the small space amidships which was free of crates and luggage. Thank God it was not that terrible dazzling moonlight which turned night into day, thought Sivert, pulling his cap down over his eyes. Now both the first mate and the helmsman would take him for one of the watch. Cautiously he glided forwards. Each time the first mate was facing him in his pacing, he stood still or crouched down behind one of the crates, and then, when he turned, he took a couple of long steps.

In this way he reached the door of the cabin. Previously it had not been quite closed at night, but now the weather had suddenly turned cooler; no doubt that was the reason why it was fully closed tonight.

His heart thumping, he took hold of the round brass handle, and after listening for a moment he turned it. Straight away he stuck his hand in and got hold of a pair of trousers, which he gently lifted from the hook and pulled out through the opening. At that moment there was a muffled cry from inside the cabin; the door was pushed right back against the wall and Monsieur Pierre stood in front of him in his nightshirt and grabbed the trousers from him. Sivert stumbled backwards, knees and hands shaking, and dropped the coin at once; it fell jingling to the deck. Monsieur Pierre bent down after the sound and found the gold coin immediately; it was glinting in the pale starlight on the dark deck.

The subsequent events happened in a great rush. Monsieur Pierre shouted some unintelligible words, Monsieur Jean, also in his nightshirt, pushed his way to the doorway and waved his hand for quiet, and the first mate came over and asked what was going on.

It seemed to Sivert that he was plummeting backwards into a pitch-black abyss, and that something cold had closed over his head with a great rushing sound. He raised his arms and planted claw-like fingers in his hair, tugging fiercely. Then he sank almost to his knees, emitting a half-stifled groan through gritted teeth, and suddenly burst into a run with his chest thrust out, jumped up onto the boom to leeward, grabbed hold of the hammock netting, heaved himself up with a kick to the boom and pushed himself out over the gunwale.

'Sivvert! Sivvert! Mon Dieu, qu'est-ce que vous faites?' yelled Monsieur Jean, who with the two others had run after him and had got there just in time to seize Sivert's ankle with both hands, as he fell forwards and tumbled to his knees on the boom with his face pressed against the side of the ship.

In the couple of seconds which passed before they managed to haul him back on board, Sivert did not utter a sound, but kicked and struggled with all his might to get his foot free. When he was once more standing on the deck, he swayed, his limbs gave way, and he collapsed in a heap onto the boom between the two Frenchmen, who were holding him one by each arm.

'In God's name, what's wrong wi' you, lad?' asked the mate, who had not understood a word of what was happening.

Sivert made no reply. His head fell back, and his arms hung down slackly.

'Apportez le lampion,' said Monsieur Jean, upon which Monsieur Pierre in his airy attire ran on bare feet to fetch the lamp, came back and shone it on Sivert's face, which was yellowy-white with dark scratches on his forehead and temples, as he bled copiously from the nose. His eyes were closed, and it looked as if he had fainted.

'I'd best go an' wake t'capt'n,' said the mate.

'No, no, non!' exclaimed Monsieur Jean urgently, grabbing the mate's arm to stop him. 'Not le capitaine.' On that he addressed a few words to Monsieur Pierre, who then gave the lamp to the mate, and the two Frenchmen together carried Sivert into their cabin, where they laid him in the top bunk. Then Monsieur Pierre went to fetch some water, and Monsieur Jean washed his face, staunched the nosebleed and put plasters on his wounds. After that he pushed his arm under Sivert's neck, raised his head and poured a glass of cognac into him, muttering the whole time between his teeth: 'Pauvre garçon, ah mon pauvre petit garçon,' and stroking his hair caressingly at intervals.

Sivert, who kept his eyes closed the whole time, let himself be treated like a helpless child. Awareness of what had happened filled him with a dull, paralysing pain. He had been branded a thief, and that by Misser Jang and Misser Pierre, who had showered him constantly with kindness and friendship. How could he bear all this – it was not to be borne. Suddenly the idea leapt into his mind that he had actually drowned after all, and that it was just his corpse which had been hauled on board again. Sivert Gabriel Jensen, cabin boy, jumped overboard from the bark *Two Friends*, Captain H.J. Hansen, in the Atlantic, on a voyage from Kingston to Marseilles, 16 ½ years old. Slowly the tears began to gather under his eyelids. Poor unfortunate boy, his thoughts continued. Short was his earthly pilgimage, and his young life was swallowed abruptly by the faithless waves. His time on this earth was not happy, alas. Thorns and thistles choked his path; at home he was unjustly treated, and on board he was persecuted, until he met two Frenchmen – and now the tears streamed down over his cheeks, and his breast heaved with shuddering, sobbing breaths. They took care of him, they were his benefactors, his best and only friends. He loved and honoured them and aspired only to lay down his life for them. But then one night it happened that he went into their cabin in order to return a gold coin which belonged to them. At that they raised the alarm, because they thought he was going to steal from them. He could not live with that, and that was why he leapt into the sea. Here his sobs became so violent that his breast creaked and heaved.

Monsieur Jean and Monsieur Pierre, who were both bending over him, hushed him tenderly and spoke calmingly to him. In the end they poured more cognac into him.

After that his sobbing quietened somewhat. Suddenly he sat bolt upright, seized firstly Monsieur Jean's hand and then Monsieur Pierre's, and pressed his lips on them with passionate force. Then he lay back on the pillow, closed his eyes again, slowly grew calmer and eventually fell asleep.

The Frenchmen, who were still watching him, regarded him with concern. Around his tightly compressed lips there was an expression of bitter suffering which moved them deeply. After a while Monsieur Jean laid a plaid over him and said to Monsieur Pierre that he would have to share with him. The latter nodded, and then they both crawled into the narrow lower bunk and lay down side by side, close together, back to back.

14

When Sivert woke up the next morning, he could at first not understand why he was lying in his old cabin and not in the forecastle with the sailmaker. He felt so dizzy and his head was heavy, and his forehead felt tight and prickly. He felt automatically with his hand and discovered that he had a bandage around his head. Then he sat up in the bunk and caught sight of the small yellow suitcases marked with the Frenchmen's names which were standing on the floor. At that moment he remembered everything, and was overcome by shame and hopelessness. Oh, why had they not let him go overboard last night! His life was destroyed, and there was nothing more for him in this world. Suddenly it occurred to him that he had slept too long, that the captain must have asked after him, and that he knew everything. Now he would of course be interrogated, be reviled as a thief and whipped in full view of everyone; perhaps they would put him in irons and lock him up in the paint store in order to deliver him to the law when they put ashore. Oh well, the worse it was the better, he said to himself. He felt ready to endure anything that followed, and besides it was all the same whatever they did with him, and whatever happened to him. Quickly he crawled out of the bunk, straightened his clothes and went out on deck.

Up on deck the Frenchmen were busy moving a crocodile crate which they wanted to place in the sun. From early morning when they had got up, Monsieur Pierre had been popping into the cabin constantly in order to check whether Sivert was awake. He was bursting to let him know that the whole thing had been a misunderstanding, and ask him just to forget it. When he looked more closely he had discovered that all his gold coins were still in his possession after all. The one he had plucked from the deck last night must have been the one he couldn't find earlier. It had of course been there in his trouser pocket, had slipped out of his purse and then fallen out of the pocket as Sivert picked up the trousers. What he had wanted to do with them, he really didn't want to know. He was so shocked by the events of the night, so full of sympathy for Sivert and of remorse concerning himself. He felt an intense desire to believe in Sivert's complete innocence, and therefore he had made up the idea that Sivert had wanted to brush the trousers, or perhaps sew on some buttons which he had mentioned were missing. Monsieur Jean had supported this assumption, and triumphantly reminded him that he had been convinced that Monsieur Pierre's suspicions were unfounded. The fact that Sivert had actually had the marked coins in his possession was something they both refused to acknowledge. Sivert had not stolen, had not thought of stealing. He was the soul of honesty and integrity, and they would make amends.

When Sivert came out on deck the Frenchmen had their backs to him. He hurried forrard to go into the forecastle and change his shirt, which was stained with blood. But as he was passing by, Monsieur Pierre caught sight of him and took hold of his arm with a friendly: 'How do you do today, Sivvert?'

Sivert turned his head away with a disparaging gesture.

'Look here Sivvert, Monsieur Pierre talk to you. Oui sure?' said Monsieur Jean, imitating Sivert's way of replying, and bent his smiling face down to Sivert's to look him in the eye.

'You come with me,' Monsieur Pierre walked aft and pulled Sivert into the cabin after him.

'I beg pardon, mille thousand pardons,' he said to Sivert, grabbing his hand. 'You pardon me, oui, sure?'

'How you say pardon?' he asked when Sivert made no answer.

'Forgiveness,' said Sivert with eyes downcast.

'Ah so! You forgiveness me, oui sure?'

'Oui sure,' said Sivert, with a melancholy smile. 'Thank you, merci beaucoup, Monsieur Pierre.'

'You good kind boy,' went on Monsieur Pierre. 'I have all moneys, no moneys lost, no moneys lost!' He shook his head energetically. 'You understand, oui sure?'

'Oui sure,' nodded Sivert.

'All right, many thanks, not talk of money, jamais, never, you understand?'

'We'll never mention that money again,' replied Sivert.

'Yes, yes, never talk of that money again, capitaine not know, mate not know, everyone not know.' He brushed his palms together in a dismissive gesture. 'That is right, many thanks, Sivert.' –

'What in the name of all the devils in hell did you get up to last night?' asked the captain when Sivert came down an hour or so later to set the table for dinner.

Sivert stood for a moment hanging his head and twisting one foot. Then he looked up and said in a low voice and with an embarrassed smile: 'I were sleep-walking, capt'n.'

Right up to this moment Sivert had been cudgelling his brains in vain to think how he might answer the captain when he had to account for last night's exploits. He was convinced that neither the captain nor the mates had heard a word from the Frenchmen, and he could tell that the crew had no idea as to why he had tried to leap into the sea during the night. Now, when he heard his own voice explaining that he had been walking in his sleep, he almost shocked himself. The idea had occurred to him so suddenly that he had not had time to consider whether it would work. The thought fleetingly crossed his mind that he should perhaps have said something different, and he felt painfully uncertain as he stood there looking surreptitiously at the captain.

'I see,' said the captain as he raised his eyebrows and leaned his head back, 'so you walk in your sleep, do you? When did all that start?'

Sivert realised he was saved.

'I've not done it the last two or three years, capt'n,' he said candidly, 'but I were real bothered by it when I were a littl'un.'

'Ri-ight, well, we'll not 'ave mad capers like that, so you better get used to it, lad. If you sleepwalk any more, you'll get a good hiding.'

Sivert felt an inexpressible sense of relief at having emerged so well out of that wretched affair. All things considered, it had worked out far better than he could have expected, if it had to be found out at all.

Despite that, however, he no longer felt happy. From that day on, the relationship between him and the Frenchmen was no longer the same. It is true that they went to great lengths to resume their old easy interchange, but all their efforts failed in the face of Sivert's shyness and reserve. He became careless and negligent in his dealings with them, avoided them as much as possible, stayed in the forecastle when he had free time, answered only what was necessary when they spoke to him, and pretended he did not understand when they spoke 'Norvegian'. To the crew, who noticed the change and wanted to know what the problem was, he professed that he was tired of being a nursemaid. It was much more rewarding to do proper sailor's work. Without asking the captain for permission, he took his turn on watch for the rest of the voyage, and was always extremely busy when the Frenchmen came anywhere near him.

After a six-week voyage they crossed the Strait of Gibraltar with a fresh westerly breeze, but that night the wind shifted to a northeasterly, so it was not until seven days later that they reached Marseilles harbour. Here they were lucky enough to be allocated a berth at once, so they could tie up at the quayside without further delay.

When the Frenchmen, after having got all their baggage safely ashore, had said goodbye to the captain and first mate, they asked after Sivert, but he was nowhere to be found. The ship was searched from bow to stern, and his name was yelled out countless times, but all in vain. So the Frenchmen had to leave the ship without saying farewell to Sivert. The baggage was loaded onto waggons, and they had to hurry to the train station. They asked the first mate to give him their greetings and thanks and left two five-franc coins with him to give Sivert as a tip.

But in the bows, over the side, hunched into a ball, or rather hanging down with both hands around the jib boom and his feet in the jib topsail which they had not had time to make fast, Sivert was hiding. As the moment approached when he knew that the Frenchmen would come over to him, place their hands on his shoulders and say their goodbyes, he had fled. A feeling of sorrow, remorse, love and desperate longing was gnawing at his heart. It would be unbearable to stand there before them, fighting back his tears and forcing himself to look indifferent.

Now, from his hiding place, he watched as they instructed the waggon drivers on the quayside. He registered Monsieur Jean's familiar figure with the hunched shoulders, hollow chest and black hair and beard, which had grown so long on the voyage. He could clearly hear the sound of his rapid, jerky speech, and saw him waving his hands and arms as he usually did when he spoke. Sivert stared at him and felt his breast swelling, and he blinked repeatedly in order to banish the tears which blinded him. Monsieur Pierre stood beside him, now and then interjecting a word into the conversation, and pointing eagerly several times to an extremely long, narrow street with tall warehouses of pale yellow stone. Then the baggage waggons set off slowly, and Monsieur Jean signalled to a cab which was waiting nearby. Before they got into it they both turned around and looked intently back at the ship. Sivert knew that it was him they were looking for, and he felt as if his heart was bleeding. Then they both took their hats off and waved them towards the ship, where the two mates and a couple of the crew were looking after them, got into the taxi and drove away. For a further moment Sivert could see them from the side. Then the taxi turned the corner up into the long narrow street, and he could see them no longer.

Then Sivert sighed so loudly that he was afraid someone might hear. He ducked further down and listened, but there was no-one nearby. Like a thief he stole out into the forecastle, jumped down onto the deck, and hauled up a bucket of water to clean the cabin.

15

'Heave away, shipmates, put your backs into it! Don't give up now!' The captain yelled as loud as he could, trying to make himself heard over the howling of the storm and the roaring of the sea.

'We can't keep goin' any more, capt'n!' shouted the bosun in reply, as he let go of the pump rope and grabbed hold of the bench around the mainmast to stop himself being thrown around.

'No, we can't keep goin'!' repeated several voices, 'we'll 'ave to stop, capt'n!' With a gesture of hopeless surrender the others also let go of the pump ropes and crouched down on deck, each finding something to hold on to and hunching their shoulders up over their ears to protect their heads from the crashing waves.

The ship was heading out of Lisbon, where they had called after unloading in Marseilles, and was loaded with salt for Bergen. A couple of days after they had set sail they had been overtaken by a hurricane-force storm, accompanied by a sea swell so violent and threatening that the captain could not remember having seen a worse one. As the ship had been tossed about helplessly the cargo had shifted, and the ship had sprung a leak. To begin with it had taken on six inches of water in an hour, then eight, and now it had risen to a foot.

The captain went over and sounded the pump. He looked dark and worried. 'Three feet of water,' he muttered, 'with nine we'll sink, in a couple of hours we'll have five if there's no pumping. But it's no good, the crew must have a short break.'

'All hands turn in!' he shouted after a short discussion

273

with the first mate. 'I'll keep watch for now.'

The crew looked towards the captain, their eyes stinging with seawater and a sleepless night, and then towards the bow, where half of the forecastle and a section of the port bulwarks had been washed away by the waves.

'Down in the main cabin with you,' said the captain cheerfully. 'Take my bunk and the sofa, and those who can't fit there'll have to sleep on the floor.'

Once more they looked at the captain, shaking their heads slightly as if to say: 'We know you can't possibly mean that.'

'Get a move on,' the captain went on. 'The sooner you get to sleep, the sooner you'll get to pumping again. The boat can take on a deal more water yet afore she's full.'

Slowly and hesitantly the crew moved aft. They had to duck down constantly, clinging on in order to avoid being thrown in the air and swept out to sea. They were so weary and exhausted that their knees were buckling. They had been hauling on the pump ropes with hardly a break for two whole days, night and day.

At the wheel stood Sølvfest. His head was swathed in a scarf which was dark with dried blood. His face was waxy and blueish like that of a corpse, and his eyes were dull. The previous evening, when the forecastle had been smashed by a breaking wave which buried half the ship beneath its seething foam, he had been hit by some splintered wood which had inflicted a gaping wound on his temple. Despite being confused and only half conscious he had had enough of his wits about him to throw himself flat on the deck and cling on to the forward hatch with both arms. When he got to his feet again and looked round for the cook, who had been hauling on a brace with him, he had disappeared.

'Man overboard!' he had yelled at the top of his voice. It was only then that he realised that the two mates and the captain were holding him up, and that one of them was mopping up the warm blood which was running down the side of his face. Later the second mate had told him that he had seen the cook's legs straight up in the air, high above the railings, as he plunged headfirst into the sea. There was no hope of rescuing him.

'I'll take the tiller, Sølvfest,' said the first mate, coming over to him. 'You need an hour's rest like the others.'

'I'm surprised the captain don't hoist distress signals,' said Sølvfest in a hoarse voice, holding his chest as if it hurt to speak.

'Well you c'd ask where we're to hoist 'em, now the riggin's gone,' answered the mate.

'The mizzen top an' mast stumps,' mumbled Sølvfest, 'they'll stick up from the hull a bit.'

'Aye, it'll be soon enough when we clap eyes on a sail, but 'tis as if they've all gone to't bottom. – You'd think we was down by Cape Horn an' not in reg'lar sea lanes. – Go in an' rest in my bunk, Sølvfest, it'll be full up down below.'

'Thanks for that, first mate.' Sølvfest held on to the front of the deckhouse with both hands and pulled himself round the corner and into the mate's cabin, where the second mate had just toppled into the lower bunk. His and Sivert's cabin had been badly damaged. A breaker had shattered the door and torn away a piece of the outer wall, the bunks were full of water, and spray from the waves kept washing in.

Down in the main cabin, where the windows and skylight were covered by shutters and tarpaulins, the lamp was burning night and day all this time. It looked as if it might at any moment turn a somersault up in the skylight, where it was swaying to and fro and smoking, its glass blackened and cracked. The air was filled with an acrid, musty smell, and the floor was awash with puddles, sloshing a half-empty tobacco packet to and fro.

Inside the inner cabin the bosun and sailmaker had climbed into the captain's berth, soaking wet just as they had come down from deck, still wearing their seaboots, oilskins and sou'westers. Head to foot on the sofa lay an able seaman and a deckhand with a shaggy cap, the wet lining of which was plastered to his forehead. The water was sliding in droplets off the oilcloth-covered sofa, leaving narrow, gleaming stripes. Four men lay side by side on the floor to leeward, with a leather-covered bench cushion under their heads and some sea jackets and oilskins covering them. Amongst them was Sivert.

Hardly had they arranged themselves before the captain appeared. He went in to the inner cabin, the door of which stood open, pulled out a chest drawer and took out a large-sized hymnbook with tarnished pewter clasps.

'I thought I would read the prayer for those in peril on the sea,' he said, in a voice which sounded strangely unfamiliar and embarrassed. 'Not because – not that I think there's any immediate danger right now, but doesn't hurt to think a bit about such things too – I suppose none of you has anything against it,' he went on, when no-one said anything.

'We say thank you, capt'n – for my part at least,' answered the bosun, sitting up.

'It's allus good to hear the word of God,' said the sailmaker, sitting up too.

'Just stay put, Our Lord ain't fussy about such things. He well knows how tired you are,' said the captain, propping himself up against the table under the lamp, and placing his feet well forward on the floor to keep his balance. 'It'll not take long,' he continued, leafing through the book, 'such prayers aren't normally very long, if I remember aright, it's not the length that matters.' When he had found the right place he took off his cap; the crew followed his example, and then he began to read in a sing-song tone as if at a prayer meeting, waving his arms to and fro as if the hymnbook was a balancing pole:

Prayer to be said in storms and mortal danger at sea.

Heavenly Father, almighty Lord and everlasting God!
Thou who hast created all things in the beginning
for the good of mankind, but after our sinful fall from
grace dost punish us for our sins, especially when
Thou sendest terrible thunder and lightning from the
heavens and raging storm and winds over the earth
and the sea: we miserable sinners, who are here in this
raging tempest, storm and distress, confess that we
have deserved this torment, and much worse, if Thou
wert to treat us according to Thy strict decrees. Have
mercy, we humbly beseech Thee, according to Thy
merciful will, look down upon us with pity and kindness
now and always, and in Thy infinite power command
this terrible and raging storm and tempest to be still,
lest it threatens us with death and destruction. Preserve
us with our ship and our goods as Thou didst preserve
Thy servant Noah, when Thou didst destroy the whole
world with water in Thy rightful wrath. Oh Lord, help
us, as Thou didst help Thy disciples when they were
in distress on the water, else we perish. But if it be Thy

will, Oh Father, that our time has come, that we should
not survive this peril at sea, then we beseech Thee that
Thou wilt save and preserve us in everlasting belief in
Thee, until we have breathed our last, and accord to
us on the Day of Judgement a joyful resurrection and
entry to eternal life with all Thy chosen creatures! To
Thee, Oh Lord (here the captain raised his voice and
spoke in a slow lilting tone) we commend our ship and
our goods, our lives, souls and spirits, and all that we
own; whether it be to live or to die, we are Thy children.
Praise everlasting be unto Thee! Amen.

He closed the book, held it between his folded hands
and carried on without pausing to recite the Lord's Prayer.

When he had finished he stood for a moment with closed
eyes, and then heard deep snoring breaths all around him.
He shook his head with a sigh, and caught sight of Sivert,
who had got up during the prayer and knelt down with his
arms round the corner of the bench under the windows.

'I'm glad to see you listening with devotion, Sivert. The
others didn't manage to stay awake.' He went into the
cabin again to put the hymnbook away. 'As the good book
says, the spirit is willing, but the flesh is weak,' he went on,
looking at the bosun, who was lying on his side, snoring
with his mouth open and his piously folded hands over the
edge of the bunk beneath his chin.

'D'you think we'll founder?' asked Sivert, as the captain
came into the outer cabin again.

'That's in God's hands, my lad. Just you carry on praying,
it can't do any harm.' With that the captain hurried up on
deck again.

Sivert remained kneeling where he was and searched for

words to pray with, but he couldn't think of anything but: 'Dear Lord, help us or we perish.'

Up until now he had been quite calm during the storm, with no thought that there might be any real danger. Since they had got through that time up north, surely they would be able to cope with this one too. He knew now that it would take a great deal for a ship to capsize, and as long as the others kept their spirits up, he did too. It was true that he had been badly shaken when the cook went overboard, and Sølvfest had been so close to following him, but one man drowning was a frequent occurrence, and didn't mean that there was any danger to the ship. Similarly it had been a fearful shock when the mainmast and the foremast split almost simultaneously, and the rigging came down with a thunderous crash over the lee railings. But then when the captain had shouted that they should cut loose the rigging, and everyone had rushed across with axes and knives, he had grabbed the meat saw without more ado and chopped at a rope so resolutely that it had snapped in two. It was only now when the captain was reading a prayer over them that he felt a stab of fear. If the captain was turning to religion, things must be in a bad way. He had seen him in so many different situations, but never had he heard him utter the name of Our Lord, and it didn't seem to have been in his thoughts either.

And now his voice had become so gentle and kind, it was unrecognizable. The way he had said: 'That's in God's hands, my lad' – it was so unlike the captain that that alone had been enough to scare the life out of Sivert.

He stayed on his knees, holding on to the bench, with his face bent over his hands, whilst his body was twisted here and there, now and then being lifted so high off the floor that he had to fight in order not to be thrown backwards up onto the bench. Every time there was a shudder like that the whole ship was shaken, as if it was going to split at the seams, and the crashing of the waves sounded like a thunderclap in Sivert's ears. 'Dear Lord, help us or we perish, we perish!' he called in a loud voice. Was he really going to perish on this day, at this hour, perish – what was it to perish? It was to die, to die, to die, – and then came the judgement. He who was so full of sin – 'Dear Lord, help us or we perish!' But he could attain forgiveness – yes, forgiveness – but then he would have to confess. 'Oh Lord, I want to confess that I …' – but then he couldn't remember his sins, they were so dreadfully many – it was everything. Everything he had done and thought and said, all his life, but if he repented then he could be among the blessed despite that, that was what they said, and that must be something really special.

But then he ought to welcome death. Welcome it, welcome it – 'Dear Lord, help us or we perish!' No, he couldn't welcome it, even if he knew with absolute certainty that he was going to be among the blessed. He was afraid, dreadfully, frantically afraid – 'Dear Lord, help us or we perish!' Yes, here he lay in anguish; it was a different matter that time he had stood in front of the mirror and relished the thought of beating up the cook. – The cook, he was no longer among the living – where might he be now, would they finish up in the same place? No, the cook had not had time to repent, so he was not among the blessed. There was that day he had invented the story about the ghost, and he had not been able to confess his lie to the second mate – 'Dear Lord, help us or we perish!' How dreadful a liar he had been; he didn't mean to, but he always did it nonetheless, it was like a part of him, he wasn't aware of it until he heard himself lying, and then he forgot it at once. Like that time he had written home that he was the one who had saved the ship. When he read about it in the letter from his parents which had reached him in Marseilles, he didn't understand what they meant. He had not been able to work out some lines about the fact that he would be recognised and get his reward in the end. It was not until they were moored in Lisbon loading salt that it suddenly occurred to him what he had written. Then he had felt so sorry and ashamed, but now it had become a millstone around his neck which would drag him down to damnation.

Oh, if only he could live, if he could avoid dying now, in the midst of his sins – , he would walk in the sight of God for the rest of his life. The Lord could not mean to let him die before he had tested him for longer. – He had hardly lived at all yet, God could not be so unjust – . 'Dear Lord, spare my young life!' he called out. God, who could read his heart, would see that the reason he wanted to live was to repent and atone, so he would have to grant his prayer. Although that was not certain – so many had been snatched away in the midst of their youth and in the midst of their sins.

'Dear Lord, save us or we perish!'

Up on deck the captain had managed after a superhuman effort to get the stove lit and boil up a kettle of water for tea. Neither he nor the crew had tasted anything hot for the last three days and nights. Now when the crew woke up they would have a mug of tea with their biscuits, that would give them heart.

Every fifteen minutes he went over to check the pump. The ship was still taking on the same amount of water, so things had not got any worse.

The captain looked at his watch and calculated that the

crew could sleep for another half hour, then they would have to get up and man the pump.

In the meantime the storm was raging with undiminished force. The sky was like a grey-black wall on all sides, with patches of strange watery paleness here and there. The waves surged to and fro, boiling into frothing foam before they poured across the deck. The wind howled and screamed around the naked mast stumps; it seemed at times that all the monsters in the world were bellowing in fear and lamentation.

'As long as the rudder holds, and the pump is working, we have a chance,' said the captain to the bosun, who was still at the wheel, 'and there's one good thing, she's not taking on more water than afore.'

'I was jus' thinkin', it's amazin' wha' she can take,' answered the bosun, turning the wheel.

The captain carried the teapot down to the galley, placed it on the table between the fiddles and lashed it fast to the mast. Then he went into the foodstore and collected a smoked ham and a large whole cheese, which he had bought to take home for his own household, and put both on the table. He then put out bread and butter and went in to awaken the crew. However, they were sleeping so deeply that his calls had no effect. He had to shake each one in order to wake them up.

When they finally began to stir, they were so frozen in their wet clothes that their teeth started chattering.

'Here you are, men,' said the captain, opening all his cupboards, 'here are socks and trousers and shirts, change into dry clothes – just take what you need, don't stand on ceremony. On the table out there you'll find food and drink, some good hot tea, so don't tell me the captain can't be a cook when it's needed. So just see that you get a move on and get out there to the pump.'

Half an hour later they were all out on deck again, pumping with ropes around their waists. The sleep and the good food with hot tea and dry undergarments had refreshed and strengthened them so that they worked with a greater will.

Yet after a short time it began to get dark again, and with that the feeling of hopelessness returned. The prospect of yet another night like the two previous ones on this wreck of a ship with a sinking cargo made them almost desperate. The booming from the hold, where the sodden masses of salt were being hurled against the sides of the ship, was as loud as the crashing of the waves. At any moment they expected the ship to break up and be torn to pieces. During the day it was more bearable, but these nights with no glimpse of a star, no glimmer of light – black, terrible, impenetrable darkness both above and beneath, both fore and aft! –

'Set someone to hold a lookout, bosun, while I turn in for an hour,' said the captain, coming over to the pumpers. 'I can't stay on my feet any longer, my eyeballs are stinging as if they've been dipped in acid.'

'Aye, it's not surprising you need rest, capt'n,' answered the bosun, who was hauling on the pump rope along with the others. 'You've been on the go longer than any of us.'

'If anythin' happens, wake me up,' continued the captain, 'but if it carries on like this, you can let me sleep till twelve. It's nearly ten now.'

'Aye aye, capt'n.'

The captain walked aft and peered at the compass.

'How's it goin' with you, Sølvfest?' he asked.

'I don't rightly know what to say, capt'n, there's no point complainin', you 'ave to keep at it till you drop.'

'Does your head ache?'

'I'll say it does, and there's a heavin' an' a churnin' goin' right through me,' answered Sølvfest. 'One minute I'm shakin' with cold, an' the next I could collapse wi' fever, an' there's sparks in front of me eyes the 'ole time.'

'You're better off at the wheel than standing there pumping,' said the captain.

'Aye capt'n, but she won't rightly answer.'

'When I've had a rest I'll take over, Sølvfest, just see you hold out till then. Keep her up into the wind.'

'I keep thinkin' about the cook, capt'n,' Sølvfest went on. 'His struggles are over now, but we've got ours to come.'

'Aye, one day we all have to die,' replied the captain, 'but many a ship has weathered worse storms than this.' With that he went below, clambered up fully clothed into his bunk, which was still damp from the bosun and the sailmaker, turned towards the wall and murmured: 'Into Jesu's hands we commend ourselves.'

He must have slept for an hour or so when he was awoken by a terrific bang, and at the same moment he was flung out of his bunk and out through the door of the cabin onto the floor of the outer cabin, which was almost perpendicular. It all happened so fast that he didn't come to his senses until he was lying against the aft cabin wall, clutching on to it. The lamp had gone out and smashed against the ceiling, and the captain heard the shards of glass raining down around him.

His first thought was that the ship was going down, and that he wouldn't even make it up on deck before it was all over, but straight after that he could feel the ship righting herself again, though she was not able to settle on an even keel. It was as if a force the size of a mountain was pressing on one side of her, sending her down and down, further down each time she tried to recover.

The captain crawled along the wall in the darkness and out into the forecastle; he made his way up the companionway, which was almost upside down because of the violent tossing. Then all at once the hatch was ripped open; a stormy gust met his bare head and hit him like a blow; his hair streamed back as if someone was pulling it, and at the same time a knee struck him full in the face.

'Get back!' he yelled, 'you're kicking me in the face.'

'Rudder broken, wheel smashed!' called the first mate's voice.

The captain seized hold of the edge of the hatch and was on deck with one bound.

'Christ Almighty, it's rough!' he said, gasping for breath. 'Wheel smashed, you say, what happened to Sølvfest?'

'I dunno, capt'n, the whole deckhouse has gone.'

The captain looked towards the place where the deckhouse had stood, straining to see in the dark, and fighting to take a few steps aft as he held on to the hatch.

'Then I guess Sølvfest has gone the same way,' he muttered. 'Haven't you shouted for him?' he said more loudly.

'Aye, shouted and searched,' answered the mate in an unsteady strangled voice. 'I reckon we've seen him for the last time. – Look out, capt'n!' The mate suddenly grabbed the captain by the shoulder, pulled him down into a crouch and clung on to the hatchway; an enormous wave crashed over it, tore off the hatch cover and washed it over the leeward railing.

'We must find a tarpaulin, otherwise the forecastle'll be full of water on the spot. Come on, first mate!'

'Things don't look good for us, capt'n,' said the mate a little later, after he and the captain had lashed the tarpaulin fast over the hatch.

'As long as there's life there's hope, first mate,' answered the captain. 'There's nothing else to do but wait for daylight.'

'If she lasts that long,' muttered the first mate.

'So long as the pump keeps going. – How long since you took a sounding?'

'Just before the deckhouse went, she's not takin' in any more water than before.'

'Aye, there you see – . No reason to complain - - - What's that they're shouting over there?'

'Pump failed!' The shout now reached them clearly.

The captain ran over. 'Can't you pump more water?' he asked.

'Not a drop, capt'n, you c'n hear it.' The words were accompanied by a dry grating sound.

'There went our last anchor chain,' muttered the captain, wiping the cold beads of sweat from his brow.

'Shall we launch the boat, capt'n?' asked a voice.

'Where are the crew?' replied the captain, straining to see them.

'Here, capt'n,' answered several voices. 'We're all by the pump.'

'Listen, men,' said the captain, 'if we put out in the boat it means certain death, so we might as well wait for it here.'

'But the boat is watertight, capt'n,' said one.

'Aye, as long as it lasts, but I reckon the sea would soon break it up.'

'The ship'll sink in three hours at most,' said the bosun.

'Get some lamps and let's look aft below deck and see if she's sprung a leak above the waterline,' said the captain to the first mate after a short pause. 'The stern has dipped badly this last while.'

When the captain reappeared on deck he ordered the crew to split into two halves. The first group, led by the first mate, were to go down below deck aft and use whatever they could find of wood, oakum, tarpaulin, metal plates and anything else to try to seal a leak to starboard where you could see the water streaming in. The others were to go down into the hold with the captain and investigate whether anything could be done about the pump. The captain himself didn't really believe that these activities would be of much use, but as he said to the mate, it was a good idea to keep the crew busy for as long as possible. Before long they had all disappeared from the deck, with the exception of Sivert, who had been ordered to keep a lookout and give a shout if he spied any sails.

Sivert crawled forrard and took his place to windward with his arms around the foremast, staring out into the darkness and the sea spray, his eyes burning and blinking. The ship laboured and heaved beneath him, so that he had to hold on tight to remain on his feet, and the waves dashed over him ceaselessly. The storm howled around his ears, and the whole time he thought he could hear dreadful shrieks of terror. What if it was the cook's damned soul returning to haunt his old quarters, writhing in torment without rest. What if he suddenly saw him standing threateningly before him in the darkness with that scar on his nose. He had a feeling that the cook was standing behind him. He did not dare turn around, not at any price, nor move, nor look sideways – he just had to keep staring ahead into the thick darkness. Oh, if only he had been with the others. Standing here on his own was the worst thing of all. He was continually drenched with fear, like a hot torrent, and there was a weight on his breast which forced his heart into his throat. Now and then a yellow fog appeared before his eyes, and his temples were throbbing fit to burst. He wanted to cry out to God for help, but he was unable to. He could not even summon the strength to whisper: 'Dear Lord, save us or we perish!'

He felt as if everything in his head was gradually turning into a sodden, seething mass. Finally he sank into a semi-conscious stupor. He didn't really know any longer why he was standing there, or what was going on; he just had a vague impression of something wretched and ominous, and his limbs felt as if they were clamped in a vice. But he remained mechanically staring ahead and clinging on. Each time the spray hit his face, he came to for a moment, but then the next moment he slipped back into semi-consciousness.

A faint dawn light began to show, but Sivert did not notice it. Suddenly he sank down beside the mast, but at the same moment a burst of spray hit him full in the face; he straightened up and realised his head was completely clear. He rubbed his eyes and discovered that day was breaking around him; it seemed to him as well that the storm had abated a little. Then he glanced behind him and saw that the stern was trailing in the water, lifting the bow up at a steep angle. As he turned his head back he saw a gleaming red point ahead to windward. Like an electric shock the realisation hit him that this must be a ship. Quickly he crawled up onto the forecastle, lay on his stomach and shaded his eyes with his hand. – Yes, there was no doubt, it was a red lamp. His breast filled with a blissful feeling of joy and hope. In a moment he was over by the main hatch and tore open the door. 'Sails ahead to windward!' he yelled with all his might, and at the same moment he burst into tears.

Subsequent events later remained in an hazy mist for Sivert. People were laughing and crying, someone put an arm round his neck and kissed him, the bosun flung his arms round the sailmaker, and several people were shouting and talking all at once. Then suddenly there were flags hanging on the mizzen top and on the stump of the mainmast, and then it was full daylight and a large steamship was heading straight for them. He untied a rope and a boat was hoisted into the air, and right after that he was sitting in the boat, which was rocking up and down, between the bosun and the second mate, and then it seemed to him that the boat was so full of people that it was going to sink. He was so terrified that he must have screamed, because someone put a hand over his mouth and pushed him down into the bottom of the boat. Then he saw the back of the captain as he climbed down into the boat with the ship's log under his arm, and it seemed to him that at the same moment he felt a rope around his waist and was being hauled up over a ship's railing and felt the deck beneath his feet. He turned his head to look for their ship, but couldn't see it, and then the bosun shook his fist at the sea and said:

'Look now, there's only the bowsprit of *Two Friends* stickin' up. Farewell comrade, rest in peace, blessed be your memory.'

Then everything went black. His knees buckled and he knew no more.

Notes

Chapter 1

Ladegaardsbakken: now Ladegårdsgaten. Ladegaarden was probably originally a farm, and 'bakken' means the hill.

Stølen: a residential area in the east of Bergen.

'The Farmer Wants a Wife': in Norwegian this is 'Munken går i enge', 'The munk walks in the meadow', a similar game of choosing a partner.

Stril: a derogatory term for fishermen from communities north-west of Bergen.

Smedesmugalmindingen: 'Almindinger' (nowadays 'almen-ninger') in Bergen are the wide sloping avenues, often with planted areas, which in many places lead from the higher streets down towards the lower ones (author's note). 'Smedesmug' means blacksmith's alley.

Madam Davisen i Påtholle: 'Påtholle', or Potthullet, was the name of a drinking den in Nøstet in Bergen, quite a long walk from where Tippler Tom and Oline had met. A 'pott' is just under two pints of beer.

Kvarven: the entrance to the harbour (author's note).

Chapter 2

Dræggen: a district of Bergen around Bergenhus Fortress, close by Stølen but lower lying (author's note).

woven hat: this is a hat woven from thin offcuts of wood or shavings.

gammelost: a matured sour milk cheese, highly pungent.

Hollændergaten: so called after the Dutch traders who had stalls there from the fifteenth century onwards. It remained a sought-after address until the 1860s.

An' she's only an 'ousemaid!: she is employed 'i Månes-kondisjon', i.e. for a month at a time, so she can be fired at short notice.

Chapter 3

bark: a three-masted sailing ship. Amale Skram had sailed round the world on such a ship with her first husband August Müller, and she knew the layout and the function of the various pieces of equipment intimately.

fiddles: raised borders on a table which prevent objects sliding off.

Chapter 4

T'ship's doomed: 'skuten er fejg'. The word 'feig' (normal meaning 'cowardly') can also mean that there is some kind of evil fate hanging over a person or object.

to go berserk: 'å gå berserkergang' – like Viking warriors who became possessed and tore off their shirts as they charged into battle.

Chapter 6

hanging over the fire: it was hanging on a 'sjerring', which was an iron construction fastened inside the chimney, for hanging heavy pots on (author's note).

What good is there in rising early: part of the second verse of a hymn by the German writer Lazarus Spengler, a friend and supporter of Luther.

Dræggen: see note to Chapter 2.

yer bread: author's note remarks that this is bread from the baker's ('Stom'brø'e' in the original), not the homemade unleavened crispbread.

Here they are all Blak in White cloths: although this description, and some of the subsequent references to the local culture, will offend twenty-first century sensibilities, the author is here reflecting widespread European assumptions and biases of the period in which she was writing.

Consul: this is not a diplomatic consul, but someone in charge of a shipping company, who enjoys a high social standing. See also Chapter 7.

Speciedaler: before 1875, when the modern krone was introduced, the monetary system in Norway consisted of speciedaler, ort and skilling. There were 24 skilling in one ort, and 4 ort in one speciedaler. When the modern system took over, one speciedaler was converted into 4 kroner.

Chapter 7

folded up the dry washing ready for rolling: the washing would be stretched over a roller and smoothed with a rolling board rather than ironed.

Chapter 8

Oh my lady come down below!: the author quotes this song and the one a little later in English.

most brilliant workmen: these phrases are again in English.

pokkenholt … logwood: pokkenholt is also known as *lignum vitae*, an extremely hard wood native to the Caribbean. Logwood is an American tree used in dyeing, transported in the form of logs.

quicksilver: this is a mistake by the author. The silvering on mirrors is not quicksilver (mercury) but a mixture of silver nitrate, sodium hydroxide and other substances.

Appartements to be had: author's spelling. Amalie Skram's

English was uncertain, so it is not clear if the misspelling was intentional.

Something to drink?: the girls all speak English (which the author translates into Norwegian in notes). I have occasionally normalized the spelling.

Bethelem school: Betlehem was founded as a school for the poor, but by Amalie Skram's time it had become a normal primary school. It is now a museum, in the district of Bergen where she grew up, Klosteret.

Skansen: a place on Fløyen mountain outside Bergen.

Chapter 10

sour milk: 'Melkeblanne', a mixture of soured milk and water used as a refreshing drink.

some vessels are created to dishonour, others to honour: the text refers to the New Testament, II Timothy 2:20: *i et stort hus er det ikke bare kar av gull og sølv, men også kar av tre og ler, og nogen til ære, andre til vanære.* (In St. James' version: but in a great house there are not only vessels of gold and of silver, but also of wood and of earth; and some to honour, and some to dishonour.)

Chapter 11

Lourdaud: lout, oaf.

Kalfaret: Kalfarveien was for hundreds of years the main road linking Bergen with the countryside to the east. In the nineteenth century it was the town's most elegant promenade street.

the Ash Lad: i.e. Askeladden, the hero of many Norwegian folk tales, a poor peasant lad who always proves to be the smartest and defeats the troll or marries the princess.

AMALIE SKRAM

Lucie

(translated by Katherine Hanson & Judith Messick)

This novel from 1888 tells the story of the misalliance between Lucie, a vivacious dancing girl from Tivoli, and Theodor Gerner, a respectable lawyer from the strait-laced middle-class society of nineteenth-century Norway. Having first kept her as a mistress, Gerner is so captivated by Lucie that he marries her, only to discover that his project to turn her into a demure housewife is continually frustrated by her irrepressible sensuality and lack of breeding. What had made her alluring as a mistress makes her unacceptable as a wife. His attempts to govern her behaviour develop gradually into a harsh tyranny against which she rebels in a manner which brings misery and despair to both.

Lucie
ISBN 9781909408081
(Paperback, 170 pages)

AMALIE SKRAM

Fru Inés

(translated by Katherine Hanson & Judith Messick)

Fru Inés is a city novel, vividly evoking the sights, sounds and smells of nineteenth-century Constantinople. The city is a hub, a meeting point of East and West, where privileged Europeans enjoy a cossetted existence screened from the tumult and misery of the streets. One of the privileged is Inés, a Spanish Levantine from Alexandria, whose marriage to a Swedish consul has brought her a life of enviable luxury; but behind the polished façade she is lonely and unfulfilled. Her yearning for passion leads her to embark on an affair with a naive young Swede, Arthur Flemming; but their love is threatened from the start by portents of disaster and the threat of discovery, and Inés is inexorably drawn to seek rescue from the sordid dealers from whom she had been so careful to keep aloof.

Fru Inés
ISBN 9781909408050
(Paperback, 170 pages)

AMALIE SKRAM

Betrayed

(translated by Katherine Hanson & Judith Messick)

With high hopes, Captain Riber embarks with his young
bride Aurora on a voyage to exotic destinations. But they
are an ill-matched pair; her naive illusions are shattered
by the realities of married life and the seediness of
society in foreign ports, whilst his hopes of domestic
bliss are frustrated by his wife's unhappiness. Life on
board ship becomes a private hell, as Aurora's obsession
with Riber's adventures as a carefree bachelor begins to
undermine his sanity. Ultimately both are betrayed by
a hypocritical society which imposes a warped view of
sexuality on its most vulnerable members.

Betrayed
ISBN 9781909408494
(Paperback, 136 pages)

Caught in the Enchanter's Net: Amalie and Erik Skram's Letters

(edited and translated by Janet Garton)

This selection of letters exchanged between two Scandinavian authors, the Norwegian Amalie Skram and the Danish Erik Skram, during the last two decades of the nineteenth century, presents a lively picture of cultural and political ferment during a decisive time in the development of the two states. Both had access to the leading figures of the time, from radical writers and critics to politicians. The letters provide a wealth of information about contemporary issues, from parliamentary procedure to the price of hatpins. They also tell of a passionate attachment between two very different personalities, from seduction and marriage, through literary partnership and childbirth, to the final despairing separation.

Caught in the Enchanter's Net: Amalie and Erik Skram's Letters
ISBN 9781870041522
(Paperback, 461 pages)

www.ingramcontent.com/pod-product-compliance
Lightning Source LLC
Chambersburg PA
CBHW052007020726
47501CB00004B/1041